THE STONE HOUSE

Everything changes for Kate, Moya and Romy when they receive word that Maeve, their mother, is critically ill. They return from Dublin, London and New York to Rossmore and the old stone house where they grew up – Moya the beautiful, Kate the brains, and Romy the bold one. For Kate it is time to consider her life as a high-flying lawyer and single parent. Moya must take a hard look at her marriage to the charming but unfaithful Patrick and consider her own worth – and wild child Romy has to find the courage to stop running and face her family.

THE STONE HOUSE

THE STONE HOUSE

by

Marita Conlon-McKenna

Magna Large Print Books
Long Preston, North Yorkshire,
BD23 4ND, England.

British Library Cataloguing in Publication Data.

Conlon-McKenna, Marita
The stone house.

A catalogue record of this book is
available from the British Library

ISBN   0-7505-2418-9

First published in Great Britain in 2004 by Bantam Press
a division of Transworld Publishers

The right of Marita Conlon-McKenna to be identified as the
author of this work has been asserted in accordance with
sections 77 and 78 of the Copyright, Designs and Patents Act,
1988

Published in Large Print 2005 by arrangement with
Transworld Publishers

Magna Large Print is an imprint of Library Magna Books Ltd.

Printed and bound in Great Britain by
T.J. (International) Ltd., Cornwall, PL28 8RW

Maria Grech Ganado's poem
'Relative Time' is taken from the
Ribcage collection and is reproduced
with permission from
Minima Publishers.

For Mandy, Laura and Fiona,
my own three wonderful daughters.

ACKNOWLEDGEMENTS

Maria Grech Ganado, for the use of her wonderful poem 'Relative Time'.

The two men in my life who are each so good in their own way: my husband James for his constant belief and support and my son James for making me laugh and smile every day and for being one of the kindest young men on the planet.

Mandy, Laura and Fiona, my three daughters – all so different and wonderful!

My sister Gerardine, it is so good to have you home.

Sarah Webb for being one of the nicest people I know and for always giving the best advice.

'The Irish Girls' who help make being a writer so much fun. Martina Devlin, Claire Dowling, Mary Hosty, Julie Parsons, Deirdre Purcell, Marisa Mackle, Jacinta McDevitt, Ann-Marie Forrest, Catherine Dunne, Tina O'Reilly, Suzanne Higgins, Cauvery Madhaven et al. – thanks for all the dinners, drinks and chats.

'My 'Irish PEN' friends, especially Christine Dwyer-Hickey, Patricia O'Reilly, Denise Deegan, Nesta Tuomey and Kathleen Sheehan O'Connor.

My agent Caroline Sheldon.

My wonderful editor Francesca Liversidge.

Nicky Jeanes and all the team at Transworld.

Gill, Simon, Geoff, Declan and all the team at 'Gill Hess', Dublin.

The Irish booksellers for all their support over the years.

Lastly to all my readers, especially those who have grown up with my books, thanks for making writing such a pleasure.

RELATIVE TIME
(for my mother)

Towards the end, my mother would
 regularly
bid me wind the clocks she couldn't
 reach–
how little time I felt I had, how slow
to respond, bipolared like a pendulum
 that's stopped.

Younger, I'd rushed to do it, directing
 from the stool
the ticking and the tocking with a wave of
 each hand,
gleefully flitting with each ding and dong
as I had paced them, clock succeeding
 clock.

When time ran out between the chores
of my own motherhood and my lost name,
all it became was the tighter twisting of
 keys
in yet more faces without doors, each
 effort
a rehearsed piece played for my mother

who thought me younger than she.

She's gone. As has my own young family.
And I've inherited the clocks, and the time
to wind them in. I keep their faces
within reach of mine. Sometimes their
  chimes
bring memories of lighter days.
  Sometimes
all they can say is GONE GONE GONE.

Maria Grech Ganado

Maeve Dillon walked down the gravelled driveway and across the main road, before turning through the gap in the hedgerow on to the narrow lane that led to the Strand. She savoured the solitude and quiet of the empty beach as she kicked off her flip-flops and wriggled out of her loose grey tracksuit. She loved to swim at this time of the morning and she walked across the bleached sand to the beckoning curve of swirling foam. The tide was in and she waded out to the tops of her thighs, her screams like that of a five-year-old as the freezing chill of the waves enfolded her and she dived in. The water was so cold it almost took her breath away. A good swimmer, she took long even strokes as she swam along the shoreline. Back and forth, five times, six times, the sea water invigorating her, sending the blood coursing through her veins, making her feel young, alive. She floated, letting the rhythm of the waves take her. There was nothing like it. Ever since she was a small girl she'd been swimming on this stretch, and now that she was getting older it was one of her great pleasures. Light and ageless she floated. Her daughters fussed and told her it was dangerous to swim alone but she ignored

17

their concerns – it beat going to a gym or aerobic classes any day! Two more stretches, backstroke, overarm. She ran out and grabbed her towel, scrubbing at her limbs and shoulders, trying to dry herself, warming as she pulled the fleece sweatshirt over her mottled blue and pink tinged skin as she set off back up the beach, nodding to Philip Doyle, who was walking his two golden Labradors.

She walked briskly, turning towards home.

She crossed the road to the Stone House, the granite-clad house, where she had grown up, and where she and Frank in turn had raised their own family. The house built by her grandfather was set on a slight slope overlooking the beach, and provided magnificent views of the Rossmore coastline and the shipping lanes, the sound and smell of the sea a constant in the lives of its inhabitants.

A shower, then breakfast, for she had a busy day ahead.

She pottered around the kitchen. Porridge oats, milky tea, and some toast with bramble jelly. A solitary breakfast; she was still unused to this empty kitchen, children grown, Frank gone. She sat inside the window perusing yesterday's edition of the *Irish Times*, Jinx, the cat, mewing for attention. She let him out and watched him chase a daring robin across the patio.

She loved this house, this garden, and drew comfort from them. Since she had been widowed she had resisted pressures to sell it and to move somewhere smaller. This was her home and she had absolutely no intention of selling it. The place held far too many memories for her to even consider leaving it. Growing up, her daughters had filled the house with their laughter and stories and parties and Frank and herself had hatched so many plans together at this very table. They had fought and cried, loved and grieved under this roof, struggled at times to keep their marriage together. Good and bad times, all shared between the bricks, roof, floors and polished wood of this old house. But now Frank was gone, her daughters caught up in their own lives and she was for the most part alone. She did her best to keep herself busy, create new routines, enjoy simple things: the garden, the church choir, lunches, the bridge club.

Maeve stirred herself. She had a few things to do before meeting her sister for lunch.

Chapter One

Kate Dillon considered the notes, letters and stacks of files on her desk. She'd been far too wrapped up in the Bradley and Hughes merger, and look where it had got her. A backlog of cases to deal with and a senior partner breathing heavily down her neck, looking for some kind of date and time strategy that he could use to appease his mighty corporate clients. She rubbed at the back of her neck, hoping the circular movement of her fingers might ease off the tension of her impending headache. She stretched and, moving her head sideways, gazed from the tinted windows of her office to the quays below. A soft sunshine speckled the dark waters of the River Liffey, the late-afternoon traffic already building up. Like a princess in a shimmering glass tower Kate looked down over the city below her. She loved Dublin with its mix of old and new, ancient streets and modern contemporary architecture. Patterson's, the huge law firm where she worked, was situated right in the heart of Dublin's busy International Financial Services Centre in the redeveloped docklands. Old warehouses and derelict buildings and yards had given way to glass and steel and concrete; the dollars, pounds, euro and yen of banking and finance had created an artistic landmark. She had fought hard to work in such an environment and soon hoped to reach the level of junior partner, a title few women of her age had achieved.

'Kate, have you looked at that paperwork for Hughes's yet? They want a contract drawn up now!' interrupted her boss. Bill O'Hara, a former Irish rugby star, was now an eighteen-stone legal powerhouse who usually had the charm and wit to soft-soap the most truculent of clients. 'Colman Hughes wants it all wrapped up by next Monday.'

Kate let out a whoosh of breath. There was at least twenty-four hours' solid work in it and she had to collect Molly from the crèche in an hour and a half.

He looked down at the pile of work on her desk.

'Just leave the rest and concentrate on this. It's too important,' he said.

'I know.'

At Patterson's, everyone knew that even the best and most loyal client could be fickle as hell if someone didn't jump through hoops to get their work done and on time. Their competitors were waiting with open arms.

'Promise I'll do my best but...'

'Good girl, Kate. I knew I could rely on you.' A smile lit up his broad face as he walked away from her in his immaculate Louis Copeland suit.

'I'm out to dinner with those two Americans but I'll be home by ten, so you can e-mail me with a draft.'

Kate cursed her own ambition and need to be appreciated as she phoned Derry to tell him yet again that she had to work late and to ask him if he could possibly pick up their three-year-old daughter.

A smile relaxed her face as she heard his calm and unhurried voice.

'It's all right, Katie. I was just in the middle of some designs. But it's no problem. I'll see you later.'

'I'm sorry, Derry. Really I am. It's Bill, he's put me in a spot. I'll try and get home in time for bedtime, OK?'

'Sure. Molly and I will mind each other so don't worry, and I'll make her pancakes for tea.'

Kate laughed. Molly was going through a pancake stage, demanding them at every opportunity

'Save me some!' she said.

Putting down the phone she said a mental prayer of thanks for Derry's easy nature and the fact that he was self-employed. He worked from a small mews office close to her apartment, designing yachts and boats for a number of clients, including boat-builders and yards. Their three-year-old daughter was the result of a passionate fling. Derry was a good father who paid her some support money and had insisted on playing his part in raising Molly, a wild bundle of mischief who was a perfect balance of their two separate personalities.

Kate, a single mother, had fought hard to develop her legal career and establish her financial independence. She had seen too many of her colleagues put their career on the back boiler as they gave in to the demands of self-centred husbands or demanding young families. She had worked too hard to throw in the towel and give up the position and respect she had earned in Patterson's. She had no rich husband or family to support her: everything she and Molly had, she had earned. She had learned the hard way when she was younger not to rely on men and had no intention of ever being dependent on anyone. No, she was quite capable of taking care of herself and her child, but at this minute was very glad that Derry had agreed to help out.

Free to concentrate, she cleared her desk and opened the file on her laptop, making notes on the yellow pad as she read through the minutiae of the agreements of undertaking that were to form part of Colman Hughes's latest acquisition. Funny, it reminded her of something she had worked on three years ago... Leaving her desk she headed down to the third floor to the company's library of back cases and legal opinions, where she hunted for the exact documents she needed and the letter from the inspector of taxes she had dealt with.

Vonnie Quinn sat snug in the window seat of Lavelle's, looking out over the seafront and harbour.

Putting on her reading glasses she studied the menu, noticing the daily specials written in chalk on the blackboard over the busy serving counter as Sheila O'Grady the owner ambled over.

'How are you, Vonnie?'

'I'm fine, Sheila, fine. I'm just waiting for Maeve.'

'Can I get you something while you're waiting?'

'I'm sure she'll be along in a few minutes.'

'Then I'll give you time to make up your minds. How's Joe and the family?'

'They're all grand. The boys are big as houses now, all grown up. What about your own children?' enquired Vonnie.

'Lisa's doing her finals and Anna's just started working for one of those fancy French banks in Dublin as an economist.

Deirdre and Tommy are in the business here with me, and Brian's just moved back from Manchester.'

'Brian's the married one?' said Vonnie. She wondered if Sheila had any grandchildren yet. She could sense a reticence in the other woman at the mention of her older son. Years ago Brian had dated her niece, they'd been childhood sweethearts, mad about each other. Then all of a sudden it had broken up. She couldn't remember why, but perhaps it had been for the best.

'Brian and his wife divorced a while back.'

'Oh, I'm sorry to hear that.'

'Well these things happen nowadays. He works for that big engineering firm Jameson's. They're doing all the work on the new bypass road and motorway.'

'That's a big project.'

'Aye, but he seems to like building roads and bridges, and it's good to have him back home.'

Vonnie smiled. She was full of admiration for Sheila, who had worked so hard in Lavelle's over the years to put her children through school and college and given them every opportunity. The two women had both attended Rossmore local Convent of Mercy and were classmates. Sheila, a bright girl, had married young, too young, and by the time she was thirty had been left a widow with five small children to raise and no income. She had never complained and instead of whining about her misfortune had gone to Hazel Lavelle's looking for work. Rolling up her sleeves she'd set to, her hard work and intuition a huge factor in turning the small coffee shop into one of the finest restaurants in the county with a huge local trade, and the humble bakery into one of the main suppliers of gourmet breads and pastries and desserts in the South-East.

Vonnie settled down to watch the passers-by and hoped to catch a glimpse of her younger sister. She smothered a flicker of annoyance. It was so like her sister. Of late, Maeve always seemed to be delayed, caught up in something. Ever since the death of Frank over four years ago, Maeve was constantly trying to lose herself in things. Bridge, book clubs, gardening, the choir. No doubt she was attending to her plants or typing up a letter for one of the charities she volunteered for, had forgotten the time and would arrive in a few minutes, hair flying, all flustered.

The restaurant was filling up and a queue was forming for tables as she lifted up the hand-painted menu. Carrot and parsnip soup with a hint of ginger, that sounded good, then perhaps the vegetable bake and a side salad with a glass of wine.

'Still no sign,' smiled Sheila as she took her order.

'You know Maeve!'

She watched as Sheila walked back to the kitchen, envying her trim figure and her short hair, a subtle shade of highlighted ash blond. She was an attractive woman and yet had never remarried. No wonder there were still so many rumours about her. Years ago the small town's gossips' tongues had wagged and she'd been linked with a local married businessman: Vonnie's brother-in-law's name was among those mentioned. Maeve had steadfastly never said a word to deny or confirm the accusation and had kept coming to Lavelle's for coffees and lunches until gradually over time the innuendoes were forgotten.

The soup was delicious, served with freshly made brown bread, and she tried to stifle her annoyance with Maeve as she began to eat. She hated sitting alone while all around her people were immersed in conversation. Sheila diplomatically brought her over a copy of the *Irish Independent*. She called Maeve's number: no reply. At least she must be on the way.

Annoyance gave way to alarm as her main course was served, and she ate the leek, mushroom and pepper mixture, not even bothering with coffee as she paid the bill.

'Maybe she just forgot?' consoled Sheila as they said goodbye.

'Maybe.'

As she got into her silver Volvo, a feeling of concern overwhelmed her and shifting her car into gear she turned out of the Rossmore Road instead of heading home, determined to give her sister a piece of her mind for standing her up as she drove towards the Stone House.

Forty minutes later Lucy, the senior secretary in Patterson's Mergers and Acquisitions Department, broke the peace and quiet of the Research Library room.

'Kate, there's an urgent message on the phone for you. I didn't know where you were and thought maybe you'd gone home early.'

Home early! Kate raised her eyebrows. Some chance. She jumped up. Maybe something had happened about collecting Molly.

'Was it Derry?'

'No. It was a Mrs Quinn. She's insisting on talking to you.'

'Did she leave a number?'

'She said she's not at home in Rossmore but will phone you straight back. It's urgent.'

Aunt Vonnie. What was her aunt doing phoning her at work? Her aunt hated going through switches and secretaries and much preferred long rambling calls at night with a cup of tea or a glass of wine as they chatted. She was barely back at her desk when the phone went again.

'Kate, is that you?'

'Auntie Vonnie, what is it? Is everything OK?'

'No, love. I'm sorry. It's your mum. We were meant to meet in Lavelle's for lunch today. She never turned up so I drove out to the house. She's unconscious, Kate. They're not sure if it was a fall, some kind of bleed into her brain, a stroke even. She's in the Regional.'

Kate felt the coldness in the pit of her stomach as she asked, 'Is she breathing? Has she regained consciousness?'

'She's on oxygen. And no. The doctors are with her. They want to do all kinds of brain scans. They're very worried about her, Kate. They asked me to contact her next of kin.'

'God, Vonnie. Don't say that. Mammy's going to be fine.'

'I don't know, Kate. You need to get down here. See her. Talk to them.'

Kate gripped the phone, not believing. Her mother was as strong as an ox, and never got sick. She hated hospitals and doctors.

'Kate, you'll come immediately! Your mother needs you.'

'I'll be down straight away. I'll phone Moya and Romy, so don't worry.'

'I'll stay with her, but you just get here as soon as you can, pet.'

'Thanks, Vonnie. Thanks.'

Kate put down the phone. Lucy was staring at her.

'Are you all right, Kate? Is it bad news?'

'It's my mother. She's been taken to hospital. My aunt is with her. I have to leave for Waterford immediately.'

'Don't worry. I'll look after things at this end.'

Automatically Kate began to clear her desk of sensitive documents and switched off her computer. Realizing she'd better tell Bill she had to leave early, she went to his office. He'd already gone and the sun was beating on his high-backed leather chair.

She'd go home, grab a bag and some things before heading to Waterford, thanking God it was *en route*. Pulling her diary from her handbag she searched for her sisters' numbers as she began to dial the 044 code for London. She cursed her sisters, wondering why they couldn't be more like other families who supported and cared for each other. What had happened to them all? Moya so wrapped up with her own life in London and Romy who had simply taken off when she was not more than a kid and turned her back on the family. She'd never even bothered to keep in touch. Selfishly she had broken their parents' hearts years ago. Worst of all, her youngest sister had made absolutely no effort to come home for their father's funeral, something that Kate would never forgive her for!

Moya had her mobile turned off, so she tried her home number instead, leaving a simple message telling her what had happened and promising to phone later.

Kate eyed the row of modern silver and steel clocks on the wall. Hong Kong, Tokyo, New York and London. It was midday in New York, Romy should at least be up, she thought as she began to punch in the international code.

Romy Dillon whisked the free-range eggs together, fluffing them up as she turned them into the hot pan. A little cheese, tomato and onion and she had the perfect breakfast. Outside the daylight teased her as New Yorkers rushed to work and shops in the bright sunshine. She would eat, work for a few hours and then call on her friend Diana. She switched on the coffee-maker just as the phone in the living room shrilled. Barefoot she raced across the bleached floorboards to get it.

'Romy?'

She almost dropped the phone, recognizing the voice instantly.

'Romy, please don't put down the phone. I need to talk to you.'

'Is it Molly?'

'No, Molly's fine,' answered Kate. 'It's

31

Mammy. She's in hospital, in the Regional. Vonnie just phoned me. She's unconscious. They're not sure what it is but the doctors told her to contact us. It's serious, Romy.'

'I heard you.'

The distance between them lay empty, desolate.

'Romy!' screamed her sister. 'You are a cold-hearted bitch. I don't give a damn about you and what's going on in that crazy head of yours. Mammy's sick, dying, and the least you can do this time is to come home and see her.'

'Don't you dare tell me what to do!' Romy said coldly, the pain ripping through her, for she had no intention of getting into an argument.

'I'm not telling you what to do. I'm simply informing you about Mammy. It's up to you if you want to come home or not to see her.'

Romy's mind was racing. She couldn't think, didn't know what to say. She would not make promises she couldn't keep. Be pressurized by her sister into a knee-jerk response. She wasn't going to be pushed into an automatic reply. She tried to gather her thoughts, protect herself.

The silence lay heavy between them, harsh and cold as the Atlantic Ocean, worse than any distance.

'Thanks, Kate. Thanks for letting me know,' she said slowly as the phone went dead on the other end.

Back in the small galley kitchen she scraped the burnt eggs into the sink, pouring herself a cup of coffee as she curled up on the padded window-seat. There had been no pleasantries, no niceties between them. How could she go back home? Return to the place she had left so long ago! Nothing had changed, so why should she even consider going back and dragging up the hurt and pain of the past and a time she still tried so hard to forget?

Chapter Two

The rush-hour DART was crowded and Kate was fortunate to find a seat. The commuter train seemed to take an age as it crossed the river and pushed out along Dublin's coastline passing Ringsend and Sandymount and Booterstown, Kate almost jumping out at her usual Monkstown stop. Molly had already been collected and the minute she entered their apartment she was greeted with a flying hug.

'Mummy! Mummy, you're home. Look what I made today.'

Her daughter disappeared into the kitchen

and emerged with an enormous painted pink and yellow butterfly that looked like it still might be wet.

'It's beautiful, pet. You're a great little artist,' she said, scooping her up and burying her face in the curly dark hair. Molly giggled as Kate pretended to bite her.

'I have to get changed, darling, and drive down the country to see Granny.'

'Can I come too?'

'Not tonight, pet. Granny's sick. She's in hospital.'

'I want to see her,' pleaded Molly, putting on her begging face.

'No, I'm sorry, Molly. Little girls aren't let in the hospital. You have to stay home with Daddy. OK?'

She could see the look of consideration pass over the child's face as her lip wobbled and she decided whether to cry or not.

Derry looked up from working on his laptop, papers spread out around the table. 'Just trying to catch up. I've a big meeting tomorrow. Listen, I'm sorry about your mum.'

She felt guilty for dragging him away from clients and his own work at the design yard, but was relieved to know that Molly was so well taken care of as Derry doted on their small daughter. Emotion washed over her as he wrapped her in one of those big bear hugs that still unsettled her. She clung to him for a second, almost wishing that they were something more to each other than Molly's parents and that she could stay exactly where she was for the rest of the night instead of driving down to Waterford.

'You get changed and I'll make you a cup of tea and something to eat before you leave,' he offered.

'Thanks.' Tears welled in her eyes and she rubbed at them so Molly wouldn't get upset too.

In the bedroom Kate kicked off her shoes and hung up her black suit, pulling on a pair of beige corduroys, a long-sleeved T-shirt, a wool zip-up jacket in a creamy white and a pair of comfortable decks for driving. She grabbed a change of clothes, her pyjamas, some toiletries and her toothbrush, shoving them all into the green overnight bag. Molly was engrossed in the TV when she came back in the room and she slipped into the kitchen.

'Don't worry about anything, Kate, honest. Molly and I'll be fine,' reassured Derry. 'You just stay with your mother. She's the one who needs you. I'll be able to collect Molly tomorrow if need be, and I can reschedule the next day if I have to. The O'Reillys might be a bit annoyed, but they can wait! I'll have their brief finished next week.'

She drank the hot sweet mug of tea, and

ate the thin golden pancake with a shake of sugar and squeeze of lemon quickly; Molly came in to sit beside her. She watched Derry wipe Molly's sticky hands, his sandy hair bent down over hers, infinitely patient. Not minding that his beige chinos had a layer of sugar on them. Minnie and her friends were always telling her that she was lucky to have Derry on the scene and that he was so different from most guys. He wasn't one to shirk the responsibilities of fatherhood. She knew that, but sometimes she longed for more. Perhaps to feel that his weekly visits to her apartment and his involvement in her life were not just because of the dark-haired bundle of mischief the two of them had managed to produce. Funny, the only female that he could totally commit to was a three-year-old!

She got up to go and made Molly swear to behave.

'Listen, I'm sorry having to call on you like this. Are you sure you're OK about it?'

'We'll manage.'

'I don't know what I'll do if she dies!'

'Hey! Come on, don't talk like that. Maeve's strong. She's a tough Dillon woman. You'll see, she'll get through this.'

'I'm not sure if she will,' Kate said, trying to compose herself as she grabbed her car keys and kissed Molly goodbye.

She cursed the heavy traffic and over-crowded roads and prayed that she would soon reach Waterford's main hospital and find her mother much recovered. Aunt Vonnie wasn't usually an alarmist but sometimes falls and head injuries looked a lot worse than they were. Her mother could be sitting up in bed talking by now, for all she knew.

At the Wexford lights she checked her phone: still no reply from her older sister. Putting her foot on the accelerator of the Golf she passed a slow truck hauling cattle for the ferry, the animals staring balefully at her.

She eased the car into fifth gear as she followed the Dublin to Waterford road hoping she would make good time. She put on the radio but couldn't concentrate on the news so she switched to her Coldplay CD, the familiar music soothing her.

It was almost dark by the time she reached the city. The shops and banks were shut. The streets were empty as she drove through it and out past the college and the glass factory to the Tramore road to the hospital, where she easily found a spot in the almost empty car park.

'Kate! Oh, thank God you're here.'

Her aunt looked as if she had aged ten years in a few hours. Her naturally curly dark hair was standing on end, her face pale and strained as Kate hugged her tight.

'How is she?'

'There's no change. I keep asking but that's all they'll say.'

'Can I see her?'

'There's a nurse in the station there. Nurse Kelly. She's expecting you.'

The nurse was calm and gentle as she explained how they still had not fully ascertained what had happened to Kate's mother. A massive bleed to the brain but the extent of the damage, and her chance of recovering, it was still far too early to say.

'Can I talk to her doctor?'

Dr Healy had gone home for the night but would be on again in the morning when her mother would be fully assessed by a neurologist and the team.

Nurse Kelly passed Kate a gown and led her into the intensive care ward where her mother lay.

Kate felt a chill pass over as she entered the long narrow room. She was unable to ascertain which of the high narrow beds held her own mother. Fear choked her as she realized they all almost looked like corpses attached to machines that forced air into lungs and monitored every minute change of rhythm and pressure. The nurse led her to the woman in a bed down on the right. It was her mother, her face calm, eyes closed, her skin cold to touch. She looked so different with the colour drained from her skin, her hair brushed back off her face, her grey roots showing. She was wearing a simple printed tie-back hospital gown. Kate automatically bent forward to touch her.

'Why is she cold?' she blurted out, trying to rub her mother's arm and shoulder and warm her.

'It's better she is cool than hot with a temperature. The air here is kept at a regular temperature to make it easier for the patients.'

'Mammy! Mammy!' she whispered. 'It's Kate.'

There was no response. She watched her mother's face: closed, her effort now concentrated on breathing, the machine making a slow whooshing sound beside her. It scared her. She had never seen her mother like this.

'She just looks like she is asleep. How long will she stay like that?'

'We'll know better tomorrow, be able to judge. For the moment she's best left quiet, totally still. The brain is delicate, there's still swelling.'

'How much?'

'We're not sure of the extent of it yet.'

Kate looked at her mother and wondered how she could have taken her life so much for granted. Her mother was never sick.

Everyone in Rossmore knew that. Maeve Dillon was a woman with a fine constitution who kept herself healthy and fit with walking and cycling and swimming all year round. She didn't smoke, didn't overeat and only drank the odd glass of wine or pint of beer. She'd always looked after herself and following their father's death had kept occupied with the Vincent de Paul work as well as playing bridge and helping with the local meals on wheels. Kate struggled to compose herself.

'Can I stay with her?'

'You can sit with her for a few minutes if you like, but as you see the nurses and doctors need to be able to get easy access to patients here quickly so there aren't the same facilities for visitors as in another ward. There is a special waiting room just outside the door with coffee and tea and a place to put your feet up. Your mother is being totally monitored and if there's even the slightest change in her condition you'll be informed.'

The nurse left her for a few minutes. It felt unreal balanced on the narrow stool waiting for her mother to wake up. When Kate was small she would grab at her mother and shake her and roll on top of her to wake her when she needed her, and her mother would reach and pull her daughter into her arms even when she was asleep or having a nap, the two of them laughing.

'Mammy, I'm here with you. You're in the hospital but you're going to get better. I promise.'

All around silence, except for the machines. She wanted to scream and shake her mother. Rouse her.

'Mammy, please wake up.'

Nurse Kelly appeared silently at her shoulder, suggesting it would be better if Kate wait outside for the moment. She followed the nurse out, hanging the gown on a hook.

'Did you contact Maeve's other children?' the nurse asked.

'Yes, I left a message for my sister in London and I spoke to Romy in New York.'

'They realize the seriousness of your mother's condition!'

'I told them what my aunt said. I'll phone Moya again.'

'I'm sure you've done your best,' smiled the tall dark-haired nurse. 'You go and have a seat in the waiting room with your aunt and I promise to get you if you're needed. You'll be tired after the drive.'

'I'm bunched,' she admitted, feeling that every ounce of energy had drained out of her.

'A cup of tea'd do no harm. Your mother is in the best of hands.'

41

Aunt Vonnie sat pretending to read an old copy of *Image* magazine in the magnolia-painted room.

'Well what'd you think, Kate?'

'I don't know,' she admitted honestly. 'I just don't know. Do they think she's going to die?'

Her aunt's pale blue eyes welled with tears.

'I hope not,' she said firmly. 'Maeve's a fighter. She won't give up easily.'

'But they were saying about swelling in her brain, what does that mean?'

Her aunt shook her head. 'We must pray for her. Prayer is what's needed now. We must ask the Lord to spare her.'

Kate didn't know what to say. She hadn't the same faith or belief as her aunt.

'Would you like some tea or coffee?' she asked.

'A mug of tea would be grand, pet.'

In the far corner of the room there was a sink and an electric kettle, mugs and cups, spoons and plates, and an assortment of different types of teas and coffee, packets of biscuits and milk and sugar.

Kate was glad to busy herself, wiping around the sink with a cloth and cleaning the worktop.

Her aunt looked wretched, she thought, as she passed her the hot mug of tea. 'It must have been a shock for you finding Mammy like that,' she said.

'All I can say is thank God we'd arranged to meet for lunch and that I was so mad with her I drove over, otherwise God knows what would have happened!'

Kate couldn't help but feel the reprimand in her aunt's voice. Her mother lived on the outskirts of the town and if it wasn't for her friends and activities could go for days without seeing anyone.

'I'm so glad you were there,' she said, squeezing her aunt's hand.

Her mother would be lost without her older sister, the bond between them still strong.

'When I got to the house it was too quiet – you know your mother, she always has the radio or music blaring – then I found her. I thought she was dead at first. I came with her in the ambulance. Once we got here they all took over, but I kept talking to her. You know Maeve, she loves talk.'

'I don't know what we'd do without you, Aunt Vonnie. You and Mammy are so close.'

Her aunt took a packet of tissues from her bag and blew her nose. She looked absolutely exhausted, her face drawn, a ladder in her tights, and her pale blue and cream suit crumpled.

'Maybe you should go home for a while and have a rest,' Kate suggested gently. 'You've had such a shock today, and contacting me and the ambulance and everything.'

'Maybe you're right,' agreed her aunt, rubbing her eyes. 'I'm all done in.'

'I'll stay here with Mammy.'

'What did the girls say? Are they on their way?'

'I spoke to Romy, but,' she shrugged, 'I don't know.'

'This time she has to come home, Kate. Give me her phone number, I'll phone her when I get home and tell her to come immediately. Your mother needs her!'

'I know.'

'And what about Moya?'

'She's probably getting a flight. I don't know.'

'A mother needs her children around her at a time like this, and you girls should be together if anything were to happen.'

'Please, Aunt Vonnie, don't say that.'

Kate was too tired and upset to get into any kind of argument or deep discussion with her aunt, who was far too overwrought herself.

'There's a payphone outside the door. I'll go and phone Joe. I won't be long.'

A few minutes later her aunt reappeared. 'He's on his way. He's so good he'd already left to come and get me.'

Kate smiled. Her uncle was one of the nicest men put on the planet: caring and protective and still mad about her aunt after thirty years of marriage.

'He wants to look in on Maeve anyways. Maybe you should try Moya again?' Vonnie said.

'I'll use my mobile. I've got the number in that.'

'You'll have to go outside or downstairs where we came in to use it. There's signs everywhere here.'

Kate sighed. Her aunt wasn't going to give up on it. Getting up from the low, tweed-covered couch she made her way down in the lift and out past the night porter's desk to the automatic doors.

She redialled Romy's number. No answer. She didn't bother leaving a message. She went down through her address book and called Moya. The number rang and rang and was finally answered by her niece Fiona. Rock music pounded in the back-ground.

'Hi, Fiona. It's your Aunt Kate, is your mum there?'

'She's out.'

'Oh, is your dad there?'

'He's out too,' she said slowly. 'They're together.'

'Did your mum get the message I left earlier about Granny?'

'I don't know.'

Kate could almost hear the uninterest and confusion in the teenage voice.

'Listen, did she check her messages?'

She fell silent. It was no use.

'Fiona, I need to speak to your mum, urgently. Where is she? I need the number.'

She knew that Patrick would insist on privacy and not being disturbed, mobiles switched off, but that her sister was the type of mother who always left the number of where she was going pinned up somewhere in case her children needed her.

Her bet paid off. Minutes later she had the number. Dinner party or not, she didn't give a damn. She was phoning Moya and telling her to get herself home as soon as possible.

Chapter Three

The house in Ovington Gardens was warm, hot even, for the Mitchells always seemed to have the thermostat of their heating turned up and the boiler at full blast. A huge fire burned in the magnificent Adams fireplace and Moya Redmond thanked heaven that she was wearing a Synan O'Mahoney scooped-neck black-frilled top and figure-hugging black skirt, a classic with a little bit of oomph that she'd picked up the last time she'd visited Dublin. If she'd worn wool she'd have expired.

Patrick looked handsome as ever but a bit warm about the gills and she hoped by the time they sat down to eat that the men would be able to relieve themselves of their jackets. Why, even the champagne was warm!

Moya knew almost everybody at the dinner party so she should be able to relax and enjoy the night.

'Moya, don't tell me you're hiding yourself!' joked Hilary Mitchell their hostess, her plump face red with excitement.

She was fond of the older woman and hugged her warmly.

'I was wondering where you were.'

'I was just in the kitchen checking on things.'

They smiled, both knowing that checking on things meant checking on Poppy and Rachel Belling, the caterers. The girls ran a polished operation from a small shop on the corner of Granville Street, and with word-of-mouth recommendations now needed to be booked almost a month in advance.

'Everything is in hand and we should be ready to sit down and eat in about twenty minutes or so.'

Moya smiled. Ken Mitchell was a stickler for not eating too late, claiming it caused ulcers, and usually liked to entertain at home rather than in expensive restaurants.

'Have another glass of champagne,' insisted their host, topping up her glass. 'You look beautiful tonight, my dear, as always.'

He was a nice man but she wondered if he ever said such nice things to his wife. Patrick had worked with him in the busy accountancy firm for the past ten years, ever since they'd moved from Ireland.

'Thank you, Ken. You're looking pretty good yourself,' she joked.

He was a short, stocky man with a thatch of almost white hair and in a few weeks' time he would be sixty-five. He had announced his intention to retire from heavy practice work and vacate the position of head partner but would remain on as director.

'Hilary tells me that you are going to South Africa in a few months,' said Moya.

'Well we haven't seen Vanessa and her brood for almost two years so we reckon it's high time we made the trip to Cape Town. It's hard for her to get away now with the four kids.'

'Hilary's very excited about it.'

'To tell the truth so am I. We'll play a bit of golf, and Vanessa's organizing a safari trip for us to one of the big game parks. I haven't looked forward to anything so much for years. Retirement might be the best thing ever, it's now time to pass on the baton.'

She smiled. She could see it in his face. He'd worked hard for so many years building a huge practice and list of clients and had more than earned his time off. God knows how many missed dinners and good-night stories and school visits had happened under this roof, Hilary managing somehow to hold the family together. She glanced over to see her husband deep in conversation with Simon Clifford, the head of Tax.

Caroline Clifford looked bored, her mind somewhere else as she chatted with Ruth Taylor, Tom's wife.

She liked the Taylors and always found them good company. Their son Max was in the same school as Gavin, their twelve-year-old.

Moya walked over to join their conversation, Caroline excusing herself as they talked of the forthcoming Easter holidays and the school play.

'I'm going out to the terrace for a fag. Don't tell Simon where I've gone.' The tightly fitted black sheath dress made Caroline look like a tall whippet as she slipped through the terrace doors.

'How does she keep that figure?' sighed Ruth, enviously; she'd put on about two stone after her last baby and never managed to get it off. 'Do you think I should try smoking?'

'Don't be mad. Smoking would be bad for you and the kids.'

'I guess so.'

'You know so,' joked Moya.

There were two other couples due: Susan Owens their corporate finance specialist and her husband James who worked in stock-broking and Dudley Palmer and his wife. Moya loved meeting Eleanor Palmer; the sixty-year-old was a rather well-known crime writer and loved annoying her stuffy husband by regaling those around her with gruesome details of the crimes that the police were working on.

Another glass of champagne and Ken called them in for dinner. Moya was delighted to be sitting near Hilary and Tom. Patrick cast his eyes to heaven when he realized that he was sitting between Caroline and Ruth and would be expected to keep the peace. At least he was near enough to Ken to be included in his conversation, thought Moya. This dinner was more than just a cosy get-together of colleagues and wives. Patrick was convinced that Ken was taking his time and sussing out his future replacement.

'He wants to leave the place in good hands,' he'd told her on the way over. 'So remember, tonight is very important.'

Moya could sense her husband was tense and wished he would just relax and enjoy the easy company of those around him and forget office politics for one night. She smiled over at him, rotating her shoulders ever so slightly, which was her secret 'relax' signal.

The food was excellent, the girls working a treat as per usual. Hilary was at ease, knowing everything was in the capable hands of professionals as one course was served after another. Moya gave up worrying about Patrick and concentrated on enjoying the night. She was stressed and tired at the moment and a few hours of interesting conversation and a few glasses of red wine would no doubt work wonders.

There was a fillet of lamb with all the trimmings. Ken, not comfortable with newfangled fancy food, had insisted on a simple menu.

'The lamb is very good, Hilary, just perfect.'

She helped herself to baby new potatoes and minted peas and the carrot and parsnip bake, noting the men were enjoying the good food. There were roasted onions and a piping hot gravy, the smell making her realize just how hungry she really was.

The talk turned as usual to golf and holidays and property. Moya put on a smile, pretending she was interested as Simon and Caroline bragged on about the two new apartments they had just purchased as an investment.

'They should double their price over the

next ten years,' smirked Caroline.

'Think the property market's overheating, myself,' murmured Ken as he helped himself to more lamb. Moya felt like hugging him for his good sense.

The food and the wine worked and she felt relaxed and at ease, noticing Patrick ditch his jacket on the back of his chair as he unwound. Sometimes she forgot how handsome her husband was. Seeing him every day it was easy to take his six-foot-five-inch height and good looks for granted. It was only the reaction of other women to his sheer physical presence that reminded her. Looking around at all the other men, there was no competition. Patrick was just Patrick. He smiled at her and for an instant it was as if they were the only two at the table. He was a master at that – turning on the charm and making whatever female he had his eye on feel special. She had seen him do it so often and was conscious of the effect he had on women of all ages. Just because he was playing the adoring husband, faithful and true, in front of his colleagues, it meant nothing. She ignored him and turned her attention to Hilary who was asking about the children.

'I heard your eldest has just started in St Andrew's. How is he liking it?'

Moya flushed. Gavin going to an expensive private school so far from home was a bone of contention between herself and

Patrick. She would have preferred him to be educated at one of the good boys' schools close by.

'It's taking time, Hilary, but he's settling in,' interrupted Patrick. 'He played rugby last term and I think next term it will be cricket.'

'So he's sporty!'

'Look at your boys, how well they turned out,' he added. 'Gavin is very privileged to have been accepted by St Andrew's and, all going well, Danny will follow in his footsteps.'

Moya said nothing. She was the one who had dealt with Gavin's pleading to stay with his pals and not to move to a new school where he knew nobody. To her mind there wasn't the remotest chance of sending Danny, their youngest, there. Patrick had notions about what was the right and correct thing to do without taking their own family needs into consideration. He worked so hard – long hours in the office, after hours, at weekends, entertaining clients, touting for new business – that it was no wonder he was remote from the family, a distant father who expected to control things.

She was relieved when the dinner talk turned to the gory details of Eleanor's new book and the possibility of it being turned into a television series.

'That would be wonderful,' gushed Ruth,

who was a big fan.

'You never believe those film and TV types till the deal is done,' added Dudley.

'I was thinking I might be like Hitchcock and ask for a walk-on extra role,' teased Eleanor, deliberately. Poor Dudley cringed at the thought of his wife on TV. The rest of the dinner table was in absolute kinks of laughter.

'Don't mind her, Dudley,' soothed Hilary, knowing full well that her best friend was quite capable of such an eccentric request.

Moya secretly hoped she would as it would drive the senior partners in the firm crazy.

The plates were just being cleared when Moya was called to the phone.

She jumped up immediately and Poppy showed her to the phone in the hall. Out of politeness, all their mobiles had been either switched off or left at home and she prayed there wasn't some absolute calamity at home.

'Yes,' she said as she grabbed at the receiver.

'Moya, it's Kate. I've some bad news about Mum.'

She flushed. She hadn't spoken to her sister for an age and she leaned against the wood panelling as Kate told her about their mother.

'I'd left a message but you hadn't replied

so Fiona gave me your mobile number and the number of where you are. You are coming?'

'I'll get a flight as soon as I can and hire a car. You just stay with her, Kate, and I'll get there as soon as I can, promise.'

She closed her eyes, unbelieving, getting her breath and trying to think. She dialled the operator and got put straight through to the airline, the words tumbling out as she told them her situation. They could put her on the last flight from Heathrow to Dublin but she would have to be there in just over two hours and fifteen minutes. She booked it and stood trembling at the dining-room door. Patrick came out to join her.

'Is it the kids? What's happened? Is one of them sick?'

She shook her head.

'We have to leave right now. Mammy's in hospital, Kate says she's in intensive care, and they are doing everything they can to save her. I've got to go straight away, I can get a seat on the last Aer Lingus flight from Heathrow.'

'We can't just walk out on Hilary and Ken like that.'

'It's my mother, for God's sake!'

She could see it in his face. He was torn between staying at the party and getting her to the airport.

'You bastard!' she screamed at him. 'You

stay here if that's what you want but I'm going home to Ireland!'

Hilary and Ken appeared, and Moya quickly explained the situation. Hilary hugged her close.

'I remember the day I got word about my mother, Lord rest her. Ken and I drove to Scotland like two maniacs. No, you've got to go and get on that flight, get home as soon as you can.'

'I'm sorry for ruining your party,' she apologized.

'Don't even think like that, my dear,' insisted Ken. 'Family must come first.'

Three hours later she had boarded the flight, a small bag stuffed with essentials by her teenage daughter stored in the overhead rack. Moya closed her eyes and silently prayed.

Chapter Four

Romy stared at the ceiling, listening to the distant hum of traffic from Lexington and 57th Street below and the night sounds of the city as Greg lay snoring slightly beside her, his arm flung across her chest, his naked body close to hers. She stroked his skin: it was soft and warm and she loved the way he smelled. Wholesome and manly, he didn't douse himself with colognes and body sprays and deodorants like some of the guys she'd been with. He didn't need to. She pushed herself into the curve of his shoulder wishing she could snuggle there and drift into sleep. She needed to sleep, forget her aunt's call and the lonesome thought of her mother lying in a hospital bed. Going home was something she didn't even want to think about. Where did Kate and her Aunt Vonnie get off with telling her what to do!

Vonnie had even threatened never to speak to her again if she didn't fly home immediately. She'd had a bellyful of them all and the very thought of returning to Rossmore and seeing the Stone House where she'd grown up made her feel panicked and nervous. She had no wish to revisit that part of her life, and as far as she was concerned there was no going back.

Guilt tormented her as she tossed and turned, rebuking her, forcing her to confront the possibility of her mother dying without her presence. A sound of utter despair escaped from her.

'Hey, Romy, are you OK?'

She was too choked to speak, too wrapped up in her own misery.

'You're thinking about your mother.'

She nodded in the darkness.

He rolled over towards her, and Romy

was glad of his comforting warmth as she buried her face against his shoulder, wanting to erase the anxiety and dread within her.

'You know, I wasn't there when my dad died,' he confided. 'I was away at college when he had his heart attack.'

'That wasn't your fault!'

'I know, but they'd sent word to the dean. But, I'd skipped lectures that day. Took off with a few of the guys and was busy skirt-chasing and downing beers when my old man passed on. He'd been fit and healthy up till then.'

'You being there wouldn't have changed a thing,' she reasoned. 'Not a thing.'

'I know, but sometimes I wonder if there was something he might have wanted to say to me, I can't help myself.'

'Don't beat yourself up over it,' she argued.

'Yeah well I sure know about it now. Tom and Julia are always on about it! They get to recall the way he looked and the last thing he said to them. It still cuts me up.'

'You're a big softie. Anyways, families are different. My mother's unconscious. She probably won't know who's there or not, and me turning up might even make things worse.'

In the near darkness she could feel his eyes on her.

'Romy, you don't believe that's true.'

'Just leave me alone. This is my family, my problem! Keep out of it!'

'OK. Message received loud and clear. But I want to say something, based on my experience. I'm just warning you that you might regret it, that's all.'

She lay beside him fuming at his daring to interfere in her life. Just because they were lovers he had no right to tell her how to live her life and what to do. None!

They lay in silence beside each other. After a few minutes, Greg rolled over on his side and turned his back to her.

'You have it your way, then.'

She didn't want to get into another argument with him. She just wanted peace and quiet for now and passion and good sex and the feel of his body beside hers later. She liked the nights he stayed over and made the effort to be a part of her life; they could pretend to be a couple. She knew not to expect much, make demands. He had the office, the ongoing acrimonious divorce from Jen, and his kids. She came in somewhere after those three. She had her own life, her own friends and interests and had made room for him, given space to a relationship that might happen if she didn't push too hard.

Greg had been upfront with her, telling her he'd had enough of tears and histrionics and wanted 'something easy'. Easy – that was sure something she was good at!

Diana had had a go at her too this afternoon in the studio, telling her to take a cab to JFK and buy a flight home immediately. Perhaps she should have listened to her friend, instead of lying here in the dark thinking about her mother, the smell of her skin, and the way she laughed at silly things. Maybe it was only a machine that was keeping the breath in her body now. She remembered the way her mother used to hug and dress her and tickle her until she'd nearly wet her pants. Hot tears scalded her eyes as she lay in bed thinking of her as night slipped to day.

'I can get a cab,' she insisted.

'I'll drive you,' offered Greg, pulling on his shirt and tie.

'What about the office?'

'What about them? I'm paying enough they can manage without me for an hour or two!'

She felt shaky with relief as he grabbed her bag and toted it downstairs then flung it on the back seat of his car, holding the front passenger door open for her. Awake at 3 a.m. she had gone online and booked a flight to Dublin, almost instantly regretting the impulsive act but determined not to change her mind.

'Will you make sure that Diana takes the cat?'

'Yeah, sure.'

'And you'll notify the landlord to keep an eye on the place.'

'It's done.'

She fiddled with her purse, nervous as they drove through Manhattan and out towards JFK. Greg, frowning, concentrated on the traffic as they passed through the toll booth. He looked tired. She guessed neither of them had got much sleep and when they yawned in unison he took her hand.

'You'll sleep on the flight.'

She usually didn't as she ended up in conversations with her fellow passengers or got glued to the in-flight movie or whatever book she was reading, but today was different. Today she wanted to arrive calm and relaxed, in control of her feelings.

'Ask the hostess for a blanket and pillow,' he suggested, 'and try a nap.'

She gritted her teeth. She had flown to every continent in the globe, worked in many countries and had clocked up far more air miles than most.

'What about you?' she asked.

He shrugged, cursing under his breath as an old lady in an ancient Volvo pulled out in front of them. 'I've too much on today and it's my night for Amy and Jack.'

Romy tried to smile.

He was obsessive about his nights with his kids, over the top doing things with them, bringing them to new places, in a constant quest for fun and entertainment as if that would cover up the massive split in their family. Meeting Greg Anderson had been great, he was fun and loving and good company, but from the beginning he had been quite clear about his level of commitment and his family obligations. Over the past five months Romy had managed to steer clear of letting herself fall totally in love with him, knowing that as usual her timing was out. She always seemed to meet either the wrong men or the right man at the wrong time! Greg definitely could have been a Mr Right. But she knew, looking at him, that in a few hours' time, wrapped up with his children and involved at work, she and her troubles would disappear from his busy mind.

At the airport he offered to come with her to the Aer Lingus check-in desk.

'Just drop me off outside,' she said.

Romy had her big backpack, stuffed with clothes and a few essentials, and a small holdall. She always liked to travel light.

His lips brushed hers as they kissed goodbye. He tasted of coffee and toast and she lingered for a few minutes enjoying the physical pleasure of his mouth on hers as the airport security man came to move him along.

'I'm going!' he yelled at the uniformed figure as she grabbed her things and jumped out of the car. 'Have a safe trip and I hope your mom's going to be OK.'

'Thanks, Greg.'

She knew he meant it, for underneath it all he was a thoughtful, old-fashioned, rather decent type of guy. Saying goodbye to him she wondered if their relationship would even manage to survive the separation of her return trip to Ireland, as she pushed her way through the busy terminal building.

Chapter Five

Kate dozed uneasily in the hospital waiting room, frightened to let herself sleep, her muscles tense as she waited for news of her mother's condition. She was woken by the arrival of her older sister, who stood for a second staring at her, awkward and tense, both of them unsure how to react, before flinging themselves into each other's arms and clinging together. Kate was comforted by the smell of her sister's expensive perfume and face creams and familiar lemon-scented shampoo.

'How is she?' asked Moya.

'She's on a ventilator to help her breathe

and her condition is unstable.'

'Oh, God! I don't believe it. I only talked to her about five days ago, stupid things, rabbiting on about the kids and she seemed so well.'

'She was. They think it's a sudden massive haemorrhage to her brain or a stroke. They'll do more tests in the morning to see.'

'Can I go and see her?'

'Come on, the nurse is down at the nurses' station, she'll take you in to her.'

The staff nurse led the two of them through the hush of the intensive care unit to their mother's bed. Moya was anxious.

'God, she looks so different. Mammy, it's Moya, I'm here.'

Kate tried to control herself, surprised by the intense relief she felt knowing that her sister was beside her.

'She's unconscious and there is some oedema present but she has had some sedation,' explained the nurse.

'Will she pull through this?' questioned Moya, touching her mother's arm.

'Your mother is critically ill at present and is being supported. It would be wrong of me to try to guess the outcome. Dr Healy will be here in the morning and he should be able to give you a better assessment of her condition.'

'God! Look at her, Kate, hooked up to machines and monitors. She'd hate it!'

'It's keeping her alive, Moya, helping her.'

'I can't believe it – collapsed in the garden! If Vonnie hadn't found her what would we have done? I feel so guilty living so far away.'

'Well you're here now,' sighed Kate. 'That's all that matters.'

'When you phoned we were at a big dinner party. Very important for Patrick.'

Kate bit her lip. Her sister's life was very different from hers, busy with her children, her pet project – the gallery she helped out in – and a constant round of dinner parties, supper parties and balls – all part of the social scene that being the wife of a senior partner in the corporate finance section of a large accountancy firm involved.

'Patrick was being utterly stupid about me leaving, but I managed to get a seat on the last London flight into Dublin. The poor man on the Hertz desk in the airport must have thought I was a lunatic as I flung my Visa card at him getting the rental car! Then I drove like a crazy person.'

'Thanks.'

'Is Romy coming home?'

'I doubt it.'

'She's so screwed up! Imagine not coming to see your mother.'

The hours crawled by. They took it in turns to sleep, the hospital stirring as porters, cleaners and nurses began another shift. Dr Healy was vague and pessimistic, waiting for the results of tests. Aunt Vonnie returned in the morning and insisted they eat something and have a sleep in the relations' room.

'Your mother's not going to get any better by one of you collapsing with exhaustion.'

Kate yawned; her eyes were sore and she was stiff from sitting still, doing nothing, watching her mother lying silent surrounded by the whooshing of machines, the nurse constantly checking her monitor. Minutes and hours meant nothing in this time-frozen world.

'You two go and have a hot drink and something to eat,' urged their aunt. 'I'll stay here in the waiting room.'

Moya and Kate went downstairs to the hospital's small canteen while the consultant and nurses checked their mother. As she sat opposite Moya at the small table, surrounded by hospital staff and visitors, over two mugs of creamy coffee and a toasted bacon sandwich, Kate realized that, despite being sisters, they had little to say to each other. She asked about her niece and nephews, avoiding any mention of her brother-in-law. Enthusing about Molly's new crèche and how well she had settled in, she suspected Moya disapproved of her working full time and being a single mother.

Despite looking tired, with grey shadows

under her eyes, her sister still managed to look beautiful, with her black, shoulder-length hair, and her dark smoky eyes like two smudges in the porcelain face. Her trim figure was encased in simple black trousers and a matching polo-neck. Kate swallowed a pang of envy as she watched two or three of the senior doctors stare over in her sister's direction; Moya was barely aware of the attention.

'Kate, are you listening to me?'

'Sorry, I can't even think at the moment.'

'I was just saying how long do you think Mammy will be like this?'

Kate shrugged. She had absolutely no idea and the medical team were very noncommittal every time she tried to talk to them.

'I can't stand it, seeing her the way she is. I just want her to be well and back to normal again.'

Kate felt like shaking her! Moya always wanted everything to be perfect, hated things not to be right, to be messy, broken.

'You realize if Mammy survives this, she might never be right. She's already paralysed, we've no idea what damage the haemorrhage has done.'

'Oh God, you are such a pessimist!'

'Moya, I'm not arguing with you, d'ye hear. Our mother is fighting for her life, that's what we've got to think of now. The rest we'll cope with later.'

Kate could feel every muscle in her body clenched tight with anxiety. Moya only meant her best, she knew that deep down, it was just her own stupid animosity that kicked in whenever they were around each other.

'We'd better get back down,' she suggested, ignoring her sister's calm, unflinching gaze.

The corridors were busy with visitors and staff, and they both quickened their step as they approached St Michael's intensive care ward.

'I know you hadn't been expecting your sister to arrive,' smiled Nurse Kelly, approaching them, 'but she's in with your mother now.'

For a second they stood together, silent, almost at one with their thoughts.

'She's just flown in and is jet-lagged, but at least she's here.'

'Thank God,' murmured Moya.

It's like the return of the flipping Prodigal! thought Kate, bracing herself to see her younger sister.

Romy stood beside the high narrow bed with its chemical smell and tubes and monitors, trying to quell her feelings of nausea and panic, as she stared at the figure of her mother. It was worse than she had imagined.

'She's unconscious,' explained the young nurse, 'and quite heavily sedated.'

This old woman lying as if deeply asleep, her hairline grey, her skin more lined, her eyes closed, was so changed from what she remembered. Her mother had never seemed old, never seemed frail before.

'Mammy, it's Romy. I've come home to you.'

No response. It wasn't as she'd imagined, like the scenario she had replayed in her head over and over again. There was no big wave of emotion, no torrent, just the sense of recognition and deep, deep regret.

'Mammy,' she said, kissing the cool forehead.

Kate and Moya stared at their sister, taking in the tall rangy figure in the denim jeans and white embroidered shirt, strawberry blond hair tumbling to her shoulders as she leaned over their mother. The last time they had seen her she had been pale and washed-out looking, eyes lined with black kohl, with heavy white makeup and dark lipstick, a lanky Goth kid with wild unwashed hair that she wore with an awful headband. Desperate and secretive, she had lied and tricked the two of them to get money out of them to run away. Now she was different, thought Kate. She was beautiful, stunning! Not in the same way as Moya, who was a classic beauty, but

Romy was striking. She had a look of her own, her skin glowing, her long body lean and tanned, her hair glossy and wild. Heavy silver earrings dangled from her ears, and one wrist and most of her fingers were covered in unusual pieces of silverwork. No wedding or diamond ring visible. She looked up at them both, blue eyes apprehensive as they approached.

'Romy, you're all grown up!' Moya blurted out. 'I can't believe it.'

'About time,' murmured Romy, awkward. '*You* haven't changed, Moya. You'd never believe you have three kids.'

'God, well you have totally changed, Romy. For the better! I can't wait till Mammy sees you!'

Kate didn't know what to say. She was still angry, remembering their phone call, and wondered what had made her sister change her mind. It didn't matter really. The most important thing was that she had got on a plane and come home. This was no time for recriminations or rows. For once they had to try and pull together for their mother's sake.

'I'm glad you're home,' she said.

'You were right, Kate. I had to come,' admitted Romy. 'Had to see her.'

The three sisters stood around their mother's bed, for the first time in a very long time together, united.

Mammy would be pleased to see us like this, thought Kate, wondering how it was that the three of them had grown up in the Stone House, shared the same childhood memories of Rossmore and yet somehow had let the relationship between them sour; the bond of sisterhood had managed to be stretched so tight that it was almost broken.

Romy held her mother's hand, overwhelmed as she remembered the times before everything changed and, wild and troubled, she had run away.

Chapter Six

ROSSMORE 1984

Romy ran and ran, racing all the way to the Strand ahead of her mother and sisters, who were a right crowd of slowcoaches carrying the rug and towels and the big yellow and white beach bag. She had only her bucket and spade as she flew across the grassy sandbank towards the sea.

Impatient she threw off her T-shirt and shorts and knickers and chased to the water, feeling the sand and stones run through her toes and the water lap against her skin. Her mother beckoned frantically for her to come back and get changed into her togs like her sisters. But impatient and excited she ignored her, jumping in just the way she was.

'Why don't you ever do what Mammy tells you?' Moya gave out, swimming out near her in her pink and white striped swimsuit.

'She's so stupid!' jeered Kate. 'Naked, skinny dipping!'

She had filled her mouth with sea water and spurted it at her sisters, splashing them by kicking her legs till they left her to duck and dive and swim on her own. Drying off later by lying on the sand in the sun and pretending she was a mermaid.

They were lucky, that's what her daddy always said, living in the big old house overlooking the secluded Strand, while all the summer visitors to Rossmore had to drive their cars or cycle for miles or get the train from Dublin to get to the beach. They fought for space for their deckchairs and rugs and towels on the crowded cove beach, skin turning pink, queuing for the public toilet while her family practically had the Strand to themselves.

Hungry, she trailed back to sit with them when her mother produced tomato sand-wiches and a packet of Goldgrain biscuits for lunch. She poured herself a cup of warm Mi-Wadi orange squash from the bottle in her mother's bag.

After lunch her mother dozed, lying on one side while Moya studiously ignored her and perfected her tan and Kate lay on her stomach reading a book. Bored ten-year-old Romy grabbed her bucket and spade and began to dig. Brian O'Grady had told her if you dug deep enough you would find treasure or eventually get to Australia.

Her father surprised them at three o'clock, arriving down, white shirt sleeves rolled up, sporting his grey summer trousers. He bent down and admired her handiwork.

'Romy, that's some hole you're digging. Foundations, is it?'

'I'm digging to Australia,' she retorted, 'to see the kangaroos and the koala bears.'

'Well you'll have to dig a bit deeper then,' he joked, not offering to help as he walked over to join their mother on the rug. He wasn't much of a one for the beach and although he sometimes wore a pair of big wine-coloured swimming togs, Romy had never seen him swim.

'Anyone for ice-cream?' he'd offered half an hour later.

Hot and sweaty from digging Romy had jumped up and volunteered to go with him as the others gave their orders, slipping her hand into his as they went back across the beach. He jingled the coins in his pocket as they walked along the roadway to Sissy

Sullivan's, the neighbour who lived closest to the Strand and sold ice-pops and choc-ices and Golly Bars from a big fridge in her porch. An ice-cream banner and an Irish flag hung over her front door.

'Four choc-ices, one Golly Bar and a bottle of red lemonade,' said her father. 'Did I ever tell you I was standing in line to buy ice-cream and a red lemonade at the Palace Dance Hall in Tramore when I first met your mother?'

'What kind of ice-cream?' she asked, curious.

'Choc-ice. I got talking to two lovely girls, sisters, and ended up buying them a choc-ice each. Afterwards I asked the small pretty one, Maeve, up to dance with me. And as they say, the rest is history.'

Romy liked the way he told stories and explained things and let her ride in the car with him when he was working. She loved her mammy and sisters but sometimes maybe she loved her daddy more.

'Race you back!' she dared him, grabbing two ices and her own creamy Golly Bar, screaming with excitement as he pretended to chase her back.

The week before Christmas their mother told them she was expecting a baby. 'Isn't it lovely news for the Christmas?' she smiled, her face pale and strained.

'Everything's going to change,' Romy blurted out, flinging herself in her mother's lap and burrowing into her.

'Well, naturally it will a bit,' laughed their mother. 'I'm sure things were different for Moya and Kate when I first brought you home from the hospital! But having another little person in the house to love is going to be wonderful.'

Moya had sat in the middle of Christmas lights, tinsel and ornaments, not believing. How could it be that her middle-aged mother was announcing she was pregnant? It was the most mortifying, disgusting thing she'd ever heard of. What would Cora and Niamh and all her friends think when this news got out? God, how had she not noticed the swollen stomach, the full breasts, and her mother's recent constant complaints about being tired? She had just presumed her mother was getting fat, or getting the change like their neighbour Mrs Costigan, who kept forgetting things and had locked herself out of the house only a week ago.

'Are you sure?' was about all she could manage.

'Of course,' laughed her mother, patting her stomach.

Moya couldn't believe her youngest sister's instant and honest assessment of the appalling situation they were in.

'I know I'm no young chick but you're all

getting so big that I know I'll have loads of helpers this time with the nappies and the bottles and changing and bathing the baby.'

'Mammy, I think it's wonderful news!' said Kate firmly.

Moya had to at least pretend to be happy for their mother's sake. 'It's great, honest. You and Daddy must be thrilled,' she said.

'Your father is over the moon about it.'

'If it's a girl can I name her?' begged Romy.

'It's not a kitten or a doll,' Kate said protectively.

'We'll just have to wait and see what your little brother or sister is like.'

Frank Dillon told everyone who came to the Stone House over the Christmas the good news about the expected arrival of another young Dillon.

'There's still lead in the pencil,' he'd joke as he offered glasses of whiskey and gin and beer to everyone who crossed the threshold.

Moya tried to banish the cringe-making thought of her mother and father doing it in the big bed upstairs.

'Don't mind your dad, Moya pet,' Aunt Vonnie consoled, seeing her embarrassment. 'Frank's just so excited about another baby, that's all.'

'There'll be another Dillon to carry on the family name,' he boasted.

'He thinks it's going to be a boy,' she confessed worriedly to her aunt. 'What will he do if it's another girl?'

'He'll thank God for another beautiful daughter who is almost as nice as her three sisters.'

Moya blushed. How could she be so insensitive? Aunt Vonnie and Uncle Joe had four boys – Neil, Conor, Fergus and Liam. Maybe they had wanted a girl.

'Naturally Joe and I would have loved to have had a little girl but to tell the truth I don't know how one would have survived in our household with all the men talk and sport and football and old GAA guff that goes on! That's why I love coming over here to you lot for all the tears and tantrums and stories. Why do men never know any good stories or gossip?' she pondered.

Moya laughed.

'Anyways I wouldn't be without my boys for the world.'

'I'd better help passing round the smoked salmon and brown bread,' Moya said as her aunt and mother sat down together chatting, heads together.

A month before the baby was due Maeve Dillon was brought into hospital as her blood pressure had gone through the roof and she needed total bed rest. Their father arranged for a local woman, Mary Dwyer, to come in and give a hand with the housework and ironing and to cook their dinner when they came in from school. Wearing a selection of ancient Aran cardigans and a brown tweed skirt she'd sit for hours watching the TV or doing the crossword in the daily paper, her huge body wedged in the armchair as one of her meat and potato concoctions bubbled on the cooker.

'She smells of BO,' complained Romy who was collected from school by her.

'Shush,' hissed Kate, who hated the disruption and the boiled potatoes and was trying to work on her science project, disappearing to her room as soon as she'd eaten.

Moya took it on herself to scrub and clean the kitchen with Jif every night.

'You're cracked,' jeered Romy.

Two and a half weeks later all the worry and waiting was ended when Sean Francis Dillon was born, weighing in at five pounds and seven ounces.

Looking at their new brother in the little crib beside their mother's bed in the maternity ward, they all agreed he looked tiny, with his baldy head and snub nose and wizened expression. Five days later their mother brought him home.

Sean was small, but his crying was loud enough to be heard all over the house, their mother dropping whatever she was doing to attend to him.

He was a poor feeder and after two weeks of his fussing and crying and not gaining any weight their mother had reverted to using a bottle and formula to feed him.

And as Romy had predicted everything did change. Her position as the baby, the youngest in the house, was usurped as she became 'Sean's sister'. The house was organized around the tiny person who slept in the small bedroom beside their parents' room. Maeve Dillon, unwilling to leave him till he got a bit bigger and put on weight, contented herself with staying home. Their father deserted his usual after-work pints and dinners and late-night meetings, coming home to join them for tea, checking on his son and lifting him up in his arms and parading him around the house.

The girls were bewildered by his intense affection for Sean and the havoc created by such a tiny mite. However, over the weeks they each grew to love their small brother with a similar intensity.

Chapter Seven

'Smile, girls!' coaxed their mother, looking through the camera lens as they stood at the front door step in their school uniforms. The morning sun glimmered over Rossmore's village and harbour, making them squint and fidget as the light flashed through the trees in the driveway.

'Try to look happy. It's a big occasion, Romy starting secondary school.'

'We'll be late on our very first day back,' worried Kate, glancing at her wrist-watch. 'Romy, for heaven's sake put your chin up and stop messing.'

Moya tilted her head in the bright September sunlight, pulling in her stomach and putting a wide smile on her face. She couldn't wait to be finished with this awful uniform, her last year in school over, adulthood beckoning. Poor old Romy, only starting in the convent and having Mrs Cusack as her First Year head!

'Come on, smile! You look lovely!'

Moya didn't think anyone would ever believe they were sisters, they all were so different except up close around their full lower lips and the wide spacing of their varied coloured eyes. She hoped to God Romy wouldn't be depending on her to mind her as she wasn't having a first-year trailing around the school corridors after her.

'That's it!' Maeve smiled, putting down the camera. 'A perfect photo of my three beautiful daughters.'

Romy looked all wired up, pale under her freckles and nervous. Her uniform skirt was too big and too long, right down to her knees as her mother had insisted on allowing space for growing. She had Kate's outgrown jumper and a crisp new white shirt and an impressively huge new school-bag, which weighed a ton.

Cora and Ciara had been standing patiently at the gate waiting for them during their mother's shenanigans with the camera.

'Morning, girls,' yoohooed Maeve, waving to them. Cora felt relieved that their mother never bothered taking the family camera from out of the kitchen cabinet where it had been thrown a few years ago. 'Doesn't Romy look wonderful – a real St Dominic's girl!'

Moya wished her mother wouldn't make such a big thing over an everyday occurrence. She grabbed Romy, pushing her towards the gate.

'Now you two remember to look out for your sister and help her if she needs it and Romy, I'll be waiting to hear how you got on.'

As the autumn days got shorter Maeve Dillon pushed the buggy through the falling leaves and around Rossmore, baby Sean, snug in a cosy zip-up pram suit, complimented and admired by all who knew her. He had lost the delicate look and was becoming a smaller sturdy version of his father. She was still tired with the lack of sleep and night feeding but at long last felt she had turned the corner and despite her age was enjoying motherhood again. Her sister Vonnie had been on to her about going to Dublin to do a bit of shopping.

'Come on, Maeve, you haven't a stitch of clothes for the winter! You know Brendan Butler will invite you and Frank to the Fianna Fáil fundraiser, and then you've got the Council's dinner dance. What are you going to wear to them? Buying a few new things will give you a boost and besides, I want to go to Dublin to get a new coat and a pair of winter boots for myself.'

'What about the baby?'

'Maeve, we're not trucking the baby with us. When was the last time you had a day out on your own? Think of yourself, for a change! Frank and the girls will be well able to mind him.'

It was tempting, the thought of a day away, shopping, trying on shoes, getting some new make-up, seeing the latest style.

'We'll treat ourselves to lunch in Mitchell's. What do you say?'

Maeve could feel the smile spread all over her face as she said, 'Yes, please.'

Moya looked at the list her mother had left: times for bottles, instructions for changing, teething gel, and what to feed the baby with at lunchtime and at teatime. It looked easy enough. Sean was getting to be such a good baby that he was no bother at all. He had a touch of a snuffly cold so her mother had expressly forbidden her to take him out for a walk.

'I'm going out,' called her father, grabbing his car keys. 'I've got to see Ray O'Carroll about the few outhouses and acres he wants to sell between here and Woodstown.'

'Daddy, you promised to stay home and help with the baby.'

'Listen, I won't be too long. I'll have to have coffee and a chat with him. It's a site with good potential and Martin and I feel if we got the right planning permission through we could build about a dozen houses on it.'

'Can I go with you?' pleaded Romy, getting up to follow him.

'Not today, pet. You stay home with your sisters and help mind the baby.'

Annoyed, Romy flounced out of the room as Frank Dillon left.

Moya was intent on trying to tidy her bedroom and create a study zone as Sister Breda
had advised them, clearing a place for notes
and revision and a study planner. Getting rid
of the clutter of old shoeboxes and little
baskets of old Rimmel and Revlon and 17
make-up, and the collection of stuffed dolls
and teddies she had grown out of, would
certainly help create a bit more space. Romy
could choose from them as she was into that
sort of stuff now. First she'd dust them off
and clean them up so they'd look more
appealing to her younger sister.

Kate interrupted her an hour later, calling
her to come downstairs to the kitchen quick.
'Wait till you see what Romy's done.'

The two sisters stood in utter disbelief at
the kitchen door as they surveyed the mess
and the crestfallen expression on their dog
Lucky's face.

'Christ Almighty, what have you done?'
roared Moya, taking in the damage, the wet
floor, the spilt shampoo and soaked towels
and the clumps of wet dog hair scattered
everywhere.

'His hair had got too long!' she argued.
'Mammy wouldn't bring him to Monica to
get cut because she was too tired and too
busy so I decided–'

'To do it yourself,' Kate and Moya said in
unison.

'Yes,' she admitted. 'But he kept moving

and trying to get away from me. He has far too much hair.'

Not any more, thought Moya. The poor dog looked like he'd been attacked by some mad thing, with hair and fur missing all over the place, a large bald patch on one side and one leg almost devoid of hair. His face looked lopsided, which gave him a totally different expression.

'Poor Lucky,' said Kate, running to hug him and almost slipping on the floor.

'You have the dog and the place destroyed,' threatened Moya. 'Just wait till Mammy and Daddy get back and see what you've done. You'll be in right trouble.'

'I was bored,' she muttered. 'I had to do something.'

'Well then, you won't be so bored as you'll have to get the mop and the big brush, and the brush and pan and give us a hand with cleaning this place up, and taking up all the flipping dog hair.'

It took three-quarters of an hour to restore the kitchen to a reasonable state, Moya hiding away her mother's large kitchen scissors.

'I'm starving,' murmured an unrepentant Romy, slouching onto a kitchen chair. Moya put on some tinned tomato soup and toast for them, realizing the time and that the baby was due his lunch more than an hour ago. She didn't want him sleeping all afternoon so she decided it was better to wake him.

The moment she reached the top of the stairs, she sensed it. Something was wrong. The fraction of a second it took to cross the doorway and see the small still figure in the cot, she knew. The memory of it would stay with her for ever.

She lifted him up immediately and tried to rouse him, shaking him, listening to his chest but knowing by the cold touch of his skin and the obstinately closed eyes and calm expression on his face that her small brother had stopped breathing.

She screamed and screamed for Kate and her sister galloped up the stairs to help her. All three of them were screaming and shouting at each other, panicked, disbelieving, useless in their attempts to revive him as his heart had stopped beating.

Kate ran and phoned for the ambulance and for Dr Deegan. Moya, shocked, sat holding him in her lap till they came, praying that they could somehow resuscitate him.

The family doctor gently took Sean and laid him on the bed to examine him.

'It's nobody's fault,' he assured her. 'It's what we call a cot death. He must have died a few hours ago. There's no explanation or reason for it. Babies sometimes fall asleep and forget to breathe or wake up. There's nothing you or anyone could have done.'

It didn't matter what the doctor said.

Moya had no doubt in her mind that in some way she was partly responsible for what happened. If she hadn't been distracted, tidying her room, dealing with Romy, her little brother might still be alive.

Mrs Costigan came across and brought them over to her house while Uncle Joe and Dr Deegan waited to tell the news to their parents.

Sometimes Moya found it hard to remember the church and the funeral and all the cards and flowers from the people of Rossmore, and their family friends and her father's business acquaintances and all the girls in school, the walking in the gusting wind afterwards to the place where they buried baby Sean aged only nine months and eleven days and the people back in their house afterwards drinking wine and whiskey and saying what a good baby he'd been.

The impact of their small brother's life and death was immeasurable, for none of them could or would ever forget him. Their mother had cried and cried, a torrent of tears, eyes swollen in her puffed face until her eyes were so dry and red and sore, they could produce no more tears. She stayed in bed, lost in her misery, often forgetting to get dressed or to wash her hair. For months she took tablets to make her sleep and then tablets to make her wake up, Aunt Vonnie the only one who could seem to reach her.

Moya still blamed herself. She was seventeen, the eldest, and had been in charge; over and over again she repeated the pattern of that day once her mother had left the house – her father's going off on business, her attempts to follow what Sister Breda had suggested, and Romy's crazy attempt to cut the dog's hair.

'I shouldn't have left him,' was her mother's constant refrain as she pretended that Moya had done nothing wrong, saying only, 'We have to accept it was God's will.'

Maeve Dillon found some consolation in prayer and mass-going and attending novenas and prayer meetings.

Kate said that God was a bastard and were there not enough old people dying in the world and starving children in Ethiopia and round the world to do him without taking little Sean?

At night lying in their beds they couldn't help but overhear their father pleading with their mother to come and lie with him and give him another child, but Maeve Dillon firmly closed the door on him. Months later she moved into Sean's old room, leaving their father to sleep in the big bed on his own.

Their father was lost and lonesome, and soon reverted to his old ways, staying out late, going to meetings arranged in local bars and pubs and hotels and coming home late smelling of drink. Moya hated it when he began to cry and talk of 'the little fella' and what might have been.

'You know you still have us, Daddy,' she'd gently try to remind him as she made him tea and scrambled eggs on toast.

'Moya girl, you'd not understand what it feels like for a man to lose his son,' was all he'd say, staring into the bottom of the blue and white mug. Moya pitied him. Witnessing his raging grief, she felt that she was partly to blame for what had happened and the awful sadness that Sean's death had caused.

Chapter Eight

The summer of the wasps was one all of them would remember. Instead of their parents coming together in their grief and sorrow, a gaping void of anger, blame and coldness had grown between them as Maeve and Frank Dillon went through the day-to-day small family rituals unable to comfort or be kind to each other.

Moya distanced herself, as she studied for her Leaving Certificate, closing her bedroom door as she focused on French and

English and Art, losing herself in the works of the Renaissance artists, Michelangelo, Raphael and Donatello. Kate knew that Moya still blamed herself for what had happened, that no matter what anyone had said, she still considered herself a part of the domino-like chain of awful events that resulted in her small brother's death.

Her mother visited Dr Deegan every few weeks and was on small yellow pills that calmed her and helped her to sleep and bury the rage that still engulfed her from time to time. Aunt Vonnie patiently listened to her talk and encouraged her to go for walks and drives and get some fresh air as she began to take tentative steps back to normal life. Their father, withdrawing from family life, lost himself in projects, developing the Old Mill, putting in a tender to bid for building a new area health clinic, and investing in a raft of businesses, including shares in a racehorse.

'He's gambling and drinking and never home,' their mother complained. 'He won't even sit in a room and talk to me.'

Kate sensed her father's fear that, if he did sit down to talk about little Sean and how he felt, like a tall tree he might topple over and end up on the same yellow pills from Dr Deegan that her mother was on.

'Men always feel they have to be strong, and bottle things up,' Aunt Vonnie said, shaking her head. 'It does them no bloody good, but they do it anyway. Joe's the exact same!'

July was sweltering hot. Romy, wanting to stay out till midnight and hang around the town like a stray, was packed off to Connemara to Irish college with three friends.

'It's not fair,' she'd complained. 'My Irish is crap and I won't be able to speak to anyone for nearly a month.'

'That's why you're going,' insisted Maeve, as she packed Romy's underwear and spare jeans and a rain jacket into the navy suitcase. 'Living and talking constantly with the other students and going to the classes is bound to improve it. Besides, you'll enjoy yourself.'

'You'll have a great time,' promised Kate. 'I loved the Gaeltacht and the ceilis at night are great crack!'

'And good kissing practice,' confided Moya. 'That's where I met my first boyfriend.'

'I suppose,' agreed Romy. 'Anyways it'd be good to get away from this morgue of a place.'

'Don't let Mammy and Daddy hear you say that!'

'Why not? It's the truth!'

The South-East basked in glorious summer weather. Rossmore's holiday cottages and hotels were packed with visitors, the beach and cove crowded with families in swimsuits and shorts sunbathing and jumping in the sea. Most mornings Maeve Dillon walked down to the church to ten o'clock mass, going into the graveyard to say prayers on her way back. It was the routine of some of the elderly and the widows of the parish. Kate wondered why her mother had opted to join them. At home, she donned a sloppy T-shirt and a pair of beige trousers and spent the day in the garden, weeding, tidying, planting and pruning. The garden was a myriad colours and shapes, climbing full-headed roses tumbling from the walls as delphiniums and lupins burst from the flowerbeds. She broke for lunch, which was salad and brown bread served on the round wrought-iron table on the patio, even for visitors. Kate helped by mowing the lawn and at night hosing the garden and watering the parched plants. Moya refused to get her fingers and nails dirty with garden work.

John Joe, the local handyman had been down to the house removing a wasps' nest from the overhead beam at the corner of the french windows, and had spotted another one hanging from the eaves above Romy's window.

"Tis the heat, Mrs Dillon, has brought them all out this year. I've never seen the like of it. McHugh's discovered one in an air vent for the pub and sent one of the young barmen up on the ladder to try to do it. Drove the wasps crazy! And Cyril McHugh had to stand two rounds of free drinks for the customers after the swarm invaded the place. There was even one under the deck in the tennis club. They're bloody everywhere!'

'Well you just get rid of it safely, John-Joe, before my daughter comes back,' she instructed.

As the heat wave continued Kate swam and played tennis in the evenings with a few school friends. As often as she could she went sailing with Uncle Joe and the boys, who kept a small yacht moored off the pier. Lying in the grass half dozing and reading she watched lazily as her mother set to with the secateurs on an overgrown pyracantha bush in the corner of the garden, clearing away branches, and the undergrowth. Moya, spreadeagled, lay in the full sun in a tiny bikini trying to tan herself.

She remembered the heat and the haze and her mother's sudden *'Oh!'* of surprise as the paper-like rugby ball shape tumbled from a spiky overhead branch, floating for a second before splitting and shattering in the air, the wasps flying in every direction, falling on her mother's hair and head and face and covering her bare arms as she frantically tried to brush them off her. Moya jumped up screaming, wrapping the towel she was lying on around herself as Kate flayed uselessly at the wasps with the cushion she'd been sitting on, her mother screaming trying to escape them.

The wasps moved *en masse*, clinging to her skin, the buzzing loud in the still summer air as her mother screeched and yelled. Kate grabbed the towel off Moya and whacked crazily at them, desperate to get them off their mother, ignoring the stings on her own hand as she tried to knock them off with the towel.

'Get the hose or a bucket of water!' she shouted.

Moya raced back with the hose, then rushed to the kitchen door to turn on the tap, as Kate sprayed her mother with the water, the force managing to loosen some of the wasps, that dripped soggily in clumps onto the grass, others taking off into the air. She sprayed the wasps off her mother's clothes but others were left in her hair and her ears and around her neck. She looked awful, barely able to speak.

Moya ran into the house to phone the doctor, but Mary Deegan told her it was her husband's half-day and that he was out on the golf course and uncontactable. Their neighbours the Costigans were gone to France for a month: Moya and Kate were being paid to feed their cat and water Mrs

Costigan's potted geraniums. The octogenarian Lily Murphy who lived beside them was deaf and couldn't drive.

'We have to get her to the doctor or the hospital,' said Moya, worried.

'Phone your father. He can drive me,' murmured Maeve Dillon through lips that were already swollen.

There was no reply from their father's office but it could be that he was talking to someone and didn't bother picking up.

'I'll go and get him, Mammy, I'll only be a few minutes,' shouted Kate, grabbing her bike and flying off down the gravelled driveway, pedalling as fast as she could, heart racing, to the village. She couldn't believe it – his office was shut, the key turned in the lock. She ran into Paddy Powers bookmakers but there was no sign of him; McHugh's public house hadn't seen him either. She'd spotted his big silver Mercedes parked down a laneway. He must be in the town, but where? She looked up and down the street panicking. Half the place was shut as it was Wednesday half-day. Even Lavelle's café had the blinds down. She thought of Sheila O'Grady. She was friendly with her mother and had an old Renault 4, maybe she could drive her or help her. She raced down the lane to O'Grady's narrow two-storey house and knocked on the front door, then chased around to the side, calling Mrs O'Grady's name. She'd been in the house a few times before, collecting Romy or bringing messages from her mother, and now she could hear the radio blaring as she pushed down the handle of the back door. 'Mrs O'Grady, please can you come up to the house and help my mammy?' she called.

The kitchen was warm, with the windows wide open and two plates and two cups on the table. She started to walk towards the hall, stopping suddenly at the curve of the staircase where two large men's leather shoes were neatly placed, the laces open, the brown leather familiar. A beige suit jacket was hanging from the banister. It was her father's: she recognized it from the tear at the corner of the pocket, which he'd kept asking her mother to mend.

She stood in the hall listening. What was her father doing in O'Grady's? They were upstairs, she could hear talking, laughing and other sounds. Sounds she couldn't believe. She wanted to run away and hide, close the back door and disappear, but she thought of Moya back in the wasp-filled garden with her mother and called his name.

'Daddy!'

She could hear the sudden silence, the whispers.

'Mammy's hurt. She needs you!' she

shouted urgently. 'You've got to come now!'

'Jesus, Mary and Joseph!'

Mortified, she escaped and stood out in the lane beside the door waiting for him.

'What the feck are you doing here?' he demanded.

'The wasps attacked Mammy and I came to get help.' The words came out in a torrent as she watched him fix his belt and pull on his shoes. 'A wasps' nest fell on her and she's covered in stings. She's real bad, Moya's with her but she needs to go to the doctor or the hospital.'

She flinched at the image of Sheila O'Grady in a flowery dressing gown, her hair loose around her shoulders, passing him his jacket and pushing her father out the door.

'How did you know where I was?'

'I looked everywhere for you. I saw your car.'

'It's better you say nothing to your mother about this, do you hear me, Kate? You know how she is.'

In the heat and sun and quiet of the lane she saw the expression on his face, the wary look in his dark eyes, the threatening stance in his heavy shoulders.

'You'll say nothing about this to your mother! Promise.'

She nodded.

'It's between us, then.'

He was trying to make her his accomplice. He need not have worried, because Kate was determined that nobody should know what an utter bastard her father had become, least of all her mother.

Unwilling to get into the car with him, she went to retrieve her bike and cycled home, slowly. She stopped for a few minutes to get her breath back and to quell the awful feeling of nausea and nerves that almost made her fall to the ground. How could her daddy do this? She had always believed him to be a bit blunt and rough in his ways but at least hardworking and honest and now she had caught him out in a lie! Her mother had no idea he was involved with another woman, least of all someone she knew. Kate didn't know what to do. She was sixteen years old and already disillusioned. She had always trusted and looked up to him and now she felt disgusted by him. She tried to compose herself as she cycled the rest of the way home.

Luckily her mother and father were already gone, had left for the hospital and Moya, standing in the cool of the kitchen in her bikini, made Kate sit down as she put Caladryl on the stings on her arm and hand. Momentarily she was tempted to confide in her sister, share the burden of unwanted knowledge about her father's sexual behaviour and expose his affair, but the thought

98

of the impact of such a disclosure on their fragile family was too much to bear and instead she decided to keep it quiet, keep it secret.

They returned a few hours later, her mother's face and arms and hands and legs swollen. Her eyes, half closed, were so puffed she looked like a prize-fighter. She'd had injections and been treated in the local casualty department, all the stings removed.

'She's shocked and she needs to rest,' said their father, helping her upstairs. 'You girls make her a cup of tea and some toast.'

She felt like a traitor as she watched him put his arm around her mother, her body against his, totally dependent on him as they slowly climbed the stairs. Kate knew at that precise moment she hated him and would never trust him again.

Chapter Nine

'Clever Kate', that's what her mother had always called her, branding her the brainy one of the family. Kate however wished that she was beautiful, like Moya who drove the boys crazy with her dark hair and wide eyes and perfectly proportioned body with her long legs and natural grace. Instead she had been gifted with a round face and pale blue eyes and wavy light brown hair that was the very devil to control and came from the Dillon side of the family where the women were noted for their strong wholesome looks and big feet and hands. She was considered fair and sensible and totally reliable and at least not given to the crazy mood swings and behaviour of her younger sister Romy, who didn't believe in rules and timetables or doing the right thing!

From the minute she could read, Kate had stuck her face in books, driving Mrs O'Donnell the local librarian mad with her constant filling in of request forms for new books. At St Dominic's Sister Goretti and the rest of the nuns had encouraged her academic abilities as she found study and learning so easy. She often ended up helping her friends Sarah and Aisling with their maths and science homework. For fun she played hockey and sang in the school choir, which meant forty girls got to jaunt around different parts of the country in a rickety school bus singing their hearts out before ending up in Dublin competing in the final round of the annual Feis Ceoil. On prize day, at the end of the school year, Maeve and Frank Dillon would sit bursting with pride in the packed school hall with the rest of the parents, clapping loudly as she went up to receive two or three prizes, Maeve's eyes sparkling as the nuns complimented her on Kate.

'Aye, she's a bright girl!' her father would say.

'And a wonderful daughter and friend,' beamed her mother.

Kate, embarrassed, felt a strange mixture of guilt and relief as she saw them standing together, still a pair.

Nuala Hayes, the school career guidance teacher, had called Kate in with her parents to discuss her options for when she left school. She had already made up her mind as to what she wanted to study and where. She had toyed briefly with the notion of medicine as she enjoyed biology and chemistry, but knew she lacked the constant dedication to the well-being of others to be a good doctor. Law would be her first choice. Her grandfather James Ryan had been the head of a busy solicitors' practice in Waterford. He had a keen legal brain and the love of a good court story and she could still remember him even in his old age sitting discussing legal challenges and precedents with his elderly friends in the front drawing room. Kate was curious as to what could keep her grandfather so entertained and interested for most of his life. He used to tease her about her sense of fairness and justice when she insisted that even a bag of sweets be divided up equally or that the washing up be shared.

'Kate will follow in my footsteps,' he'd joke, producing a mint humbug from the tin in his desk for her, 'mark my words.'

She had done aptitude tests, and read every information leaflet and booklet in the careers part of the library, researching what she wanted to study.

'She's always worked hard and done her homework,' her mother said proudly, patting her knee.

'Law in Trinity College is what I want to do,' said Kate, relishing the challenge and exciting prospect of studying in Dublin.

'Are you sure?'

'A hundred per cent,' she replied.

Nuala Hayes smiled. Kate Dillon was a wonderful student who would do the school proud. It was good to see a young girl with her career decided, compared to half the students who were a bag of nerves and hadn't a clue what to do and had parents who were planning on them being brain surgeons and teachers when they would be lucky to scrape through the Leaving Cert exams. She smiled as she stood up to see them out. Frank Dillon was a self-made man who was determined his daughters would have the opportunities he hadn't, and was keen on sending them all to third level.

Kate and her family were proof positive of the benefits of good parenting.

Her mother had cried in September when Kate packed up her things and got ready to go to college. She'd worked in the hotel on the harbour as a waitress for eight weeks of the summer holidays, going to Salthill in Galway with her friends for a week to celebrate the Leaving Certificate results.

'Mammy I'm only going to Dublin, for heaven's sake,' she'd joked. 'Moya's already there and I'll be home as often as I can, promise.'

'I know, it's just that you are growing up so quickly,' admitted her mother ruefully, hugging her.

She'd landed herself on her big sister Moya and her flatmate Louise, for the first term. Moya had just finished her arts degree in UCD and was busy job-hunting.

'What kind of work do you want to do?' Kate teased out. Moya had studied History of Art and French and had her sights set on a job that would use her skills and talents.

'I'm not doing any more studying,' she admitted. 'I scraped through my finals and that's enough for me.'

'What about working in a bank or an insurance company?'

Moya had shaken her head.

'No, I want to use my degree and work

with beautiful things. There was a job advertised in a small gallery in Duke Street last week and I've applied for it. I've an interview next Tuesday so keep your fingers crossed that I get it.'

Kate's heart lifted every time she walked along College Green and through the entrance of Trinity College, an oasis of student life and academic pursuit right in the heart of Dublin city. The noise of the buses and the traffic disappeared as she crossed the cobbled college yard or sat out on the square, taking in Trinity's ancient buildings and the centuries of tradition to which she now belonged.

In Freshers' Week she was tempted to sign up to join every society and club on offer as they all sounded so interesting and exciting. Another girl with a long frizz of dark hair and huge brown eyes was in the exact same quandary as they listened to the virtues of the societies proclaimed by their forthright members.

'Drama Soc!' shouted a thespian dressed in an Elvis outfit. Kate knew she would never have the courage to dress up and act on stage.

'Chess Club!'

'I've heard they're all swots and brain-boxes and bad losers,' confided the girl with the frizz as they passed by.

Tennis, Cricket, Blackjack, Rugby, Art, Phil. Soc. and History Soc., Film, Jazz, Inventors' Club, Athletics, Swimming, Poker – the list was endless. Minnie, the other girl, introduced herself and the two of them got into a heated discussion about the merits and demerits of each society, both bursting out laughing when they agreed to sign up for the famous Phil. Soc. Minnie and Kate struck up an immediate friendship and by the second term had decided to share a flat in an old converted house in Ranelagh.

Kate liked the anonymity of university, the fact that no-one really knew her and she'd had to start from scratch again. Vying with the leading brains in the country she soon discovered she was no longer top of the class and she had to work harder than she had ever done before, the days of being the shining star of St Dominic's gone as she struggled with the Constitution, complicated European law and interpretations of various landmark legal cases. She was no longer clever Kate, just simply Kate Dillon the girl from Rossmore who hung around with Minnie Doyle.

Although she missed home Kate had no intention of slavishly getting the bus or train back there every week, like so many of the students. She loved the city with its pubs and cinemas and theatres and nightclubs and discos and hundreds of things to do. Minnie, a likeminded soul, had the ability to dance and drink till all hours and still appear refreshed the next day.

'What in God's name would I be doing back in Longford of a weekend?' she quipped, shaving her legs with complete concentration. 'Sitting in with my granny watching the *Late Late Show* while Mum is up in the golf club drinking gins and getting tipsy! No thank you.'

Minnie had confided in Kate not long after they became friends that her dad, Denis, had run off with a girl about half his age.

'She's only twenty-five!' wailed Minnie. 'And he says he loves her and wants to marry her!'

'God!'

'Mum's gone like a lunatic ever since! It's absolutely desperate.'

Kate had told Minnie about her father and catching him with Sheila O'Grady.

'In France all the French men have affairs, nobody bats an eye at it,' Minnie told her.

'Honest?'

'It's the French way. Obviously old men must get randy. At least your father hasn't gone off and dumped your mother and sold your house and bought himself a flipping sports car!'

'No.' Kate sighed. Normality and appearances had at least been kept up, their marriage maintained as her parents led a busy social life of dinner dances, socials and business outings. Maeve Dillon was keeping busy and had joined the local Vincent de Paul and the Gardens Group. With herself and Moya gone she still had Romy to look after, even though from what she gathered Romy was being a right handful and her parents were worn out trying to get her to come home on time and not stay out till all hours.

'Couldn't you have a word with her the next time you're home?' pleaded her mother. 'She might listen to you.'

'I doubt it.'

Romy had always done exactly what she wanted. A tomboy, she'd followed their father around the building sites and show houses for years. Moya and Kate had been lucky growing up to be part of a big gang of friends, the O'Malleys, the Costigans, the Dwyers and of course their cousins the Quinns. Romy, who was much younger, was often left just to follow them around, 'Mind your sister!' their mother's constant cry.

The gang of them complained at the unfairness of it, shouting 'Get lost, kid!' at her when the adults were not around. Unwanted, Romy would simply stick out her tongue or run at them with a bit of a stick before disappearing off to entertain herself.

Kate felt guilty remembering those silly acts of childhood cruelty and agreed to try and get Romy to see some sense, but suspected her younger sister would still only stick her tongue out at her.

'Will you be home on Saturday?'

Much and all as she loved going home, the thought of lecturing her surly teenage sister, versus her house-warming! Minnie and herself had planned a night in the flat, with wine and beer and cheese and crackers and chunks of heated garlic bread. Everybody they knew in college was invited, as Minnie felt they had to widen their social circle. Kate had asked a few guys from her class and Minnie had rounded up part of the rugby squad, plus her cousin Patrick and his friend.

'God, he's gorgeous!' admitted Kate, who'd met him briefly in the library one day and already fancied him like mad.

All the girls they hung around with were going crazy, dying for Saturday night. Kate and Minnie suddenly worried how they could possibly fit all the people they'd invited into their two small rooms.

'Sorry, Mum, but Minnie's organized something and I can't let her down. Maybe the following week. I promise I'll talk to Romy then.'

Chapter Ten

After much cajoling and persuasion by his wife, daughters and sister-in-law and some deliberate masculine consideration Frank Dillon had finally agreed to fund his second daughter's twenty-first party.

'Kate, there's no question of hiring a room over a pub and just drinking,' he'd warned. 'This will be a proper occasion here at home in Rossmore with your mother and I and friends and family present to celebrate your coming of age.'

'Thank you, Daddy,' she'd squealed, convinced that if she engineered it properly it would end up mostly her friends with the bare minimum of family.

Back in her flat in Dublin she had drafted and redrafted the invitation list about twenty times, having huge arguments with Minnie and another friend Dee as to who was deserving of an invitation and who was not.

'You have to have Lisa,' they chorused, 'she invited you to hers.'

'She invited two hundred and she barely speaks to me if you two aren't around.'

'I suppose.'

'She's off the list.'

'What about Patrick?'

'You don't have to invite him,' insisted Minnie. 'He's finished college and is older than everyone else.'

Kate still fancied Minnie's older cousin like mad and in the past few weeks had finally gone out with him. They had gone to the cinema, Kate making sure they got seats in the back row. Then he'd asked her to supper in Nico's, and spent the night arguing about the government and the state of the economy, Kate feeling like she was on some kind of private debating team until he'd driven her home and detoured to the quiet of the deserted Sandymount Strand, where the two of them necked for hours.

Getting up her courage she'd invited him to the Law Ball, almost swooning when she saw him in his tuxedo, and had spent the most wonderful night dancing in his arms for hours. Full of romantic intentions she had invited him back to the flat but apparently had drunk so much wine she fell asleep on the sofa. Minnie had had to put her to bed. Diplomatically Patrick had said nothing. Kate decided that not only was he tall and good-looking but he was head and shoulders above all the other guys she knew in terms of discretion and maturity.

'I don't know what you see in him. I think he's a pain.'

'Shut up, Minnie, he's on the list.'

Finally they had arrived at the figure of sixty who would be formally invited to celebrate her twenty-first birthday. College friends mostly, and a few of her old school friends and of course her cousins the Quinns. Her parents were insisting on a few more relations and their friends the Molloys and the Kinsellas. She had a second back-up list and was secretly praying that her relations or that snobby Claudia Kinsella would be hit with some bug or virus that would allow her to invite more of her Trinity crowd.

Minnie and Dee had traipsed the streets of Dublin with her looking for the perfect outfit.

'Why don't you take Moya with you?' suggested her mother. 'You know she has a really good eye for fashion and what looks right.'

Kate said nothing. This was her party and her big sister wasn't having any hand or part in running it as far as she was concerned.

They went from shop to shop – Brown Thomas, Switzers and Richard Allen's, trying on one dress after another. Undecided, Kate hadn't a clue what look she actually wanted: sexy, classic, floaty and feminine?

'I'll know it when I see it!' she insisted, try-ing to jiggle into a slinky red backless dress in Pamela Scott's.

Minnie preferred the clingy pale blue halterneck dress, which showed off her curves and shimmied in the light.

'The black is better,' insisted Dee.

Kate studied herself in the simple black scooped-neck dress that fell to the floor, a high slit on either side revealing her thighs.

'It's so classy and it makes you look like you've dropped at least a stone.'

Kate sighed. She wasn't sure about the black, maybe it made her look too old.

The quest resumed and they made a quick sortie across the Liffey to Arnotts and Clery's. Disappointed, they headed back up towards the Green.

'What about Powerscourt?' suggested Minnie, who was ready to collapse and had developed a blister on her heel from the new shoes she was breaking in.

'Agreed.'

They walked down past Clarendon Street church and entered the magnificent old Georgian townhouse that had been transformed into high-class boutiques and expensive gift shops with a Design Centre, art gallery and restaurants too.

'There's got to be something here.'

The Design Centre was fabulous but she knew her father would have a heart attack if she told him she had paid that sort of price for a party dress. She just couldn't afford it.

Down near the big carved wooden staircase she gazed at the window of Ritzy, one of the smaller designer shops, and was entranced by the unusual party dresses that hung from wires as part of the display.

'Is this it?' screeched Minnie, leading the charge inside. They went through rail after rail, pulling out three possibilities. Minnie collapsed on a stool in the corner as Kate pulled on one dress after another. Sweat clung to her brow as she struggled with zips and straps in the tiny space.

Suddenly she knew it. This was the one. The perfect dress. Minnie forgot her blister and almost wept with relief as Kate let the pale pink dress down over her body. It fell smoothly over her tummy and hips, flaring out ever so slightly and ending just above her knees. Two narrow straps held it on her bare shoulders and a slight glimmer of glitter traced the low neckline.

'Wow!' shrieked Minnie, calling Dee to get into the fitting room.

Kate stared at herself in the long mirror. It was exactly what she was looking for. It made her legs look long, her tummy disappear and she felt beautiful in it. Judging by the reactions of her two friends the decision was made. Five minutes later the dress was wrapped in tissue in the striking purple Ritzy bag as they headed to Bewley's for a reviving coffee and cream cake.

'We'll do the shoes next week,' joked Dee.

Kate licked the cream from the chocolate éclair, imagining herself pirouetting in front of Patrick, looking absolutely gorgeous.

She went home on the Friday night to help with the organization of the party. Her mother was in her element, the kitchen stacked high with plates and glasses and cutlery.

Maeve Dillon was one of that rare breed who enjoyed entertaining. There were two huge honey-baked hams, a turkey and a side of salmon. Tomorrow there would be salads, savoury rice, baby potatoes and crisp white freshly baked bread rolls, and for dessert the Black Forest gâteau and a pavlova that had been ordered from Lavelle's.

Kate was furious that her mother was actually paying her father's mistress to make the desserts for her party!

'Can't you order them from somewhere else?' she'd pleaded.

'But where, pet? Everyone knows that Lavelle's are the best.'

Kate didn't know what to say. Obviously her mother still hadn't a clue about her father and his amorous goings-on. Kate hadn't the heart to tell her and spoil everything, but swore that, twenty-one or not, she would not eat one bite of the dessert that Sheila O'Grady delivered. She could see a frown on her mother's face, the worry that everything might not be perfect; after all, she was the one who'd cajoled and persuaded Frank to let Kate have a party.

'Listen, Mum, thanks a lot. Everything looks great and I'm sure the pavlova will be perfect.'

'Imagine, this time twenty-one years ago I was all out pregnant, ready to burst,' joked her mother, 'and now look at my baby all grown up, almost finished college, my clever, clever Kate.'

They held each other in the warmth of the kitchen.

'It will be wine or beer,' interrupted her father. 'That's what we are providing. No gin or whiskey or vodka for young people under my roof. We don't want any drunkards.'

'That's grand, Daddy.'

She resisted the impulse to retort that it was the older guests that might need watching on that score, as he disappeared off with the *Irish Times* to the peace and quiet of the living room.

'He'll be fine tomorrow, don't worry,' added her mother as she washed some more plates and cutlery. 'You should go to bed and have a bit of an early night so you'll look refreshed tomorrow.'

Kate yawned. She hadn't realized just how tired she was. Preparations were well in hand so she could safely disappear to her room.

All night she'd tossed and turned, dreaming of disasters that could befall her family and friends within the next twenty-four hours. Excitement and nerves ensured she barely slept a wink.

She was greeted with breakfast in bed and her sisters singing 'Happy Birthday' to her. Kate puffed up her pillows and roused herself as the present-giving began. A beautiful gold chain for her neck from her mum and dad, an embroidered clutch bag from Moya and a pair of dangly silver moon-shaped earrings from Romy.

'They're all beautiful,' she smiled. 'Just beautiful.'

She lay back and ate tea and toast as out on the landing her mother and sister screamed at each other.

'Why do I have to hoover the hall and the stairs and the landing?'

'Because I said so,' argued her mother.

'It's her party. She should be doing it!'

'Romy, I'm telling you to do it! Later on you are to have a bath and wash your hair and put those filthy jeans of yours in the machine. D'ya hear?'

Kate turned over, ignoring them. Romy could do her worst! She was not fighting, today of all days. Being twenty-one meant something. It meant being too grown up to bother with a lippy seventeen-year-old kid

116

who drove you crazy. She closed her eyes and tried to relax.

People had started to arrive and she was barely finished dressing. Minnie had done her nails for her and lent her a pale mauve eyeshadow that looked great with her dress. Romy had borrowed her mascara and given it back with bits of fluff from the carpet stuck to it. She'd kill her. The dress looked even better than it had in the shop and her mother's eyes welled with tears when she came in to see her.

'You look stunning, darling.'

She put on the delicate strappy gold high heels she'd found, destroying one nail in the process. Minnie demanded cotton wool and nail-varnish remover straight away. Downstairs she could hear the doorbell and laughter as her father and Moya greeted the first arrivals. 'Hurry on, Minnie,' she begged, not wanting to miss any more of the party.

The house was packed – the living room, the kitchen, the hall, the stairs even – but Kate could feel the tension ease from her as she realized everyone was enjoying themselves and mingling. Romy looked like some kind of Gothic avenger with her eyes heavily lined with kohl and a pale blue denim skirt almost up to her thighs and black leather boots as she passed around the drinks as the Quinns arrived. Moya was in the kitchen helping, and even her mother's apron couldn't take away from the stylish simple black sleeveless dress she wore with black pumps which, with her pale skin and straight black hair, made her look like something out of *Vogue*. Her father was fussing around looking for more corkscrews and a top-up from his secret stash of whiskey while Maeve Dillon regaled everyone with embarrassing stories of the night Kate was born.

'You scrub up well,' jeered her cousin Conor, swinging her up and giving her a big birthday kiss.

'Put the poor girl down,' ordered her Aunt Vonnie, pushing a huge present into her arms.

What in heaven's name was it?

'Guess!' yelled her four male cousins.

She hadn't a clue.

'We are sailing, we are sailing...' they began to sing in unison. Kate blushed.

'It's not what I think, is it?'

'It is!'

'Oh my God, my crew gear!'

'Life jacket, waterproofs, boots, over-jacket and mate's hat,' they listed off. 'Salty Dog crew gear.'

Kate grinned. Ever since she was twelve she'd loved hanging around boats and was always looking for the opportunity to go sailing with her cousins. She usually had to cadge stuff off them, and now she had the whole lot.

'That's just the perfect present,' she giggled, hugging them all.

She spent half an hour politely introducing her friends to her father and then gave up, knowing that he would never remember any of them anyways. Patrick was being very mannerly and was deep in conversation with him about the local Chamber of Commerce. Phil and Rob and James and Charlie and some of the guys from her class were already engrossed in a drinking game, which she was tempted to join in but which ended abruptly with her mother's invitation to pick up a plate and eat. There was food galore, and then the cake with twenty-one candles flickering as everyone in the room sang 'Happy Birthday' to her. Her father stepped forward to make a short speech.

'I would like to welcome you all, especially Kate's college friends from Dublin, for coming to join the family here in Rossmore to celebrate Kate's twenty-first birthday with us. Kate was always a grand girl, the high flyer of the family, the daughter who was destined for big things! She always had her head stuck in the books, but it paid off, and her mother and I are proud now to have such a promising lawyer in the family. One of these days Kate's probably going to pass out her old man, and be one of these high-powered career women you read about.'

Everyone laughed and Kate squirmed with embarrassment, catching a sympathetic glance from Minnie as her father rambled on. Her mother added how glad she was that so many had come to the party.

'Speech! Speech!' called her friends and family. Kate took a deep breath. She glanced around the room, and could feel the goodwill towards her. Mentally she said a thank-you to Professor O'Kelly, who insisted all his students were capable of standing up and expressing themselves.

'Thank you, everyone, for coming and joining us here in the Stone House, the house where I grew up. I would like to thank my mum and dad, for just being that, being the kind of parents who encouraged me and loved me and believed in me. Thank you to all my friends from college who helped me to settle in Dublin, and especially to my best friends Minnie and Dee who helped me to organize the party. Thanks again of course to my mum and dad for the wonderful food and the bar. Being twenty-one is really crazy because all of a sudden now I'm meant to feel grown up! Anyway I'm just so happy that all the people I love and care about are here with me – my family, my cousins and my friends – because tonight is the best night of my life!'

'So far,' added her mother, as Kate began to cut the cake, to shouts and applause from everyone.

Afterwards, Romy started up the music. The mahogany dining table was now pushed back against the wall, and the dancing started.

Kate looked around the room: no sign of Patrick. Phil caught her in his arms and began swinging her round to Abba's 'Dancing Queen', Kate keeping an eye out for the tall, dark-haired figure. The boys from her class danced with her one after another, admiration in their eyes. Rob tried to coax a kiss from her, telling her he'd fancied her from the first minute he'd set eyes on her in the Buttery Bar. The room got hotter and hotter as it filled up. Even her mum and dad had taken to the floor and were acting like *they* were twenty-one.

Conor helped Moya to open the french windows and some of the dancers spilled out onto the patio, glad of the cool air.

Dee was involved in some kind of argument with John, her on-off boyfriend, and Kate vowed not to get tangled up in it. Desperate for a drink of water she decided to go into the kitchen and cool off for a few seconds. Aunt Vonnie was busy putting away the leftovers, wrapping them in tinfoil.

'There's enough eating there to do you all for the next two days,' she joked: 'Are you having a good time, Kate?'

'The best.'

'Well I'm glad to hear it. Being twenty-one is real special. You look so grown up, so beautiful.'

'Thank you.'

She liked her aunt because she was always honest and direct.

'I'd better get back.'

She peeped into the sitting room. Her cousin Liam and Uncle Joe were busy chatting to a group of relations and friends of her parents. The music was blaring from the dining room and she decided to slip outside to chat. Minnie and Phil and James were enjoying cold beers and offered her one.

'Where's Patrick?'

'Beats me.'

'Maybe he went home!'

Patrick was too much of a gentleman to leave without thanking her and her parents.

'Relax, Kate. He'll turn up,' soothed Minnie.

Kate felt suddenly very grown up standing out under the night sky with her best friends, glass in hand as her parents made eejits of themselves inside. She looked good, her light brown shoulder-length hair still straight, the expensive perfume James and Charlie had given her dabbed erotically on all her pulse points, her toenails painted and peeping from her high heels, as all around her friends and family enjoyed themselves.

After a while she decided to go inside, as she didn't want to get a chill. She passed through the hall and stopped suddenly. Patrick was leaning against the bottom of the stairs, beer in one hand, rapt with attention, talking to someone. She was about to rush over and grab him, drag him off to dance with her, when something about the way he was bending down stopped her. She walked over slowly, fixing a smile on her face.

He was talking to Moya. The two dark heads and eyes were wrapped up in each other. Moya's long legs were pulled under her, as they chatted.

'Patrick, where were you? I was looking everywhere for you!'

He looked up, puzzled.

'I've been here talking to your beautiful sister for the past hour.'

Kate swallowed hard. It had always been the way. It didn't matter what she wore or did, Moya had only to smile with those full lips of hers and bat those big brown eyes and boys fell at her feet. Ever since playgroup it had been happening.

'Were you looking for me?' apologized her sister. 'Does Mum want me for something? I gave out drinks and slices of the cake like she asked earlier on.'

'Couldn't resist the black cherries and

cream myself,' teased Patrick.

Kate cursed her mother for making Moya go around offering cake. She was bound to get talking to Patrick that way. Boys and men were mad on cake. Why the hell couldn't she have asked Romy to do it instead?

'Will we have a dance?' she couldn't stop herself from begging.

'Of course I'm going to dance with the Birthday Girl, I wouldn't miss it for the world.' He excused himself to Moya, and taking Kate's hand led her back into the other room, pushing into a space near Conor and Minnie. He'd taken off his jacket and was wearing a gleaming white shirt. Pressed close to him, he smelled lovely, Eau Sauvage.

'Great party, Kate. Thanks for inviting me.'

She smiled. Why wouldn't she invite the one man in the room she adored?

She longed to put her head on his chest and feel his arms around her, have him kiss her neck and without thinking she reached forward to pull him closer to her. Embarrassed she stopped as he pulled away. They danced for another fifteen minutes, Kate talking too much as Phil and Dee and the rest of the party crowd filled in.

'You look very pretty tonight,' he told her. 'Pink suits you.'

She knew she'd get him to notice her. She twirled and danced, disappointed when after a while Patrick excused himself and Rob pulled her into his arms as the slow set started.

As the crowd began to thin, she went in search of him again, still hopeful. She spotted him out on the terrace, near her father's rose bed, his black jacket across Moya's shoulder as they leaned against each other, his head bent down over her, his lips touching hers as they kissed.

Kate couldn't help staring. They looked so perfect together that she wanted to run over and drag them apart. She felt a restraining hand on her arm.

'I told you not to invite him,' slurred Minnie. 'He's such a womanizer.'

She felt giddy and sick watching them. Patrick was just like her father, didn't care about anything but suiting himself. The fact that she had invited him was irrelevant now as he held Moya in his arms. As for her sister! Angrily, Kate turned to go back inside. This was her birthday night, her party, the most important night of her life and stupid Moya had to go and ruin it all. She'd never forgive her. Never.

Chapter Eleven

The next morning Kate's head throbbed and her mouth was dry from all the wine she'd drunk. It was her first big hangover and she turned around in the bed praying that in a few hours she would somehow feel better. Minnie and Dee and Susan had slept in the spare bedroom and her Aunt Vonnie had put a few more of her friends up in her house. The rest of the partygoers dispersed to Rossmore's various B&Bs and landladies. Oh God, she groaned, hearing the Hoover going downstairs and her mother banging around in the kitchen tidying up. She prayed that the place wasn't in too bad a state and that no-one had destroyed any carpets or bit of furniture. She closed her eyes and drifted back to sleep.

The party post-mortem was held around the kitchen table at midday. The girls sat in their dressing gowns, while her mother scrambled eggs and grilled bacon and made huge plates of toast as the gossip began. Her father glanced in briefly and, judging the lie of the land, gathered up a bundle of Sunday papers.

'Great party,' said Minnie who looked as fresh as a daisy despite dancing till four o'clock. 'Thanks a bunch for inviting us, Mr Dillon.'

''Tis great to be young,' he said, grabbing a cup of black coffee.

'We all had a wonderful night,' added Dee, 'and you and Mrs Dillon seemed to be enjoying yourselves too.'

'It was a lovely night,' said her mother, 'having you all here with us to celebrate Kate's birthday.'

Her father had already dosed himself with Alka Seltzer and was in no humour for reminders of the previous night. He disappeared off to the sanctuary of the small sun-room at the side of the house.

'He's always grumpy in the morning,' Romy declared, plumping herself down in the middle of them all, her eyes like a black panda bear, smudged with make-up.

Kate yawned. Tea and toast would hopefully make her feel better.

'The food was brill, Mrs Dillon, honest and we've all had a lovely time.'

'Well that's what parties are for! Frank and I were glad to see you all enjoying yourselves.'

One by one they went through every stage of the night: who wore what, who danced with who, and who paired off with who.

'Your cousin Conor is real nice,' mumbled

Minnie, layering egg and bacon on her slice of toast.

'Well you danced with him most of the night,' teased Dee, 'so you should know.'

Kate had a vague recollection of them in the corner smooching but hadn't realized that her best friend and Conor had hit it off so well.

'Stop teasing the poor girl,' interrupted Maeve Dillon, passing around the teapot.

'Did you see Moya with that tall guy?' interrupted Romy, stuffing herself with toast. 'God, he's gorgeous.'

Kate sat still, wishing that God in heaven would find some way of ridding her of the torment of her life.

'What's his name?'

'Patrick.'

Kate could sense her friends' unease around the table.

'Is he one of your college crowd?'

'No, not really. I've known him a good while, though. We went out together a few times.'

Minnie kicked Romy under the table and a look of utter bewilderment crossing Romy's face, before the dawning realization that she had seriously put her foot in it.

'Oh God, Kate, was he supposed to be your date? Was that the guy you fancied?'

Kate sat feeling every one of her ancient twenty-one years.

'Yes, but obviously it wasn't reciprocated.'

'Romy,' interrupted Maeve Dillon, leaving unpacking the dishwasher. 'Go and help your father in the sitting room this minute and give Kate and her friends a bit of peace.'

Romy splayed her elbows on the table, not wanting to leave the cosy circle of chat. 'Daddy's reading the papers. He'll kill me if I disturb him,' she protested.

'The hall is full of boxes of glasses and plates from last night. Tell your father to put them in the car to bring back, and you can do a count of the cutlery on the dining table to make sure we have them all.'

'It's not fair,' she wailed. 'Why do I have to do everything?'

She flounced out of the kitchen, her fair wavy hair streeling, and banged the door behind her.

Her mother diplomatically excused herself and Kate wished she could just crawl back to bed for the rest of the day.

'Don't mind,' urged Minnie. 'Sisters can be right bitches sometimes.'

'That's an understatement.'

'We'd better start making tracks,' suggested Dee who had driven down in her mother's Starlet. 'Do you want to come back with us?' Kate had intended lolling around the house for the rest of the day, basking in the glory of the past twenty-four hours and doing nothing.

'Listen, I better not. Mum will be mad if I just shoot off now and disappear. I'll get a lift or the bus back later this evening.'

The others had gone in a cloud of exhaust fumes and honking of the horn by the time Moya appeared downstairs, washed and showered and immaculate, dressed in a pair of pale-blue jeans and a white shirt, her dark hair loose to her shoulders.

'Great party,' she smiled, helping herself to tea and toast and marmalade as Kate packed the dishwasher. 'I like your friends.'

'I know you do.'

'What do you mean?'

'Well, it was quite obvious last night.'

Moya bit into the freshly made toast, deliberately ignoring her sister's snide remark.

Kate was so annoyed and angry with her she couldn't help herself shouting.

'Why did it have to be Patrick? Why him?'

'I don't know what you're talking about.'

'You know I asked him to the party because I like him. I've gone out with him a few times, we meet up, have a drink, a laugh. We've had a few dates and I like being with him. You know that.'

'I didn't know that!'

'Everyone knows it!'

'Well, I didn't go looking for him, Kate, so don't be so bloody ridiculous! We just got talking, that's all. If you must know, he was the one who chatted me up.'

'I don't want you ever talking to him again or seeing him, do you hear? Promise me!'

'I can't promise you that,' said Moya softly. 'I'm sorry, Kate. I can't promise you that.'

'It was my twenty-first, my night,' she howled, 'and you tried to spoil it for me.'

Moya got up from the table, leaving her plate and cup.

'I'm sorry you see it like that,' she said.

Even though it was her first day as a mature adult, Kate put her head on her arms and bawled like a big baby.

Back in Dublin she threw herself into study, revision becoming all important as she crammed and crammed. She gave up going out mid-week and attended every tutorial she could. Every spare hour she was in the library going over lecture notes and case studies. The final exams were looming and she was determined to get First Class Honours. Her mother was doing a novena for her and she could hardly eat or sleep with the stress of it all. Minnie had broken out in spots and Dee had got mouth ulcers and by agreement their flat was decreed a no-go zone until after the exams. Moya had phoned her once or twice, trying to arrange to see her, but she had managed to avoid her and as for Patrick, he had no interest in swotting exam students and was caught up in his own social life. She had bumped into him briefly outside the bank one day. He had been polite, thanked her for the party and wished her good luck with her exams, but had made no mention of getting together or a night out to celebrate afterwards.

'Put him out of your mind,' advised Minnie.

'He's a shit!' added Dee emphatically, trying to memorize the Constitution.

Kate had bags under her eyes and had gained about sixteen pounds by the time the exams ended. Bread, chocolate and peanuts had sustained her brain for studying and now she was paying for it.

'We look absolutely awful,' sighed Minnie, contemplating the red marks and scabs on her face.

'I feel like I could sleep for a month.'

'Let's go out and dance and drink and get picked up by some gorgeous guys and have a laugh,' pleaded Dee.

'No-one will pick us up looking like this.'

'We can dance and have a laugh, then. We're finished college, for God's sake.'

The night was young. They'd started off in the Buttery Bar for old times' sake and then crowded onto the 46a bus and gone to Hartigan's where all the rugby crowd hung out. Rob and James and a crowd from Bective rugby club insisted on buying them pints. The place was so jammered you could scarcely move and the crowd spilled out onto Leeson Street. Kate was so hot she could feel her pale blue T-shirt sticking to her.

'James and Dave and a few of the guys are off to Boston on Monday for the summer to work,' announced Rob. 'So we have to give them a bit of a send-off.'

'Where are you working?'

'Construction. Building sites most likely,' grinned James.

They stayed there till closing time, the barman lifting their glasses from the counter to get rid of them. The night was warm as they stood outside deliberating.

'Where to, ladies?'

'Dancing,' insisted Dee.

They considered a few of the nightclubs and discos close by, eventually settling on Annabel's, which was within walking distance and had a late bar and disco.

Rob held Kate's hand as they walked along Leeson Street past the empty offices and basement nightclubs. It was such a lovely night she was glad she'd made the effort to come out instead of collapsing into bed with exhaustion. Rob and herself avoided all mention of the exam papers and what they had written. The die was cast as far as she was concerned and there was no point going back over it. It was so hard to believe she was no longer a full-time student and would soon be out in the working world trying to make a living.

'Did I tell you I got accepted by Carroll and O'Riordan's for my articles?' she boasted.

'That's great, Kate.'

'What about you?'

'I'm hoping to do King's Inn.'

Kate blinked. She couldn't imagine Rob in court as a barrister.

'The old man wants me to follow in his footsteps.'

She hugged him. He was kind and soft and very intelligent and not like some of the arrogant, self–centred men she'd come across who treated the courts like their stage.

'So in a few years you can pass me on some of your clients,' he said.

She giggled. The two of them mature enough to sort out other people's legal problems. It didn't bear thinking about.

Annabel's was packed with final year students, Minnie waving wildly at a crowd from Arts. Kate pushed her way onto the dance floor as the guys promising to buy them drinks made a beeline for the bar. The music was throbbing and it felt good to relax and just let her body follow the beat. Within an hour the whole place was jumping as everyone danced off the weeks of tension, the noise and the music deafening.

'I'm taking a break,' she signalled to the girls as she made her way up to the sitting area, collapsing into a chair beside James and taking a sip of her beer. Rob was down on the dance floor with Dee trying to strut like John Travolta.

'He always does that when he has a few pints in him!' joked Minnie.

Kate shrugged. She looked around. There were a few lecherous old guys smarming their way around trying to pick up someone, their wedding rings hidden away for a few hours. The girls gave them short shrift.

'Jesus, they're pathetic.'

Over at the far end of the bar a group of American tourists, who were probably staying in the hotel and automatically got free passes to its nightclub, were trying out pints of Guinness.

'They'll be paying for that in the morning,' James joked.

She liked James, he was tall and easygoing and, she supposed, good looking, if you were into red hair. His eyes crinkled when he laughed. It was a pity he was going to be away for the summer, she thought as he slipped his arm around her.

They all agreed it was the best night ever as they walked back to the flat. The city streets were empty except for taxis hunting for fares. Rob and Dee were arm in arm. 'Coffee, tea and toasted cheese sandwiches in our place,' offered Minnie as they passed a group of revellers coming up the stairs and out of Buck Whaley's nightclub. Kate stopped for a second, looking at the tall couple standing on the pavement trying to flag down a cab. She recognized them immediately. It was Patrick, his arm around a girl, her sister Moya's dark head resting on his shoulder. She prayed they wouldn't see her and wondered how it was that her prayers never got answered as Minnie screeched his name.

She could see Moya was embarrassed, and even Patrick seemed rattled at meeting them in the early hours of the morning.

'Listen, Minnie, I'm sorry,' he apologized, declining the invitation to join them, 'but some of us have jobs to go to and I've got to be in the office by eight.'

Moya said nothing. Not a single word to Kate as the two of them jumped into a black cab and disappeared.

Silently she cursed them. Moya was a bare-faced cheat who would put going out with a fella above her sister.

'You OK?' asked Dee and Rob in unison.

She shrugged. She wasn't really. Imagine being kicked in the guts by a member of her family! Men were disloyal and untrustworthy but she expected more of her own sister. Moya had let her down rotten and it wasn't something she was ever likely to forget.

Chapter Twelve

Moya was in love. She blushed remembering wearing her mother's old striped green and white apron when she first met Patrick Redmond. Her face was flushed and hot from lifting roasting trays in and out of the oven, as she helped with the food at Kate's twenty-first birthday. Who would have believed that her brainbox of a sister would even know such a handsome, good-looking guy!

Patrick had come into the kitchen looking for some ice and immediately introduced himself. Wherever she turned that night he seemed to be there, at her elbow, passing her a plate, getting her a drink.

Food served, plates cleared and birthday candles blown out, she had eventually been able to relax and enjoy the party herself, Patrick topping up her wine glass with chilled white wine.

'You look beautiful,' he'd said, reaching

and touching her hair and pushing the loose tendrils off her face.

'Mmmm.'

Moya was used to accepting compliments, to seeing men's eyes widen when she walked into a room and women reach for their partners' hands. With a passion for clothes and an innate sense of style and colour and what suited she was glad of the expensive black dress she'd decided to wear. Enjoying the flattery, she simply smiled up at him.

The wine was good and taking in his tall figure and long face and curling dark hair, she realized with a jolt, so was he. It was rare for her to meet a man who was her physical match, at ease with his looks and seemingly totally comfortable with himself He was also easy to talk to and matter-of-factly told her about his career and where he worked. Moya, impressed with his ambition, could barely believe that he was a cousin of Minnie's.

Kate was flapping around the place in her pink dress and dragged him away insisting that he dance with her.

'Come on, Patrick. It's my birthday! You promised.'

She watched the two of them twirl around the dance floor for a few minutes, before collecting some dead glasses and bringing them into the kitchen for washing. She was barely able to hide her relief when half an hour later he appeared again.

'You're not getting away from me that easily,' he'd said softly. Moya knew in that instant that she would never want to get away from Patrick, ever.

By the end of the party he had arranged to see her again in Dublin. Both of them were equally aware of the significance of their meeting.

Kate had screamed and cursed at her the next day, accusing her of stealing her boyfriend and ruining her party, and Romy gave her the cold shoulder for being so mean to Kate.

Her father was dying of a hangover and not fit to talk to anyone and her mother was in lunatic form cleaning and tidying up after the hordes. Relieved to be going back to Dublin she accepted her mother's offer of a lift to the early afternoon train, glad of Maeve Dillon's non-judgemental attitude to her daughters' arguments and refusal to get embroiled in them.

'Kate's upset about last night, Moya, but I know you wouldn't deliberately hurt her. Phone her later in the week when things between you have calmed down a bit.'

'I will,' she promised.

'Then take care, pet, and thanks for helping with the party.'

She'd met Patrick on the Tuesday night for dinner in the Unicorn and went to the theatre with him on Thursday and to a party at a solicitor friend's of his on Saturday. Her mind in a whirl, she knew by the time they drove down to Enniskerry for lunch on Sunday that she was in love with him. She felt like pinching herself to see if it was real. She had gone out with lots of boys before but there had never been anything like this. She felt overwhelmed, swept away by his charm and good looks and personality. Her flatmate Anne-Marie had declared him a 'dreamboat'.

'God, Moya, where did you meet him? He's gorgeous.'

But it wasn't just that he was handsome, it was his confidence and the way he seemed to know everything and was able to tease her and make her laugh.

After work on Fridays she began to join him in the Shelbourne Bar with some of the other guys from his office, all in their expensive suits and ties ready to unwind after a hard day making money. She could see the appreciative looks in their eyes but ignored their flirting: she had no interest in anyone but Patrick. As far as she was concerned he was the only man in the world for her.

She had tried to talk to Kate about him, be nice and friendly and tell her that they were most definitely involved. She wanted to explain to her younger sister that meeting Patrick was one of the most important things in her life and that it was a serious relationship, much more serious than the brief fling he'd had with Kate. Kate was tense, pale and tired, exhausted from studying too hard when she finally agreed to meet in the Winding Stair Bookshop, the café on the quays overlooking the River Liffey.

'I can't stay long,' insisted her sister, hanging her jacket on the back of her chair. 'Minnie wants me to meet her.'

'How did the exams go?'

'The finals were shit! I don't know how you are meant to cram years of work and case histories into a few hours. Let's hope Mam's novena to Saint Theresa worked!'

'You'll do fine, I promise,' Moya said.

'It'll take more than a few old prayers.'

'Come on, Kate. You are such a brainbox!'

They had just ordered mugs of frothy cappuccino from the waitress when Moya broached the subject of Patrick, realizing almost at once that she should have left it.

'Why are you still seeing him?' demanded Kate angrily.

'I really like him. I'm sorry, Kate, but I do.' She could see the hurt on her sister's face.

'Patrick's one of my friends, one of my crowd. I don't go trying to steal your friends and hang around with them!'

'He's still your friend.'

141

'Like feck he is!'

'He is!' Moya insisted. 'It's just that he's my boyfriend.'

'You're such a bitch! I don't want to hear about you and your bloody boyfriend, do you hear me?'

Moya had tried to remain calm, to reason with her, but instead had made things even worse by saying, 'You know in your heart, Kate, he was just a friend, never your boyfriend. Never!'

The two of them ended up in a foul slanging match.

'I'll never forgive you for what you did!' shouted Kate, grabbing her jacket to leave. 'Patrick obviously means a whole lot more to you than I do!'

Moya sat staring at the angry figure marching along by the river down below realizing the truth of it. He did. What kind of a girl was she that would put a man above her sister? Maybe Kate was right. Maybe she should break off with him.

'Don't mind her,' soothed Patrick later that night, kissing her and stroking her skin as they lay on the couch. 'Kate's just jealous. She'll get over it. There was no big romantic attachment between us. I promise.'

'But she's my sister.'

'I know, she's a nice girl, but she's not you and it's you I want.'

As their kissing became deeper and she became more aroused, she let Patrick's lips and hands and body overwhelm any traces of guilt she'd been feeling. Moya was lost in a maelstrom of physical feelings. Although she'd had previous boyfriends and big romances nothing had been of this intensity. For all her sophisticated veneer she was old-fashioned, and at twenty-three was still a virgin.

'I don't believe it! You are the most beautiful girl in the world!'

'I want it to be special,' she admitted shyly. 'I just don't want to be disappointed.'

Patrick was patient and kind and, unlike her previous boyfriend, did not try to black-mail Moya into sleeping with him. Eventually she herself could bear it no longer and wanted more than anything to make love with him.

Patrick had organized a weekend away in Hunter's Hotel in Wicklow. 'It's a quiet hideaway,' he promised, 'and we'll have all the time in the world for ourselves.'

Surrounded by summer roses and a tumbling garden Moya immediately fell in love with the place. Good food, walks on the nearby almost deserted beach and the biggest bed she'd ever seen. All her nerves had disappeared when she'd lain naked beside Patrick and felt the touch of his skin against hers. He had wrapped her in his arms and kissed and touched her and stroked every inch of her body till she was begging him to enter her, Patrick pushing his erection deep inside her till they climaxed together. Afterwards she lay awake looking at his face and eyes and knowing he was the man she loved. Sweaty and exhausted, she wrapped her legs around him and began to touch him again. Feeling him begin to swell with the tips of her fingers and the rubbing of her hands, she turned her body to his.

'Can we do it again?'

Patrick pulled her onto him this time, her long hair draping over his face as he took her nipple in his mouth and almost breathless she guided herself onto him. She groaned in pleasure.

'Are you all right?' he said eventually. 'I didn't hurt you?'

She shook her head.

'I'm glad,' she said.

'Glad?'

'Glad it was you,' she said gently, rolling over and staring at him. Patrick kissed her eyelids as she closed her eyes. She fell asleep curled in his arms, every muscle and sinew in her body relaxed and unwound.

They enjoyed two blissful days and with great reluctance returned to the city and to work. Moya was unable to disguise her utter happiness as she sat at her desk in the art gallery and began to list the valuations on the latest paintings they would show.

She was besotted with him and went around with a perpetual smile on her face.

'Are you sure you're not losing your head over him?' asked her mother anxiously.

'Mum, you met him! There isn't a woman in Ireland wouldn't lose their head if they were going out with Patrick.'

'I suppose. He's very handsome and charming and...'

'Wonderful!' she interjected. 'Mum, can't you and Dad be happy for me? I've met the most perfect man in the world.'

'No man is perfect.'

'Well, he's everything I want.'

'Then I'm glad for you, pet.'

At the end of July Patrick brought her down to his family's summer house in Clifden for a long bank holiday weekend to meet his parents. His father Robert was a retired general surgeon, and his mother Annabel even at fifty-six was a stunningly attractive woman. She welcomed Moya to their large home.

'Patrick never told us what a beauty you are,' she smiled, patting the seat beside her for Moya to sit down and skilfully proceeding to interrogate her about her family as they drank a glass of sherry before dinner.

'Wow, Patrick, you sure know where to find them!' declared his brother Andy, who worked as an intern in Dublin, as he and their sister Louise joined them. Louise, a tall and thin sophisticated sixteen-year-old, declared she wanted to be a model or a vet when she finished school.

'There's nothing like getting away from the city during the summer,' said his father, 'and having the family around us.'

Moya blushed, not sure if she was considered an outsider or part of the family.

The weekend was spent walking, swimming and making salads while Patrick disappeared off to play golf with his father and brother, leaving her to help his mother and sister with preparing lunch and dinner. Annabel was constantly on the move. Stick thin, and with lines of tension etched around her eyes, she insisted on almost every hour of the weekend being accounted for and kept up a level of incessant conversation that made Moya long for a bit of peace and quiet.

'Can't we sneak off to a little restaurant on our own for one night?' she begged Patrick.

'Mum would be insulted. She loves cooking for a crowd and big dinner parties.'

During the last day Moya lay in the sun, her skin turning gold, conscious of being watched by his mother. When they packed up on Monday afternoon, Annabel hugged her politely and begged her to come and join them again before the summer ended.

'They like you,' Patrick smiled, triumphant, as they began the long drive back to Dublin in the sweltering heat, Moya so exhausted she fell asleep.

At Christmas he had proposed, buying a solitaire diamond ring in Weirs, which looked just perfect on her long slim fingers and hands. The engagement notice was put in the *Irish Times* and Maeve Dillon burst into tears with the good news of the impending marriage of her first daughter. Her father liked Patrick and had opened a bottle of champagne to toast the happy couple.

Even Kate had swallowed her anger and wished them both well, although the situation was still awkward between the three of them.

Sitting at her desk in the gallery, Moya still could not believe all that had happened and that she and Patrick were going to be married. They were a couple and were going to start a life of their own.

Robert and Annabel generously offered to host a small family get-together to meet her parents at their Dublin home. Her flatmate Anne-Marie gave up her bed so they could stay the night in her place. 'I'll muck in with Susan and Niamh,' she said.

Moya was eternally grateful to her good-natured flatmate as she wanted to be able to keep a good eye on her parents, make sure they arrived on time at Patrick's Foxrock home and that her father didn't get waylaid in some Dublin pub or bar.

They both looked great, her mother in a black top and skirt with a slight diamanté trim and her father in his navy suit and white shirt.

'Don't keep fretting, Moya. I'm sure Patrick's parents are wonderful and we'll get along just fine.'

Her father begged Patrick to stop along the way at the famous Goat Pub so he could at least go in and wet his whistle before meeting the Redmonds.

'One pint only,' she mouthed at Patrick.

Three-quarters of an hour later they almost had to pull him out of the place.

'We were getting worried about you,' said Annabel with a smile as she ushered them into the large drawing room and took their coats.

Maeve Dillon admired the curtains and the wallpaper and the large paintings around the room, conscious of suddenly looking dowdy compared to the neat figure in the expensive designer outfit sipping a gin and tonic.

Patrick's parents were genial hosts and in no time they were all gathered around the large dining table being served with stuffed pork fillet with creamy dauphinoise and roast potatoes and a selection of vegetables.

'This is better than any of those fancy restaurants, Annabel,' complimented her father, tucking into his meal. Moya was almost tempted to go over and hug him for saying just the right thing.

Both sets of parents frantically searched for common ground.

'You play golf, Frank? What do you play off?'

'I'm a busy man, Robert. I wouldn't have time to go chasing a little ball around a field with a stick.'

'It's great for the fresh air and a bit of exercise. You should give it a try – there are some great courses down your part of the country.'

'I'm out on building sites and looking at pieces of property and farm lands most days.'

'Ah, well very good!'

Moya sighed. Golf was quickly put aside as a topic as, clearly, her father hadn't the patience for it.

Eventually they settled on their offspring. Patrick had the grace to blush as his mother described the trauma she endured trying to get him to go to school on his first day, Maeve Dillon topping it with the story of the time Moya fell off a pony when learning to ride. Moya prayed that her father would keep out of it, as he loved to embellish stories and embarrass his offspring.

At last the talk turned to the upcoming wedding.

'Moya dear, we are talking about a large wedding, aren't we?'

She smiled. They had discussed it briefly: family and close friends invited to celebrate the day in a nice hotel.

'It's just that Robert has all his medical colleagues.'

'Of course it will be a large wedding,' blustered her father. 'We all want our friends to be there. Moya is our first to get married and both Maeve and I are in agreement that she will only have the best.'

'Oh, that's so nice to hear,' gushed Annabel. 'A generous father.'

Moya could see her mother try to catch his eye, warn him to slow down, watch what he was saying.

'Daddy and Mum and Patrick and I, we all still have to sit down and discuss things,' Moya admitted. 'Nothing is booked or organized yet.'

'A word of warning,' cautioned Annabel. 'Don't leave it too late, those wonderful country houses and good hotels like the Shelbourne and the Berkeley Court get booked out a year ahead and of course you would want to organize and book a church like Foxrock or Donnybrook as soon as possible.'

Moya swallowed hard. She had absolutely no intention of letting Annabel Redmond railroad her into some big Dublin social wedding that her family couldn't afford.

'We were hoping to hold the wedding down in Rossmore,' interjected her mother, leaning across the table, a wicked sparkle in her blue eyes. 'My only brother Eamonn is a priest and I know he would love to marry Moya and Patrick in our local church, with the reception perhaps at one of the local hotels or even at home.'

Wrinkles of disappointment gathered on Annabel's forehead.

'Down in Rossmore!'

'Yes,' beamed her mother. 'It's something we'd always hoped.'

Moya could have jumped out of the uncomfortable dining chair and hugged her mother for standing up to the might of her future mother-in-law.

Patrick said nothing, as his mother glared over at him, his father breaking the embarrassing silence by proposing a toast to 'the happy couple'.

'To the happy couple,' Moya repeated to herself over again, realizing that being part of the Redmond family was at the very least going to be difficult.

Chapter Thirteen

Rossmore was the most beautiful town in Ireland as far as Romy Dillon was concerned, its long main street crammed with the supermarket and the butcher's and Scotts, the chemist, and the bank, the post office, the library, two drapery stores and a gift shop and a rake of other small businesses and offices that ensured a constant flow of shoppers. The wide main square with its bars, restaurants and craft shops overlooked the harbour and busy fishing pier where the catch of the day was landed, the fish packed on ice or frozen and made ready for sale and distribution. Hotels and guest-houses, holiday cottages and a caravan park, mostly used by summer visitors, spread along the coast road overlooking rocky shore and sandy beach. Unlike her two older sisters Romy had absolutely no intention of ever leaving the town and going to college. School and studying were bad enough without even thinking of doing a degree.

'Education is important,' her father had bellowed. 'You are not going to end up working as some sort of shop girl here in Rossmore, flirting with the local Romeos.'

Romy blazed. How in heaven's name had her father managed to guess the precise reason for her wanting to stay and take up a job in O'Sullivan's gift store or Tina's boutique? She would do anything if it meant that she could spend every spare minute of her time with Brian O'Grady, the boy she loved.

'You are going to university even if I have to drag you there, myself,' he threatened.

Romy was madly and passionately in love with Brian O'Grady! What would her father know about passion and romance, when it had died out between her parents years ago?

Brian was all that mattered to her. He was the only boy who never seemed to mind that she was so tall and skinny, he never teased her about being long and lanky or having wild frizzy light-ginger hair that had a mind of its own. He was inches taller than her with calm blue eyes, a wide strong face and a wicked smile. Half the girls in Rossmore fancied him like mad because he wrote songs and played the guitar in a band called 'The Underground'. She loved his witty sense of humour and the way he even pretended not to notice the god-awful braces that Dr Collins the local dentist had made her wear for two years. She had known him since she was four years old and they had first sat together in the junior infants' class in Rossmore's small national school. An immediate pair, they understood each other totally. It had broken her heart at eleven when Brian had gone to the local Christian Brothers secondary school and she had joined the rest of the girls in their hideous wine uniforms at the convent. He began to hang around the town with a gang of fellas, whistling at the girls, chatting them up and playing football for Rossmore's local GAA Club while she stood around street corners eyeing up the boys like the rest of her friends, the two of them joking each other about it.

During the summers she had been banished to Irish College and to Rheims, to learn French, counting the days till she was reunited with him. Meeting up with Brian the minute she got home, they would laugh and talk as if they had never been apart. Alone with him she never felt shy or awkward and could absolutely be herself as they walked down round the harbour and pier.

At sixteen he'd kissed her and the world stood still for those magic fifteen minutes as lips and mouth and tongue explored each other. They had looked at each other afterwards. Imagine finding out you were in love with your best friend. She wanted to shout it from the rooftops, holler it at the top of her voice for everyone to hear, knowing that all her school friends were cracked about him and would be mad jealous. However, something instinctive told her to disguise and hide their burgeoning relationship; she suspected that her parents were unlikely to consider Brian suitable boyfriend material for a Dillon.

On Saturdays and during the holidays he helped out in Lavelle's, the restaurant his mother managed, as money was tight ever since his father had died.

Romy had pleaded with Sheila for some sort of job there too.

'I'm sorry but we've nothing at the moment,' Sheila O'Grady had replied, noticing the way they stared at each other and how animated her son had become lately around the Dillon girl.

So, instead she had got a Saturday job in O'Sullivan's souvenir and gift shop on the harbour, but was hurt to hear two weeks later that a girl from her school, Aoife O'Connor, was working in Lavelle's. She wondered why Brian's mother suddenly seemed to have taken such a dislike to her, but it didn't matter. She was determined to earn her own money so when she went out with Brian he didn't have to put his hand in his pocket to pay for her. Twice a week they went to the Ormonde cinema or the Lighthouse disco and it wasn't fair to expect him to fork out for her Club Orange and crisps, or burgers and chips. No, she could pay her way.

A few weeks later they had gone to Tramore for the day.

'Some day, I'll be bringing you somewhere better,' he promised. 'New York or Paris or Rome. I'm not going to stay in this dump for ever.'

With Brian holding her hand, Romy didn't care where they were as long as they were together. They bought candyfloss and popcorn from the funfair stalls along the seafront, trying their luck in the shooting gallery, and going on the dodgem cars and swing-boats.

In the screaming dark of the ghost train he'd told her he wanted to make love to her, and Romy was certain she wanted it too. They had found a quiet spot hidden from view on the deserted beach. Crazed for each other, doing it for the very first time, Romy clung to him as she felt a wave of utter satisfaction and release rush through her. She had discovered sex and knew that she would want to do it again and again.

The opportunities were few and far between. One Saturday when her mother and father went to a wedding in Cork and she had the house to herself she phoned in sick to work. Brian threw her teddies and dolls on the floor of her bedroom as they made love, Romy praying they would not be disturbed.

Brian surprised her a few weeks later, announcing he had the key to one of the holiday cottages up round Rossmore Head, that his mother acted as caretaker for.

'The Sugrues are gone to the South of France for the first three weeks of August,' he told her, brandishing the magic key.

'Are you sure we can use it?'

'Cross my heart and swear to die. Mam said if they had only given her a bit more notice she could have sublet it to someone else. Anyway, she hasn't and they won't be down until the twenty-first of the month. We just have to be careful, that's all.'

Romy couldn't believe it. The cottage was small with two bedrooms and a kitchen cum living room that gave a sweeping view of the headland.

'It's perfect,' she said, flinging herself into his arms and barely able to contain herself as he began to lift off her T-shirt and unzip her jeans.

'And very private,' she added, repaying the favour.

The three weeks passed in a blur of flesh and wanting and experimenting, Maeve Dillon wondering where her youngest daughter kept disappearing to that summer.

'Brian, I have to go home to my own bed at night,' she pleaded, kissing him one last time. 'Otherwise Mam and Dad will cop on.'

They used their hideaway a few times during the autumn, Brian bringing food and extra blankets as the weather got colder until one day Sheila O'Grady stripped the beds and locked up the house for the winter. Romy didn't give a crap about her final year in school or her exams, only thinking about the time she could be with him.

'Sister Goretti says you'll fail your exams if you don't study and pay more attention in class,' worried her mother. 'Maybe we should get you a grind or Kate could help you with your maths and science.'

'Leave me alone!' she screamed. 'I'm not like Moya and Kate. I don't want to go to fecking college!'

'You'll go to college or do some kind of course, and that's all there is to it!' shouted her father. 'By God, you'll attend to your studies and like your sisters get good marks in the exams. No daughter of mine is going to be known as a dunce!'

Maeve Dillon sighed. Why did Frank have to take on so? He had barely completed second-level education himself and had somehow successfully managed to get Martin Duffy, the local insurance man cum auctioneer to take him on as an apprentice. Frank had learned the ropes of the business from the older man as he drove around the country in his Ford Capri selling life and home insurance to the small business people and farmers in the area. He heard who was sick and ailing, or had no son or daughter to leave their house or farm to, and gradually began to discover his talent for property. Much was sold on to interested clients but a percentage of the sales became the property of the Duffy Dillon portfolio. Frank had done well, building, developing sites. He was a true entrepreneur. However, as he rose up in the world he'd become fixated on the importance of a good education for the children.

Maeve suspected that the only chink in his armour was his sense of inferiority about his schooling and lack of knowledge in certain areas. She had worked for a while in her father's solicitor's practice, even contemplated studying law but had put all these notions behind her with the birth of her first child, content like all the young mothers of her day to stay home looking after their children. Motherhood agreed with her and she had no regrets about being a wife and mother and homemaker. Frank was a difficult man and it was her job to make things smooth for him, be it the children, friends or business entertaining. She had always hated rows and upsets and wished that Romy hadn't inherited so much of her father's temper and stubbornness.

'You might enjoy going to Dublin like

Moya and Kate,' she soothed, 'it's not that far away and you'd be home at weekends if that's what you want. Your father and I will still be here, I promise.'

'I'm not going.'

Maeve sighed to herself. God preserve her from teenage angst and drama. She couldn't remember herself and Vonnie being this bad growing up.

'Your father only wants what's best for you, pet, though I'd be lost without you and maybe it would be a good thing for your dad and I to have one of you willing to stay home and look after us in our old age.'

Banging the door, Romy stormed out of the kitchen and up the stairs to her room. The prospect of waiting hand and foot on her father and mother was something she had absolutely no intention of doing.

The Leaving Certificate exams over, Romy planned spending the long summer days with Brian and was devastated to find out in the first week of July that he was going to work with an uncle in London.

'I thought we were going to spend the summer together,' she complained.

'I don't know why,' he sighed, running his fingers through his hair, 'but Mam is set on me going away and has fixed up a job for me with Uncle Kevin on some big building site.'

'But can't you get her to change her mind?

We were supposed to spend the summer together,' she coaxed, reminding him of last year.

'I know, but it's all arranged, my fare is already booked and paid for. Mam says I'm not spending the summer here and that I have to go. Listen, Romy, it'll only be for eight weeks and the money is great.'

Romy tried not to cry and make a show of herself as she knew money was tight in his family.

'Brian, promise you love me.'

He nodded, pulling her into his arms.

'Say it,' she ordered as his hands reached up under her skirt.

'I love you,' he said, silencing her with a slow deep kiss that went on and on, pulling her body so close to his that they were instantly aroused. She cursed the fact that the holiday cottage was now rented as Brian in the semi-darkness and quiet of the lane behind Riordan's boat yard pushed and pushed against her, hitching up her denim skirt around her waist as he entered her. Romy gasped, clinging to him. There was no-one like him in the whole world and in only a few weeks' time he would be back with her again, she consoled herself as, putting her jealous fears about English girls aside, she kissed him goodbye.

'Listen, Romy, before you know it I'll have made lots of money. Maybe when I'm finished you could come over to England and we could go backpacking around Europe or go grape-picking, just get out of here and do something different.'

Romy knew there was zero chance of her parents letting her do that. 'Just come back home to me,' she said, reminding him of what he'd be missing.

That summer was warm and wet and Romy spent her time selling whipped ice-creams to small bold children and trying to wrap delicate Waterford glass in such a way that it would not shatter or break during the journey to whatever far-flung destination its purchaser came from.

Bored and lonely by September, she couldn't believe it when her results came and she had done way better than she had expected with an A in English, an A in French, and a smattering of Bs and Cs.

'I always knew you had it in you,' congratulated her mother, kissing her warmly. 'Just think what you would have got if you'd even bothered to study,' said her father, poring over her marks.

Grateful to the nuns in St Dominic's for her amazing academic achievement, Romy was finally willing to join the thousands of other students flocking to Dublin, leaving home for third-level education. Her grades ensured a place in University College

Dublin to study Arts.

The week before term she had stayed with Kate, sleeping on her couch as she hunted for accommodation; she was lucky to get a place in one of the student apartments on the Belfield campus, sharing with five other students.

She wrote and wrote to Brian, begging him to join her in Dublin, not believing when he told her that he had also got good results and had signed up on an engineering course in London and would work at the weekends as a barman in Fulham to help cover his costs.

'Kevin and Auntie Mary are putting me up, but I don't have a rich daddy like you,' he joked, 'so I have to work.'

Romy had reacted like a spoilt child, fighting with him, writing hurt angry words that she never should have used on the daisy-patterned paper she'd bought in Sullivan's. He still wrote and phoned her occasionally but within a few months they had drifted apart.

Deeply hurt, she could not believe it was over. She felt lost in UCD's modern concrete and glass campus, bored by constant lectures in packed lecture halls. Some lecturers were entertaining and enlightening but many were pompous old farts and she loved to raise her hand and ask them a difficult question, speaking in middle English for the fun of it! She yawned through the subtle intricacies of French grammar and concentrated on reading up on the classics of French literature. Signora Bettina, a tall Italian woman who rolled her dark eyes, was the only one who succeeded in making her fall in love with her country and its language. Romy scribbled her notes wildly and so badly she could barely read them back, trying to make sense of them in the library where she retreated to study. The three girls she knew from Rossmore had got in with a crowd of their own and had begun to exclude her.

She didn't bother going home at weekends as there was no point. Instead she went to party after party, sometimes with her flatmates, but mostly with people she didn't know or care about, telling her sisters to 'Piss off!' and 'Mind your own business!' when they told her to cop on to herself and grow up. She had absolutely no intention of listening to them. They had their own busy lives and jobs to attend to and could keep out of her hair! She was happy to be a 'wild child', as they called her, finding others like herself who did not ask too much of each other and demanded only simple companionship as they drank and smoked dope and tried to ease the loneliness.

She ignored requests to come home for

the weekends, complaining of having to study and essays to deliver, her bewildered parents accepting this new-found studiousness. Her father came to Dublin on business and insisted on treating her to lunches and dinners which, though the food was excellent, neither of them enjoyed much. They ate at the Burlington, the Westbury, Roly's and Beaufield Mews. She knew he was checking up on her and she regaled him with stories from lectures as they ate, Frank Dillon, bursting out of his heavy navy suit with an immaculately laundered shirt and regulation striped tie, trying to make sense of a world he did not understand. Romy, always ashamed at herself for belittling him, would try to make amends, hugging him when they parted saying, 'I love you, Daddy, you know I do.'

'Your mother's coming up next week,' he'd announced over the roast beef lunch in the Montrose. 'She'll be staying with Moya for a few days. There's a lot to be done with organizing this wedding so I want you to be a good girl and give her a hand.'

Romy groaned. She hated the thought of bridesmaids' dresses. Herself and Kate like two eejits in the same dress. If she ever got married she was going to elope and tell no-one. She wouldn't want the big circus that was being planned for Moya and Patrick's wedding. She would slip away with the man she loved: that would be more than enough for her. Tears filled her eyes as she thought of Brian and she pulled a tissue from her sleeve and blew her nose loudly.

'You OK?' asked her dad.

'I might be getting a cold,' she sniffed, for a second tempted to confide in him.

'Bed early then and plenty of vitamin C,' he said matter-of-factly, reaching for the restaurant bill. 'You don't want to go disappointing your mother.'

Chapter Fourteen

Kate was doing her utmost to be happy for Moya. But it isn't every day your sister announces she is madly in love and is going to get married to the man you had high hopes for. Inside she admitted to deep feelings of hurt and a weird jealousy that it was Moya that Patrick was marrying, not her. She tried to logic it out, convince herself that she would never have been able to sustain a relationship with someone like him, and that marriage to Patrick had never remotely been on the cards but her stupid heart kept letting her down. Perhaps if she had someone else in her life it might have been different but hearing her sister go on all the time about how wonderful her future husband was was enough to drive Kate crazy.

'Kate, you're so bloody picky!' complained Minnie, who was forever trying to match-make and introduce her to someone.

She worked with lots of men and – except for one disastrous night's outing at the company's annual 4th July barbecue when she'd made a fool of herself snogging a randy young legal intern from Australia – had managed to avoid the overtures of her male colleagues. Complications like that she most certainly could do without as she firmly believed in not mixing business and pleasure.

'God, Kate, you're so stupid, surrounded by all those great guys and you won't date them! What's wrong with you, woman?'

Lying alone in bed at night she often asked herself the very same question.

Her mother was coming to stay with Moya for two days in order to do the whole wedding thing properly. Huge lists had been drawn up of all the essentials to do and shop for and Romy had skipped lectures and Kate had taken the Friday off work to accompany them.

Moya looked radiant in a simple white linen shirt and beige trousers and it seemed as if every shop they went into, the staff welcomed them warmly, carried away by the enthusiasm of the bride-to-be and her mother and two sisters.

Moya's designer wedding dress was costing a fortune and was being made by one of Ireland's top designers Clodagh Connolly who was known for her simple, classic Irish lace and linen designs. The small Dublin studio was now graced by international actresses and models and wealthy young women who could afford her high prices. Kate and Romy had stood transfixed as Moya slipped into her wedding dress for the second fitting.

'Do you like it?' she'd asked hesitantly as Maeve Dillon's eyes welled with tears. The bodice was tightly fitted and clung to Moya's perfect shape and slim waist, the skirt soft and loose falling to the floor in a swirl of hand-stitched lace.

'God, Moya, you look gorgeous,' gasped Romy.

'That's the most beautiful dress I've ever seen,' admitted Kate, awed by the designer's intuitive instinct in terms of her sister's personality and sense of simple classic style.

'Look at the detail,' encouraged their mother, fingering the material carefully. 'Such workmanship. God, Moya, it's just beautiful, it's so you!'

'You look absolutely stunning,' declared

Kate honestly.

Jilly who worked with Clodagh, the designer, helped attach the simple veil that fell from a comb carved from what looked like mother-of-pearl, shining out against her sister's jet black shoulder-length hair.

'You will be the most beautiful bride she has designed for this year,' she murmured, adjusting the headpiece so that the light ripple of lace fell down Moya's back.

'What do you think?' Moya asked, eyes gleaming as she slowly twirled around and studied herself in the multi-angled mirrors.

'I think both your father and Patrick will be very proud when they see you on the big day,' her mother said, fiddling in her leather handbag for a tissue.

'Is she making our dresses too?' Romy asked hopefully.

'Are you mad! It would cost a fortune. Besides, I saw two lovely dresses in Brown Thomas and they've some really unusual ones in the Powerscourt Centre too.'

Romy and Kate had tried on five different dresses in the upstairs Brides part of the Design Centre, both of them unimpressed by colours and styles that might suit one of them but not the other. There was a plum shoestring top and ankle-length skirt, which Kate had liked and Romy hated, an off the shoulder bluebell blue, a figure-hugging aqua satin that Kate felt might make her burst if she had to sit or kneel down and two pinks, one in silk and one in satin.

'They're lovely but they're too much,' sighed Moya.

In Grafton Street they went into Brown Thomas's exclusive bridal department where they studied the rail of bridesmaids' dresses and those hanging behind the sliding glass doors. Some were absolutely disgusting, all frills and flounces, and Kate prayed that Moya hadn't her heart set on anything like that.

'What do you think of these?'

Moya was holding up two very simple round-necked dresses in a shade of pale gold which had a bodice fitting almost similar to her own style.

'I think these might look really good on you both,' she suggested, 'and they're sort of like my dress.'

'They're a bit plain,' ventured Romy, unable to mask her disappointment.

'That's what I like about them,' retorted Moya, pushing her sisters towards the dressing room.

Kate let the cool material and satin lining slide over her skin. The dress seemed a perfect fit and with the colour of her hair made her look bright and summery.

'Wow, it's nicer than I imagined,' she gasped, gazing at herself in the mirror. Romy, who was taller than her, looked even longer and leaner in the dress, its golden colour picking up the glints of gold in her reddish fair hair, which tumbled around her face.

'I didn't think I'd fecking like it,' she admitted, 'but there's something about it, it's like a glass of champagne!'

Maeve and Moya Dillon were unanimous in agreement that 'these were the perfect dresses' as they made them twirl and turn as if they were models.

'Are you sure we shouldn't try on some more?' Kate, as usual, was indecisive when purchasing clothes. She often tried on things a few times before making up her mind.

'For God's sake, Kate, you've put on the most perfect dress that suits the two of you equally well and will look amazing with my dress. What the hell more are you expecting?'

Kate shrugged. Moya was right. If something was right what was the point going off chasing after something else?

The sales assistant couldn't believe her good fortune to have sold two dresses so quickly and without all the hassle and fighting and bitching that usually went with pre-wedding outings.

Maeve, taking out her chequebook, insisted they go for a bite of lunch before they turned their attention to her outfit and the lingerie department.

'We could grab a pizza or a sandwich,' Romy suggested, her stomach grumbling.

'Something quick and easy and light,' insisted Moya, steering them in the direction of the shop's chic salad and soup eatery where crowds of well-dressed women were queuing for a snack to tide them over as they shopped.

They roamed the racks afterwards for something for Maeve.

'I don't want to look too "mother of the brideish," she joked, 'but I don't want to let you down either.'

'Mum, you'd never let us down!' they chorused, shoving her into a dressing room with about ten different outfits.

Maeve Dillon fiddled and pulled and tried on one after another, not totally satisfied. She wished she were younger, slimmer, more beautiful, that her stomach didn't bulge, that her legs didn't wobble with cellulite and that her face wasn't starting to fill with lines and wrinkles. 'Laughter lines', that's what Vonnie called them, but she suspected it wasn't laughing that had been responsible for them in her case. She sighed, looking at herself in a motherly suit.

'Mammy, get that off, it's ghastly,' ordered Romy, pushing in to look at her. 'Moya said that you're to try this on.'

Maeve put on the light lavender dress. Its

square neckline and waist-skimming skirt flowed smoothly over her figure, the matching jacket falling from her shoulders and arms. It felt wonderful and moreover she felt good in it.

'Mammy, you've got to buy it!' insisted Romy. 'It's the nicest thing I've ever seen on you.'

'You're sure I don't look like mutton dressed as lamb?'

'Not at all,' said Moya, examining it from every angle. 'You'll knock all the relations and friends for six when they see you in it.'

Kate could see Maeve's eyes light up, her face glow with the compliments and attention. 'You look so beautiful,' she declared, hugging her mother tight.

'I suppose I'd better buy it then,' joked Maeve. 'Your father'll be relieved that he won't have to come looking with me, you know what he's like in shops!'

In the lingerie department Maeve went mad treating them all to new sets of lacy bras and knickers, expensive fripperies for under their dresses.

'Mammy, this must be costing a fortune,' protested Kate as the spending went on and Moya added a hand-stitched embroidered white lingerie set to the bill.

'We're not going to wear those exquisite dresses we've just bought with any old pair of panties and bra. It's my treat!'

By teatime they were exhausted. Shoes for Moya and Romy had been found, a hat for their mother and an array of perfumes, lipsticks and nail polishes purchased.

'I'm going to collapse,' admitted Moya.

'Me first. My feet are killing me.'

'Can we stop off and get chips or something on the way home?'

'Romy,' admonished their mother. 'Today is special, all of us together here in town shopping for Moya's big day. Do you remember when you were kids we'd all go for a slap-up meal when we came up to town to shop or to go to the pantomime or the theatre? What about a meal in the Shelbourne? A drink before, and then dinner.'

The Shelbourne Hotel overlooking St Stephen's Green was buzzing as ever, as businessmen and well-heeled tourists checked in, the Horseshoe Bar crowded with groups of work colleagues and those looking for a soothing drink after a rough day, the large cosy lounge overlooking the park filled with chat and laughter. Maeve and the girls managed to find a seat and ordered drinks as they studied the dinner menu, while a distracted Romy tried to spot the celebrity guests.

Over dinner they laughed and chatted, giggling about things they did when they were little girls.

'Do you remember the time we decided to paint the shed with a tin of red paint we found belonging to Daddy?'

'He almost went crazy,' laughed Moya, 'when he saw the state of it and the state of us.'

'Or what about the time we dug up all the flowers and were selling them at the gate?'

'Or the time we had a jumble sale and by accident Kate sold his good gold cufflinks?'

Maeve Dillon ordered more wine as they reminisced, the talk getting louder, the four of them rocking with laughter at the antics they'd got up to.

'We must have been very bold sometimes. How did you cope with us?'

'I remember I laughed a lot. Moya was always putting on makeup – one time she painted herself with nail polish instead of eyeshadow. We had to make a run for the hospital! Another time she was trying to make something for herself and ended up sewing the skirt she was stitching to the clothes she was wearing! I'd to cut them apart. Kate, you were different, you were always the curious one, always into everything, drinking medicines, eating soap, trying to climb trees and rocks. You were such a little devil and were always getting lost in the shops and I'd be mortified when they'd call out on the intercom looking for the lost little girl's mother.'

'And what about me?' asked Romy.

'Romy pet, I'm still not out of the woods with you yet. Who forgot to unplug the hair-drier last month and nearly set fire to the house?'

'That was an accident. I was rushing out to...'

'You've always been my wild child. Do you remember when you were small and every time you went to the beach you stripped off naked and refused to wear your swimming togs?'

'I liked the sun on my skin.'

'You've always had a mind of your own. Every time there was a row or an upset you'd pack up your bags and want to run away. You always seemed to be running away for some funny reason or other.'

'I liked packing my bag and stealing biscuits and cake and bread and making a flask of orange squash and pretending I was going off somewhere exciting.'

'One time yourself and that O'Grady boy disappeared for twelve hours. Sheila O'Grady and I were terrified you'd fallen in off the harbour. We'd all the neighbours and the guards out looking for you. Eventually we found you about a mile out the road by Ferguson's old mill asleep on the long grass.'

'Don't remind me. Daddy took my blue

bicycle off me as a punishment.'

'You had our hearts scalded sometimes.'

'Yeah, remember the time I got the kitchen scissors and gave poor old Lucky a cut?'

Moya almost dropped the spoon of *crème brûlée* she was eating, with shock. Kate automatically lashed out with a well-placed kick on Romy's shin, incredulous that her sister could be so stupid upsetting their mother and reminding them all of that fateful day.

'God, I'm so sorry, Mum,' mumbled Romy, appalled at herself. 'I didn't mean to.'

'I have to go to the bathroom.' Maeve excused herself, standing up instantly from the table and scrabbling around for her handbag. Kate and Moya attacked Romy the minute she'd left the dining room.

'Of all the stupid things to say!'

'Why did you have to go and ruin a perfectly good day, Romy? Do you enjoy doing it, is that it?'

'I swear to God. I just wasn't thinking.'

'You know Mammy's gone to the bathroom to have a cry, don't you?'

'I forgot!'

'How could you ever fucking forget?'

'Listen, I'll go after her.'

'No, don't you think you've done enough for one night?' said Moya sarcastically. 'She's better left on her own.'

Romy sat at the table feeling miserable as

her sisters glared at her, wishing she'd kept her mouth shut.

Maeve Dillon stared at herself in the wall-sized mirror of the marble and glass bathroom. She cursed the grief that still at times assailed and overwhelmed her. She threw water on her face and dabbed on a touch of foundation to cover the blotchiness of her cheeks and redness around her eyes. Trying to compose herself she took a deep breath before heading back to the dining room, stopping in her tracks at the sight of her future son-in-law standing at the doorway of the hotel's bar deep in conversation with a tall blonde in a black suit. For a few seconds she stood just watching, noticing how attentive he was to the young woman and how she was glancing up at him, her hand resting on his arm. Smooth and charming, totally self-confident and aware of his attraction to the opposite sex, Patrick in some strange way reminded her of Frank. Physically they were very different, and a generation apart, but her future son-in-law's ways were something she was accustomed to. He might be more savvy and polished and educated but underneath the veneer he too was a womanizer.

Taking her time, she approached him.

'Hello, Patrick,' she interrupted, smiling, noticing his reaction.

'Oh Mrs Dillon. Maeve! What are you doing here?'

'The girls and I are just finishing having dinner inside. I decided we all needed a treat after a long day's shopping.'

He made a perfunctory introduction, Maeve barely catching the girl's name and noting he didn't say a word about Moya, or the fact that she herself would soon be his mother-in-law. She was in two minds about mentioning the purchase of the wedding finery, but decided against it.

'I'd better get back inside, Patrick, or they'll be sending out a search party for me.'

Back at the table she ordered a coffee, and was just about to forewarn Moya when Patrick sauntered into the large dining room, making a beeline for their table. 'The beautiful Dillon girls,' he said slowly, fussing over them all and giving them each a kiss on the cheek.

Highly embarrassed, Kate almost pushed him away.

Moya was thrilled to see him, her eyes lighting up as she stood up and hugged him.

'I met Maeve outside.' He smiled, gazing around the room and refusing the chair the waiter offered. 'I was just having a drink with an old college pal, when I heard my beloved was here so I decided I'd better come in and say a quick hello.'

'Funny the way we bumped into each other,' said Maeve. 'You'd think we were back in Rossmore!'

'Ladies, did you all have a good day's shopping?'

'The best!' said Moya with a smile. 'The dress, the bridesmaid dresses are all organized and we bought loads.'

'The very best!' agreed the others.

Kate said very little and was relieved when Patrick Redmond at last politely excused himself and returned to the bar. As their mother settled the bill, she ordered a taxi.

'What a lovely day we've had,' said Maeve. 'I'm exhausted and my feet are killing me but I had a great time. Thanks, girls.'

'Thanks, Mum,' added Moya, Kate and Romy. 'For everything.'

Chapter Fifteen

The Stone House was in a state of near frenzy as the day of Moya's wedding dawned. Uncle Eamonn, their mother's brother, had arrived from Chicago. He was a parish priest in a place called Oakland and was delighted to have been asked to officiate at the ceremony and celebrate the wedding mass.

'Sure, why wouldn't I come home to marry Maeve and Frank's eldest daughter, my beautiful niece Moya Teresa and her young man Patrick, and to enjoy the party and celebration afterwards?'

'And how's my darling girl?' roared her uncle, wrapping Kate in a bear hug the minute he saw her. 'I thought you were going to come out to the Windy City to see me last fall?'

'I'm sorry, Uncle Eamonn, but I'd just started working and I couldn't get the time off.'

'Well, next year maybe you'll come visit.'

Eamonn Ryan enjoyed visits from his family more than anything. Running a busy parish kept him occupied most of the day but at night when he sat down by the fire and cooked a TV dinner for one or ordered in he realized just how solitary his vocation had made him. He had no regrets about working in the priesthood, spreading the Word of God, but sometimes did admit to a loneliness that prayer and books and the good people of his parish could not overcome. Coming home for a big family occasion like this was exactly what he needed to restore his spirits and renew old friendships in the town where he grew up. Kate had vacated her bedroom, which had once been his, and stepping across the threshold had provoked a whole load of memories of his childhood and youth. His initials E.R. were still carved in the wardrobe door, and the old apple tree was still bearing apples outside his window.

'This place is a tip,' Kate protested as she moved her clothes down the corridor and into Romy's room. 'How can you live with it like this?'

'No problem,' jeered Romy, who had actually done a massive tidy before Kate moved her things. 'I like it like this.'

The house was full of people as their father's brother Peadar and his wife Nuala from Galway were also staying. Their mother put them in the guest bedroom while their two kids Hannah and Jack were to sleep in Sean's old room.

The house had been cleaned top to bottom, Christy the painter coming in at short notice to repaint the hall stairs and landing.

Maeve Dillon had a notepad with a list of all the things she had to do. The fridge had been stuffed with eggs and rashers and sausages, and black and white pudding and pounds of butter, and Hannah and Jack were dispatched to get fresh bread for the breakfast in the morning.

'I feel like I'm running a guest-house,' she joked, trying to remember where she'd put the last two cakes of brown bread she'd made.

Frank was in his element talking to everyone, overseeing the erection of the huge marquee in the garden by Tony Taylor and his crew from Taylor Tents.

'Mind my roses,' begged Maeve, abandoning the kitchen and grabbing a spade and wheelbarrow to move three precious rose bushes to the safety of the back bed. The caterers had been booked, the barmen organized, and her father was out shouting at the delivery driver from McHugh's pub as he unloaded beer kegs and crates of Guinness and Smithwicks and a whole range of wines and spirits and boxes of sparkling glasses.

'God, this must be costing a fortune,' murmured their Aunt Nuala, watching her brother-in-law take out a wad of notes from his trouser pocket.

'It's what Moya wanted. We looked at the Harbour and the Rossmore Inn and the Grand in Waterford, but she felt a smaller wedding at home was what she'd prefer.'

'It's a lot of work.'

'Aye, but I suppose Frank and I felt it would be nice to have it here. We got married in that old hotel in town, and well I'd always sort of regretted that we didn't have a nicer wedding. Here in the garden with some nice music should be lovely.'

After the church rehearsal the Dillon and the Redmond families joined together for dinner in the Rossmore Inn. Patrick's parents were staying in the hotel. Annabel Redmond, enquiring about the guest list, had finally come around to accepting that her son's wedding was not going to be the big Dublin social event she'd hoped for but a relaxed gathering of friends and family at home. She was keen to be introduced to the rest of the family. Romy and Kate were as polite as could be, but decided to sit down one end of the table with Patrick's brother and sister.

Moya looked a bit pale and picked at her food.

'Are you OK?' asked Kate.

'I'm fine, just a bit nervous.'

Patrick was equally quiet while Frank Dillon and his father got involved discussing property prices in the area. Uncle Eamonn regaled them with disastrous funeral stories from the people in his parish, which included a local Mafia chief asking him to say a special funeral mass for one of his dogs.

'That's outrageous, asking a man of the cloth to do that!' murmured their Aunt Nuala. 'I couldn't say no,' joked their uncle. 'The Lord would understand I didn't dare refuse a man like that!'

'Would he have shot you?' piped up Hannah.

'Well, I don't know but I'm here to tell the tale.'

Back at home, Maeve Dillon slipped into Moya's room before she fell asleep, noting how pale her daughter looked against the pillows.

'Are you feeling all right, pet?'

'Just a little nervous.'

'You're sure about Patrick, Moya? Sure he is the right one.'

'Mammy! What are you saying? I love Patrick, it's our wedding day tomorrow.'

Maeve Dillon sighed.

'It's just that if you changed your mind, your daddy and I would stand by you, you know that. No-one is going to push you into something you are not sure about.'

'Mammy, for God's sake. Are you cracked? No-one is pushing me into doing anything. No-one!'

For a second Maeve Dillon experienced that strange sense of *déjà vu*, remembering her own mother standing in front of her in her dressing gown saying almost the exact same thing. She smiled, for she hadn't listened either.

'Don't mind me, pet, I'm just a sentimental old mother hen who hates losing one of her chicks,' she apologized, kissing her eldest daughter goodnight.

The wedding morning was frantic as everyone fought over showers and the bathroom.

Moya, the only one who seemed calm and unruffled, lay in the bed relaxing as Romy and Kate and their mother screamed at each other.

The marquee was all set up, and there were fresh roses and sprigs of lavender from the garden on every table. A long narrow table was set up as a bar on one end of the patio, the other one inside the marquee.

'Well thank God for the beautiful weather,' smiled their uncle, tucking into a plate of rashers and sausages.

The girls all disappeared to the hairdresser's with their mother and aunts. Gemma O'Leary and one of her juniors busily got them all washed and dried and arranged their hair. Romy and Kate each wore a simple spray of baby's breath creamy flowers wound through a piece of finely plaited hair at the back of their heads. Cream roses were attached to the comb on Moya's dark hair, which looked so straight it was like satin.

The minute they finished they all chased back to the house to change, to find Frank and Uncle Peadar already in their morning suits.

'You two look very handsome,' admired Maeve Dillon as she ran up to change into her own outfit.

Kate and Romy sat in their dressing gowns doing their makeup, for once putting their differences to one side and agreeing that they should wear the same ivory and beige eyeshadow and brown eyeliner, plus a coral-coloured lipstick with a layer of gloss on top.

'Phew! I suppose we look kind of OK.'

They ran into Moya who was putting another layer of mascara onto her eyelashes, which she had curled to open her eyes and make them look even bigger. The three of them did their nails before finally putting on their dresses.

'Mammy, come up for the dresses!' screamed Romy.

Maeve Dillon almost fell going up the stairs, nursing a bruise on her leg as she watched Kate and Romy help their sister into her dress and fasten up the bodice. It was even more exquisite than she had remembered and Moya looked radiant. Maeve, unwrapping the tissue, helped attach the gossamer-light veil to the comb at the back of her head.

'Do I look all right, Mammy?'

Moya was trembling as she lightly touched her hair and neck.

'You look truly beautiful, darling. From the second I first saw you, you've been my darling and you always will be. No matter how long you are married, you'll still be my little girl.'

Kate blinked away the tears welling in her own eyes.

'I'm so happy, I don't know why I'm crying,' sniffed Moya.

'You'll ruin your make-up,' cautioned Romy, flopping onto the bed.

'It's your wedding day, all brides cry,' said their mother, trying to control her emotions.

'And all mothers.'

'And all sisters too!'

'What the hell's going on in here?' interrupted Frank Dillon coming on the scene. 'Is everything all right? Moya are you OK? The wedding is going ahead?'

'Frank, the wedding is most definitely going ahead. It's just it's such a big step.'

'You look wonderful, pet,' he said, kissing Moya on the cheek. 'Patrick's a lucky man.' He raised a tumbler of whiskey to his lips.

'Don't tell me you've been drinking already, Frank. Don't tell me that!'

'Leave me alone, woman. It's just to steady me, settle my nerves for the church.'

'I can't believe that you'll be drunk leading your daughter up the aisle.'

'I've had just a few sips,' he argued, 'that's all.'

'Please, Dad, don't fight!' pleaded Moya, looking at the two of them. 'I couldn't bear it if you and Mammy were to fight today.'

Kate could see her mother's reluctance to climb down and grabbed her father by the arm instead.

'Come on downstairs, Dad,' she coaxed, 'and I'll make you a quick cup of coffee and listen to you practising your speech again before we have to leave for the church.'

The local parish church was packed with the hundred and twenty guests invited to the wedding and a collection of local neighbours and friends curious to see Moya Dillon's wedding. A few of the nuns from their old school were sitting at the back of the church smiling as the family entered.

Romy and Kate had walked up the aisle of the church in their simple champagne-coloured dresses, carrying small posies of white roses and sprays of baby's breath tied in a ribbon. Kate hoped no-one could sense the shaking of her knees and legs. They walked slowly, taking steps in time with the music, coming to stand at the side of the altar where their Uncle Eamonn was waiting. Patrick looked so handsome in a morning suit with his gold–coloured cravat, standing anxiously beside his brother Andrew waiting for his bride.

Moya appeared, breathtakingly beautiful, holding her father's arm as she came up the aisle. Frank Dillon was desperately trying to hold his own emotions in check. Father Eamonn welcomed them warmly as Patrick stepped forward and took her hand.

It was a simple ceremony and as Kate

listened to them swear their love for each other she bowed her head in prayer and asked for the grace to be able to accept Patrick as her brother-in-law. She held Moya's bouquet of roses and lilies as her sister signed the register and finally became Mrs Moya Redmond.

A sea of smiling faces and flashing cameras greeted the happy couple as they paraded down the church and out into the August sunshine where the photographer was waiting to take group photos of them.

'Wasn't that the loveliest mass ever!' remarked Maeve Dillon to Patrick's mother who was wearing an elegant black two-piece and a wide-brimmed cream hat with a swirling band of black and white around the crown.

'Having your brother say the mass made it so personal and so special. You must be very pleased, Maeve.'

'Eamonn wouldn't have missed Moya and Patrick's wedding for the world. He always tries to be here for these family occasions.'

'Moya's such a stunning bride,' gushed Annabel. 'I can see how Patrick fell in love with her at first sight.'

'They make a very handsome couple,' Maeve agreed, watching the two of them smile and pose for photographs, as well-wishers crowded around. 'I'm sure they will be very happy together.'

Forty minutes later the wedding party arrived back at the house to awaiting glasses of champagne and kir royale. It was very warm as they stood on the lawn sipping their drinks and chatting to everyone, renewing old friendships with cousins and family. Moya's work and college friends looked like a group of models or actors in their designer clothes and high heels and floaty frocks. Moya in the middle of them, giggling and laughing with Patrick at her side, introduced them to the family. Her father as usual asked the age-old question:

'What do you do?'

'Are all dads the same?' giggled her best friend Anne-Marie, throwing her arms around him and giving him a big flirty kiss.

The Stone House looked wonderful, basking in the August sunshine, the door and windows re-painted, frothy pink and cream roses tumbling around the doorway and windowsills, every pot and garden urn overflowing with splashes of colour, the large floral borders at their best, bursting with tall blue delphiniums and pink and blue lupins, a riot of colour and scented nicotiana. Everyone had worked so hard at getting the place to look right. There wasn't a blade of grass out of place or a weed growing in the flowerbeds, Maeve had made sure of that.

'You have a beautiful home, Mrs Dillon,' complimented Jenny Leyden, the girl who worked with Moya in the art gallery.

Minnie and her mother were stomping around the grass in tiny stiletto heels, Minnie wearing a fuchsia-red dress which made her look cute and sexy and had attracted much attention from a few of the single males invited.

'God, do you think we're related now that Moya and Patrick have married? We're probably some kind of far-off cousins.'

Kate shrugged, though being related to Minnie was bound to be fun.

'Moya looks amazing but you and Romy look fantastic too.'

After a while the guests and family began to move inside as the caterers were more than ready to serve the meal.

Kate was seated up at the top table beside the best man while Romy was at another table with the groom's man and Patrick's sister Louise and some of their cousins. Father Eamonn said grace before they began to eat.

Wild salmon was served, and carrot soup, roast lamb and potatoes with minted peas and a roast vegetable bake and a melt-in-the-mouth raspberry Pavlova for pudding. Kate could see the tension ease from her mother's face as one course after another was a success, Uncle Eamonn, sitting near her, clearing his plate and enjoying the red wine now that his priestly duties were done.

Her father sat proudly, head high, accepting compliments from Patrick's mother. Glancing over, Kate saw that Moya was about to burst with happiness, her dark eyes sparkling, her mouth wide and smiling, relaxed now the ceremony was over.

Kate found Andrew Redmond easy to talk to: he was very different from his brother and seemed more easygoing and less driven.

'Are you nervous about the speeches?' she asked.

'A bit, but I was on the debating team in Blackrock College and still do a bit to keep my hand in with the L & H Soc. so hopefully I should be OK.'

'Snap! I was on my convent's school team too,' she laughed, 'and the team in college too.'

'So we should be able to get a bit of a debate going this end of the table,' he joked.

She told him about her career and work, listening as he talked about the trials of being a final-year medical student. He planned to work in America or Canada for a year or two after he qualified. 'Gain a bit of experience then go out and work in Africa or Asia. It's where medicine is really needed.'

'Will you eventually come back to Ireland?'

'Who knows!'

They'd finished eating when Andy called on Patrick and Moya to cut the cake, everyone giving them a rousing cheer as they stood up and joined hands holding the knife.

The speeches were great. Her father slowly rose to his feet, the piece of paper with his speech left discreetly on the table in front of him. Kate held her breath as Frank Dillon told everyone just how much he loved his darling eldest daughter and how happy he was that she had met Patrick. Kate blushed crimson when he mentioned that it was through her younger sister they had met, and that Kate should take full credit for bringing the two of them together. She could feel her mouth go dry and her eyes burn as he went on. Why had he made no mention of that to her earlier? He rambled on about their childhood and Moya and all the broken hearts there would be now that the beauty of the family had married. Everyone was upstanding as he toasted the bride and groom. Kate sipped with relief at the glass of champagne as finally with much clapping and applause he sat down, red-faced and sweating as the barman brought the double whiskey he'd ordered earlier.

Patrick's father stood up and with much aplomb warmly welcomed Moya to their family and thanked her for taking on their son.

'I know that my beautiful new daughter-in-law will be a great influence on Patrick, and that he in turn will be a good husband to her.'

Andy followed, reading some telegrams and messages of goodwill before embarking on his best man's speech.

'I am mightily relieved that my brother the Romeo of the Redmond family has finally found his Juliet,' he joked, which brought a loud thumping from the table at the back of the marquee where Patrick's friends were sitting. Then he wondered aloud how the beautiful Moya was going to put up with his brother's bad habits, everyone laughing as he listed them. Moya put on a rueful face, saying she'd put up with them. He ended by thanking Kate and Romy for being such beautiful bridesmaids.

Finally Patrick stood up, his face serious as he thanked their parents for the wonderful meal and reception and everyone for coming along to share in their special day, declaring at the end: 'I met the girl of my dreams in this house and there was nothing left for me to do but marry her.'

Kate could feel a huge lump in her throat as she remembered that night, trying to compose herself as Moya reached up and kissed him, the whole room breaking into rapturous applause for the happy couple.

Chapter Sixteen

Romy ran her fingers through her tousled hair. Her feet were killing her from dancing in the dainty little shoes her mother and Kate had picked out to go with their dresses. Larry, the groom's man, had asked her up to dance as soon as the floor began to fill up. A conceited young barrister, he'd managed to bore her all through the meal with his talk of law courts, barely bothering to ask her what she was doing. She had no intention of letting him monopolize her for the rest of the night and dumped him as soon as she could, watching as some of Moya's single girlfriends flapped around him. They were more than welcome! She wriggled her toes trying to get the circulation going as Fergus signalled her to get up again.

Aunt Vonnie was smooching with Uncle Joe on the big wooden dance floor as if they were teenage lovers and Uncle Eamonn was dancing with Mrs Redmond like they were in a ballroom dancing competition. She supposed priests didn't know a lot about dancing or get much practice. Her mam and dad had already made eejits of themselves dancing earlier on to some old Rolling Stones music while Moya and Patrick just kept staring into each other's eyes. Everyone could see they were mad about each other.

Thank God for her cousins Fergus and Conor who had at least made her laugh and had great rhythm and loved dancing. Kate had been stuck up at the top table with the old folks and Andrew Redmond, who though he wasn't a patch on his handsome brother seemed a nice guy. Kate had got up to dance with him and chatted away with him as they moved around the floor.

Her parents were enjoying themselves: her mother had three gin and tonics lined up in front of her and was lost in conversation with Rosemary Quigley and Mary Corrigan and Lucy Ryan, her first cousin, while her father was standing up at the bar with a crowd of men nursing a glass of Paddy, proud as punch because the whole day had gone so well.

'The sun even stayed out,' he boasted.

Romy was exhausted from constantly dancing – even young Jack Dillon had twirled her around the room – and talking to all the relations who kept telling her how grown up she'd got! Giddy from the wine and the music and the heat in the marquee she stepped outside to get a breath of cool fresh air. The garden looked amazing, all lit up with a mixture of fairy lights and candles, which flickered in the darkness, the scent of honeysuckle heavy in the night air.

'How ya, Romy?'

She spun around, recognizing the voice immediately. It was Brian. Her Brian. 'What are you doing here?' she gasped.

'I'm home from London for a few days and I heard that McHugh's needed a few extra barmen to cover a wedding party so I signed up for the job. I'm used to pulling pints and changing barrels. I could do with a bit of extra cash.'

'I can't believe that you're here at Moya's wedding. I didn't even see you earlier.'

'I only came on duty at seven, though I was helping back at the pub before that.'

Suddenly Romy felt shy, standing there all dressed up in her long bridesmaid's dress. 'You look beautiful,' he said as if reading her mind.

Romy grinned. Usually she was wearing jeans or shorts or old tracksuit bottoms and her runners when she met him.

'Do you like it?'

He reached forward, his hands touching the outline of her shoulder and breast.

'You know I do.'

She caught his hand in hers, tracing the length of his finger and palm, wanting to feel the touch of his skin against hers. She'd missed him so much. Without thinking she kissed his thumb, as Brian pulled her close to him.

'I'm working, Romy,' he groaned. 'Old man McHugh will go mad if he sees me here with you. I'd better get back to the bar.'

'What time are you working till?'

'I suppose about two.'

'Then I'll wait for you. I'll meet you back out here. Promise you won't forget.'

'I'll see you at two,' he promised, lightly touching her lips with his.

Sitting out on a garden chair she could hardly think as the noise of music and laughter filled the darkness. Brian home for a few days: it was too good to contemplate. If she had her way, almost every waking hour of that time would be spent with her. She'd better go back inside as Moya had to change for going away.

The music had stopped, the band packing up their instruments and amps and loading them into a small mini-van near the shed. The bar was shut and only a few hangers-on still sat in the marquee chatting or saying protracted goodbyes out on the patio. Moya and Patrick had taken leave of everybody earlier and were staying in a fancy hotel about a mile away before heading off the next afternoon to Nice on their honeymoon.

Romy tried to stop herself yawning as she looked around for Brian, almost jumping out of her skin with delight when he appeared.

'I told Mikey to take the van home, and that I'd walk. We've loaded it up with glasses and the spirits and three crates of wine. The keg is empty and we'll come back tomorrow for the rest.'

'God, they must have gotten through tons of drink. Daddy is pissed and is gone to bed. If you stand under the window over there you'll probably hear him snoring!'

'It sure was some big bash. It must have cost your old man a fortune.'

'I know. Only the best for Moya.'

'Sure it will probably be the same for you.'

She shook her head, adamant.

'If and when I get married, it will be a much smaller affair. Six or eight people, a nice long white dress and a pair of sandals or flip-flops.'

'Flip-flops?'

'Yeah, I want to get married on a beach. Somewhere quiet and romantic.'

'What about somewhere quiet and romantic tonight?' he suggested.

'That would be nice,' she replied, stretching her arms up around his neck.

'A walk, down by the beach!'

She considered. She was still angry with him for going away and leaving her but now that he was home the chance to spend time together alone was too good to miss. 'I need to change my shoes,' she giggled, displaying the red weals on her feet and toes. 'I'll be back in a minute.'

She raced upstairs and into her room, forgetting about Kate, who was lying in the camp bed.

'You're already in bed!'

'I'm exhausted. Romy, hurry on and get undressed and turn off the light!'

'I'm going out.'

'Out?'

'Brian's downstairs waiting for me. We're going for a walk.'

'Romy, I thought it was over with you two now that he's in London.'

'I did too. But with Brian and me things are so different. It's like we're two pieces of a sculpture or a jigsaw that are meant to be together. He's always been a part of my life. I can't explain it, Kate.'

'Just be careful. I don't want you to get hurt.'

'I'll be all right, promise.'

Grabbing a pair of sandals and a little white cardigan she raced back down. Brian was leaning against the wooden pergola, smoking. She could feel her heart flip as she looked at his broad shoulders and closely cropped brown hair and blue eyes. Silently he took her hand as they walked through the garden and out the gate and down the hill towards the sea, the moonlight silvering their path and skimming the glinting surface of the sea. She stopped as he bent down to kiss her, her mouth clinging to his, her body pressing against him, wanting him as always.

'I missed you,' he said huskily.

She gave in, letting his hands roam her body, her eagerness matching his. She wanted to make love just as much as he did, her body aching for the familiar feel of him. Half drunk with lust they almost staggered down to the waterfront, clambering over the low stone wall and sitting in the darkness watching the gentle swell of the tide. She leaned against him, enjoying the familiar smell of his skin, his hair. She'd been with other boys since he'd gone away, desperate to replace the familiar feeling, always disappointed by them, by her response to them. None of them could compare to him, could match the feelings he stimulated in her as he began to kiss her deeply, their breath coming together as they explored each other's mouths. She moaned as he kissed her neck, wanting to savour every moment of their reunion. She wanted him more than anything, wanted his physical touch.

'Not here.'

He grabbed her hand and pulled her across the grassy slope, back towards the headland, deserted now except for the holiday houses.

'I have the key.' He fiddled in his pocket and opened the door to one.

She watched as he put on the light and drew the curtains. The brightness high-lighted the clean but shabby interior await-ing the arrival of new summer visitors.

'The family went back to Cork today and Mam said the new people aren't coming till Tuesday.'

A smile spread across Romy's face as she reached for him and pulled him towards her. 'Then it's ours for tonight.'

She followed him into the bedroom, un-ashamed as he pulled her down onto his lap, breathless as she moved against him. He groaned as she slipped out of her long dress and turned towards him. Already aroused, Brian began to caress her naked skin and hips and thighs until after only a few minutes she was the one begging him to enter her, her body curving to meet his.

Afterwards she lay in his arms, exhausted and sated, knowing that no-one else had the power to make her feel the way he did, that her body responded uniquely to Brian's. As she lay with her head against his chest listening to the beat of his heart she knew that for the next few days being with Brian was all that mattered. She couldn't bear the thought of them being apart.

Chapter Seventeen

The college's medical office was quiet as Romy filled in a form listing all her details: home address, course, health cover, etc. Fortunately, except for a girl with severe acne, the room was deserted. Twenty minutes later the doctor had called her in.

Embarrassed, she haltingly told him the results of the home pregnancy kit she'd done five days before. The doctor passed her a jar and sent her outside to the toilet, than examined her on her return.

'Well, Romy, as you suspected you are definitely pregnant. You seem fit and healthy and I would envisage a normal pregnancy.'

'I can't have a baby,' she blurted out appalled. 'I'm only in second year arts.'

He stopped writing and put his pen down.

'When was your last period?'

She tried to remember: it was about two weeks before Moya's wedding.

He took out a circular cardboard wheel and turned it around.

'Your baby is due on 10 May.'

'My exams, what am I going to do?'

'You could defer,' he said gently, 'or repeat the year.'

The full horror of her circumstances hit her as she sat in the black leather chair opposite him.

'I don't want to have a baby. I'm too young.'

'Do you have a boyfriend?'

She thought of Brian. She loved him like crazy but she wasn't sure she could call him a boyfriend.

'Do you know who the baby's father is?'

'Yes.' She nodded dumbly, feeling humiliated.

'Is he a student also? I could talk to him if you want.'

She shook her head vigorously. She needed time to think, to decide what to do.

'Have you told him yet?'

'No.'

It was like some awful nightmare that you would see in a film or read about in a book, never imagining it could happen to you.

'What about your parents? Will they be supportive, do you think?'

She moaned aloud, thinking of breaking the news to her parents.

'Listen, Romy, don't panic. You are young and fit and healthy and we can organize to book you into a maternity hospital and arrange for you to see an obstetrician for your pre-natal care.'

'I don't want it,' she said, breaking down. 'I don't want to book into a hospital or a doctor. I don't want to have this baby. Do you understand?'

'Listen, you're scared. Many young women are nervous when they discover they are pregnant. We handle a number of student pregnancies here on campus every year. The college make allowances, there are programmes put in place, counsellors and advisers who will talk to you, lend you support.'

'I don't want their fecking help. I just don't want to be pregnant!' she yelled at him, jumping up.

'It's going to be all right,' he said, reassuring her, making her want to bawl in his arms as he passed her some tissues from his desk. 'Nurse Malone is outside. She will give you some general information leaflets on pregnancy and a bottle of folic acid tablets, which are important for you to take for the baby at this stage. Also I'd like her to do a general blood test on you, which we should get back next week.'

Romy felt sick at the thought of tablets and tests.

'She will make an appointment for you to come and see me again so we can talk about where you'd like to have the baby and the kind of cover you want.'

Like a zombie she walked to the door with him and sat in the seat beside the nurse, rolling up her sleeve, not wanting to think about what was happening to her.

She sat through a lecture on American literature contrasting the work of Steinbeck and Scott Fitzgerald in a total daze, not writing a single word on her pad, hardening her heart for the days ahead. Now she had definite confirmation she'd get in touch with Brian, and talk to him.

She got home before the others and dialled the code for England, praying she'd catch him. His uncle came on the phone.

'I'm sorry, Brian's not here at the moment.'

'Will he be back soon?' she asked, trying to keep the panic from her voice.

'Well that's just it, love. We're not expecting him back. He signed up for a six-month contract in Germany. He left for Frankfurt about ten days ago.'

'Frankfurt!'

'Who is that?'

'It's a friend of his, Romy. Romy Dillon.'

'Ah sure I've heard him talk about you.'

'Do you have an address or phone number for him, Mr Murphy? I need to talk to him fairly urgently.'

'Brian's staying in a hostel but he told Mary he'd write with an address once he got one, but unfortunately we haven't heard from him yet. You know what lads are like! I'm sure we'll hear from him soon if you want to call again, or otherwise try his mother. She might know.'

She thanked him for his help and getting up her courage phoned Lavelle's. Sheila O'Grady was surprised to hear from her but admitted she too was awaiting a letter with Brian's new address and was anxious to discover how he was getting on in work.

'Is everything all right, Romy?' she enquired.

'I just badly need to talk to him about something, that's all.'

Puzzled, Sheila began to put down the phone.

'Mrs O'Grady, if you are talking to him,' Romy struggled to control the emotion in her voice, 'will you please ask him to phone me immediately.'

Two long weeks passed and there were no phone calls, no letters, Brian unaware of the calamity of her pregnancy. Romy had never felt so isolated and alone in her entire life. She couldn't think straight and didn't know what to do. The campus nurse had made an appointment for her in Holles Street Hospital where a Dr Ryan would look after her. On a noticeboard in college she had found the number of two clinics in London that arranged terminations of pregnancies, which involved only an overnight stay. The cost was exorbitant and she didn't know how she was going to find the money. She was already beginning to show and knew she could not leave it much longer to decide about ending the pregnancy or having the baby.

Kate had arranged to meet her after work in the Bad Ass Café for pizza and to go the cinema. Romy's stomach had almost turned over at the sight of the plates of pizza and feeling queasy she had contented herself with eating the garlic bread and salad and two huge glasses of Coke.

'You OK?' joked Kate. 'I've never seen you turn down the offer of pizza before.'

'My stomach was sick during the week, so I guess I should rest it.'

Kate put down the menu and stared at her.

'Now you say it, you do look a bit peaky. Are you still on for the cinema?'

'Sure.'

They went to *Sleepless in Seattle* in the Savoy, tears rolling down Romy's face as Meg Ryan waited for Tom Hanks at the Empire State Building. She was so weepy and miserable at the moment that the slightest thing got her started.

'College going OK?' asked her big sister as they walked back along O'Connell Street afterwards.

'Why does everything always have to be about college with you?' she snapped.

'I just wondered, you seem tired. Maybe you might need a grind or some help. I don't know.'

'Yes, Kate. You don't know. I am tired but I'll get over it. We can't all be geniuses like you. Studying and lectures and all that crap gets some of us down, OK?'

Kate Dillon studied the pale face under the freckles, the greasy tied-back hair and thrown-together ragbag of dirty jeans and T-shirt. The poor kid, she thought, determined to phone her mother the minute she got in and get her to make Romy go down home for a few days' break.

Down at home in Rossmore Romy curled up in her own bed, studying the familiar pattern of the wallpaper, wishing she never had to put foot out of it again for the rest of her days. She looked around at her noticeboard full of invitations and college timetables and pictures of dogs and horses and one of Brian playing the guitar and old tickets for a few of the gigs his band played locally and for U2 – the best band in the world. Her desk and chest of drawers were covered in photos. Some were of herself and Brian when they were younger, one of the two of them in their school uniforms. She swallowed hard. It seemed like all her life she had been waiting for him, waiting to be loved by him, and now when she needed him most he had simply disappeared. She knew he'd been seeing a girl in London, Gina something or other. He hadn't hidden it from her. The night they'd had together after the wedding had been special, a reminder of times past. Perhaps that was all it had been to him and he would have no interest in the child she was carrying now.

Hot tears slid down her face, her throat aching with the hurt inside:

'Are you all right, Romy love?'

Maeve Dillon took in the tearstained face and the utter misery of her youngest daughter, who looked like every bit of wildness had been crushed out of her, as she lowered herself onto the corner of the bed.

'Do you want to talk, Romy? You know there is nothing you can't tell me. No bad thing, no trouble you're in, nothing awful you've done that I won't try and help you. I promise.'

A shudder went through the long thin frame.

Maeve tried to brace herself. Maybe it was drugs or she'd been expelled from the college, or was having some kind of a breakdown. She ran her hand along Romy's shoulder.

'You can tell me, pet. No matter what it is, you can tell me,' she urged.

The silence filled the small bedroom, stretching between them as Romy turned to the wall, hiding.

'I'm pregnant.'

Maeve stopped. Had she heard right?

'Pregnant?'

Romy sat upright in the bed, almost screaming it out.

'I'm pregnant.'

'Are you sure?'

'I've been to the doctor.'

'To Myles.'

'No, not to Dr Deegan, I went to the doctor in college. The baby's due in May.'

Maeve Dillon could feel her heart pounding, her breathing almost stop, a panicky tightening in her chest.

'May, when you have your exams?'

'Mam, I don't give a feck about those exams. They are the least of my problems!'

Maeve pulled Romy into her arms like she used to when she was small and sick and scared.

'You poor old pet.'

'Mam, it's so awful. I don't know what to do.'

'What about the father? Have you told him yet?'

She shook her head.

'Who is it?'

She was tempted to tell the truth but instead just shrugged 'I'm not sure.'

Maeve Dillon felt dizzy. How had she let Romy's behaviour get so out of hand and crazed that she couldn't even be sure who was the father of her unborn child?

'Just some guy.'

Maeve was sick with disappointment. Her beautiful live wire of a daughter, intelligent and full of high spirits, caught in the trap of an unwanted pregnancy.

'What are you going to do?'

'I don't know. The doctor has booked me into Holles Street.'

Maeve breathed a sigh of relief. It was much better Romy have her baby in one of the big maternity hospitals in Dublin than in the small local hospital where everyone would know her business.

'That's if I have the baby.'

'Not have the baby?'

'I don't have to have it, Mam, not if I don't want to. I can go to England. And then get on with my life.'

Maeve could scarcely believe what she was hearing. She firmly believed in the right to life and here was her daughter telling her she planned to get rid of her baby.

'Jesus, Mary and Joseph, Romy, you can't do that! Destroy your own child?'

'It's my decision.'

'Oh I know that, love. It's just you need time to think, to get used to the idea of having a baby.'

'I don't want a baby, can't you understand that!'

'But for the love of God, Romy, you don't know what it is like to lose a child. You might never recover from it, never.'

The tenor of the raised voices attracted her father, who had been shaving in the bathroom and was still in his dressing gown.

'What are you two fighting about?' he interrupted.

Romy clenched her lips. She wasn't saying a word.

'Tell him!' urged her mother.

'Tell me what?'

'I'm pregnant.'

Frank Dillon stumbled for a second in the bedroom doorway.

'But you're only a child. Are you sure?'

'I am, Daddy.'

He banged his fist on top of her desk, sending the photos flying onto the bedroom floor.

'Well who's the bright bucko got you in this position?' he demanded. 'I have a few things I want to say to him.'

Romy said nothing. She could have put a bet on about her father's over-the–top predictable reaction.

'Tell me who he is and I'll knock some bloody sense into him! Is he going to marry you?'

'No.'

'No!' He roared so loud that the house seemed to shake.

'Maeve, do you know who he is?'

'He's just some guy from college, Daddy, it was a one-night stand, an accident.'

'A one-night stand? By Christ, are you some kind of easy lay, the college slut?'

'Leave her alone, Frank.'

'She's obviously some kind of tramp, with the morals of an alley cat,' he blustered, his face red and still flecked with remnants of shaving cream.

'She's your daughter,' her mother reminded him. 'Don't you dare speak about her like that!'

'She's your daughter too, Maeve. What's that they say – like mother like daughter!'

Romy watched, incredulous. For one second she thought her mother was actually going to slap him across the face, as they turned on each other and began fighting. What had her dad said about her mother? She didn't understand it.

'How dare you, Frank!' screamed Maeve, jumping up off the bed. 'How dare you?'

'She's not bringing some good-for-nothing's bastard into this house.'

'Don't you dare talk about Romy's baby like that!'

'This is my home and I won't stand for it,' he ranted furiously. 'People have respect for the Dillons, look up to me. In this town I stand for something. The child won't be raised in this house.'

'Might I remind you that this is my home too. I inherited this house from my father so I have some say in what happens under this roof. Some say.'

'We'll be disgraced,' he threatened. 'We'll be the talk of the place.'

'We've survived worse scandals and rumours,' Maeve Dillon said coldly.

Her father fell silent momentarily but blustering, began again. 'She's got to go away, stay in Dublin.'

'Going to Dublin was what caused all this,' said her mother. 'Don't you think she'd be better off home here with us? We could look after her till the child is born, help out afterwards.'

Romy turned to the wall. She didn't want there to be an afterwards.

'I don't want it! I don't want a baby!'

'Stop that talk immediately!' ordered her mother. 'I won't have it in this house.'

'Listen, Maeve, maybe she's right. She's young and has made a stupid bloody mistake. Maybe she should put it behind her. Make a fresh start, not ruin her life with a child no-one wants!'

Appalled, Maeve Dillon shook her head.

'And I suppose you'd write the cheque, pay for it, you self-centred bastard. You're not thinking of Romy or the unborn child. All you're thinking about is yourself. What will people think of the great Frank Dillon with a pregnant daughter! Frank Dillon's stupid young one got herself into trouble. You're pathetic.'

'Shut up, woman!'

'This is my decision,' interrupted Romy. 'I have to decide what to do, it's my fecking life, not yours!'

'Don't mind whatever your father says. You'll get through this,' promised her mother. 'I'll help you, help with the baby, do whatever you want. Just don't rush into a decision you might regret.'

She could see the rage on her father's face. He was used to getting his own way in deciding what happened within the circle of the family, he wasn't used to being challenged, having his leadership questioned.

'Please just leave me alone, the two of you. I feel shite!' she said and rolled over, pulling the blanket around her shoulder.

'I mean it, Romy,' insisted her mother.

She only relaxed when they'd left her room. Her mind was in turmoil. This was splitting the family apart. Her mother like some kind of holy flipping Joe, spouting on about the precious unborn's right to life – she was sick of it! And as for her father, all he wanted was for her to disappear into some hole in the ground lest she embarrass him. She'd made a mistake coming home, thinking that her parents could solve her problems just like they did when she was a kid. That day was gone. For now she was on her own. She turned on the stereo, Bono's voice filling the pressing silence of her room.

Chapter Eighteen

Crazy and demented, Romy was determined to have an abortion. It didn't matter what her mother said. She didn't want the baby! She'd go to London and get rid of it. It was a nothing at the moment, a blob of jelly growing inside her. Bye-bye, blob! She'd scrounge and scrape the money together before it got any bigger. No-one would know about it. She should never have told her parents, got them involved. Somehow she'd get the money to get to London.

Kate had money. Pretending she was so behind in her work from skipping lectures, she'd arranged to meet her for soup and a sandwich at O'Sullivan's on Dawson Street.

'I just need to get a grind for the rest of term, that's all. I know it's expensive but this guy is meant to be great. One of the girls who went to him last year ended up getting a first in her exams.'

Kate reacted generously, offering to pay the full cost of the extra tutoring needed.

'I can't take it!' Romy made a pretence at protesting. 'You work so hard.'

'Maybe I think you are a good investment,' smiled Kate as she took her chequebook out of her black leather bag. 'Who will I make it payable to?' she quizzed.

'Oh just cash,' beamed Romy, hugging her. 'I can't remember exactly how to spell his name, it's French. Thank you, thank you!'

'I suppose that's what big sisters are for,' Kate reassured her, wondering how it was that Romy always seemed to get herself in a mess.

'Promise you won't say anything to Mum and Dad about this, you know what Dad's like, Kate, he'll say I'm squandering my time here at UCD.'

Kate had already decided this was another of Romy's problems her parents didn't need to know about.

Moya was different. Wearing her mankiest old sweatshirt and baggy trousers and a ribbed knitted grey cardigan, Romy had taken the bus out to her new house. She admired the carpets and the modern furniture and the pale yellow walls of the kitchen, before confiding that she had nothing nice or good to wear for an important date with one of the young medical students she knew.

'If only we were the same size, Moya, I could borrow something from you,' she murmured wistfully, knowing full well she was a good four inches taller than her sister and a dress size or two up.

'I'll help you to pick out something nice,' her sister said, offering to come shopping with her on Saturday.

'But I can't make it on Saturday. I'm helping out with something in college.'

Moya insisted on giving her the money to treat herself to something nice.

'I can't take your money.'

'Of course you can, that's what family are for.'

She would raid the savings she had in her post office account and hold back on her gas and electricity money from her flatmates. Another few weeks and she would have enough. Then the post had come and with it what she supposed was her monthly rent cheque. Romy had stared incredulous, looking at her father's large looped writing and distinctive signature. The amount filled in was for one thousand pounds. A simple handwritten note asked her to make no mention of it ever to her mother.

She had stared unbelieving, unsure whether to laugh or cry. Her father was ensuring she had enough money to pay her air fare and her expenses for the abortion at the clinic she'd chosen.

Brian had finally phoned her. Awkward, he told her that his girlfriend had travelled over unexpectedly from England to spend six weeks in Germany with him.

'I have to go to London for a few days,' Romy pleaded. 'Couldn't we meet up? I need to see you.'

'I'm sorry,' he said. 'I couldn't get the time off work, and besides, I told you Gina's here with me in Frankfurt.'

'Don't bloody bother,' she said, banging the phone down on him. She was stupid to be so upset and hurt about his involvement with someone else. She didn't own him! She didn't need to consult him about something that had been an accident, totally unplanned. She convinced herself that it would be better if Brian didn't ever know about her pregnancy.

The college doctor refused to help her with regard to the arrangements for a termination but none the less provided a medical letter outlining the state she was in. She was sorely tempted to beg Moya or Kate to come to England with her, but knew her sisters would do everything in their power to make her change her mind.

She'd opted to fly over on the early-morning flight to Heathrow and get the tube from there to Fulham where the Thames Clinic was situated. She stood on the steps outside the tall red-brick building with its discreet signage and opaque windows, nervous about going in.

Trying to get her courage up she watched other women, escorted by their boyfriends or woman friends, enter the clinic, then finally forced herself to join them. The receptionist, a pretty woman with a soft Northern Ireland accent, produced a pile of forms for her to fill in. At the other end of the room a television was on with no-one paying it any attention.

She hadn't a clue what to write. She was definitely not putting down her home address or her own GP's name, determined to maintain some sort of privacy even during this awful procedure.

A lady doctor, Dr Bennett, had called her in, questioning her about the reasons for the termination and deciding if she was fit to have the procedure. Romy was almost out of her mind with the thought of what lay ahead, and her stomach was grumbling with hunger from fasting since the night before.

'Are you sure this is what you want?' the doctor asked one last time before signing off on the pale green form and telling her that she would not be going to theatre until almost four o'clock in the afternoon.

'We're a bit backlogged so you can rest in the room upstairs and watch the TV. The nurse will administer a sedative about an hour before we call you down. When the procedure is over you will be returned to your room to sleep it off and be under observation. You will be discharged by ten o'clock tomorrow morning.'

She was grateful for the simple professionalism of the woman in front of her, who showed no curiosity or made no comments on her condition.

Four women were to share the bright pink-painted room. Romy wondered how anyone could sit and concentrate enough to do the *Times* crossword. She didn't want to talk to them. She had no interest in discovering how these women had arrived in the same circumstances as herself, she just didn't want to know. She walked up and down the corridor trying to block out the sounds of sorrow coming from the small private room at the end. Back in the pink room the *Times* reader had already been taken down to the theatre. Romy, scared, closed her eyes not wanting to think. No matter how pristine and professional the clinic seemed it was like a funfair house of horrors. She tried not to think of the blob, think of its fingers and toes and head.

The nurse came in and gave her a sip of water and a tablet, telling her she'd be going down for her procedure soon. Drowsily, Romy pulled the sheet over her, trying to blank out her mind, and was half asleep when they brought her down to the theatre, the doctor patting her hand as he gave her an injection and asked her to start counting backwards, eight, seven, six, five, four bye bye bye.

Romy woke up a few hours later, the nurse putting a blanket over her because she was cold. The television was on in the room, with someone watching it! Later there was chicken in a sauce and a boiled potato and a cup of tea. Nauseous, she barely touched it. She felt sick, sore, walking like an old woman when she went to go to the toilet. Red blood in the bowl. She flushed it. Back in the bed she rolled over, wanting to sleep, wanting to forget. They woke the women early the next morning with tea and toast. Romy queued for the shower, the hot water streaming down her face and body as she washed and washed, knowing the stain would never go away.

'Are you all right?' asked a woman with dyed-black hair in the bed near hers.

'I'm fine,' she said, putting on her jeans and jumper.

'Isn't it a great relief to get it all over!'

Dr Bennett appeared briefly, coming over and telling each of them in turn that the procedure had gone well and to take it easy for the next few days. Afterwards the nurse reminded them to make sure they had all their belongings before they checked out.

Romy couldn't wait to get out of the clinic. Not even bothering with the lift, she ran down the stairs. She settled the bill with her father's money and, taking a deep breath, stepped out in the street, traffic and noise, the world still turning as she walked down the road. Shaking with relief, she turned the corner and leaned against the wall, heart and mind racing, trying to calm down. It was over.

Ravenous with hunger she found a small coffee bar on the Fulham road and ordered 'The Works', a toasted BLT. A hostel or a B&B for the night was her next priority, she decided.

Booking into the Prince of Wales Hotel, she noticed the difference between the nightly and weekly rate and immediately decided to stay for a week. She couldn't face going home tomorrow and back to college. She needed a few days on her own to get over everything.

As she lay in bed that night in the small stuffy room, she was overcome with tears at the enormity of what she had done. Pretending she was still pregnant, she placed her hands on her stomach. The comforting bulge was gone.

She slept and slept, and walked Marble Arch, Oxford Street, Regent Street, Piccadilly and the posh streets round Knightsbridge and Kensington. Nobody bothered her for she was a stranger, and by the end of the week she had decided to stay in London. She couldn't go home, pretend that nothing had happened, go back to studying and failing exams and hanging out. She was pregnant and had chosen to get rid of her baby. She could never hide that!

Days passed in a blur. Romy stayed in bed, sleeping or watching stupid game shows and soaps on the TV. Conscious her money was beginning to run out she had moved to the Harp Hostel in Kilburn, her room a draughty box with a double bed and high ceiling and heating that barely worked. She had no energy and had to force herself downstairs to eat or to go to the shop on the corner for bread and milk and coffee. She cut her hair as she couldn't be bothered to wash and blow-dry it. Sometimes she cried for no reason when she saw families on the ads on television or strangers in the street pushing prams. It felt like she was losing her mind and she longed to see Brian again, and have him tell her he still loved her, despite what she had done. Other times, she cursed him for letting her down and her father for making it too easy for her. He'd always believed money could buy you anything, solve every problem! She should have listened to her mother instead. She had failed her! Failed every word of prayer that she had ever learned from Uncle Eamonn and Sister Goretti and all the nuns in St Dominic's. Yes, the consequences of her bought freedom were far worse than she had ever imagined.

By December she realized that she had only a few pounds left and was forced to lift herself from the spiralling depression that constantly overwhelmed her as she tried to find a job. Staring at the freaky stranger in the bathroom mirror, she washed and tidied herself and borrowed a clean white blouse from one of the other girls as she set out in search of some kind of work. All of the big stores were hiring seasonal staff and with her sales experience she managed to land herself a job in Fenton's, a busy gift store just off Regent Street, which sold among other things the familiar Waterford glass. The owner was delighted to meet someone so well versed in selling the range.

At the end of the week she bought four postcards and sent them home, one to her parents, one to each of her sisters and one to her housemates, reassuring them that she was well and living in London but not giving them a contact address or number.

At Christmas there was no question of returning to Rossmore, and she pushed all thoughts of her family from her mind as she worked late and did overtime, wrapping

china and silver and glass right up till closing time on Christmas Eve, and then joined
the sing-song that was held in the hostel that
night. She'd cried during Christmas
morning mass in St Patrick's in Kilburn; the
sherry reception and turkey and ham dinner
provided by the staff of the Harp was the
only thing that got her through the day.

The grey London January and February
skies depressed her, the rain and cold
weather chilled her soul, and in March she
quit her job and joined up with a girl called
Elise she'd met briefly in the hostel who was
going back to France to work.

Chapter Nineteen

She'd gone to Paris first, working as a
chambermaid in the Intercontinental Hotel,
making beds and cleaning rooms and bath-
rooms. Elise and herself shared a small
stuffy apartment provided for staff with
three other girls from Holland.

'Shit and sheets!' they'd joked about work
as they smoked Gitanes and Gauloises,
drinking lemon Pernod till late at night in
cheap scruffy bars and rising only a few
hours later to go on duty in their pink and
white uniforms. But the tips were good, and

after only two months Romy and Arlene Vermeulen had packed up and hit the road, heading south for Provence. *En route* they'd picked grapes and lemons, their skin covered in insect bites and stings, their fingers and hands hard and calloused. They'd trekked the coast looking for jobs – Saint-Tropez, Nice, Cannes, Antibes, the surly French waiters in their pristine white shirts driving them off, the bar owners sneering at their French accents and Romy giving them the fingers and cursing them in perfect French.

Reluctantly they'd gone back to bed-making and washing toilets in a huge white hotel overlooking the beach where the French ladies lay bare breasted in the sun.

Their own skin turned to copper and they lived on salami and fish and salad, their breath stinking of garlic and oil as they danced in basement discos and clubs with nice French boys who wanted to do bad things with them. As the season ended and the beach began to empty Romy resisted the urge to pack her bags and return home and crossed to Morocco, learning from a girl called Leilah how to make filigree silver bracelets and anklets and how to string wire through beads and shape them into pretty necklaces and belts which they sold in the crowded market in Marrakesh.

'Always price it too high, at least 100-150

dirhams more than you expect. The buyers want to haggle, the tour guides tell them to. They expect to wear you down and to get a bargain. It's part of coming to the market.'

Her hair grew long so she braided it and wore leather sandals and loose tie-dye caftans. At night she slept in a low white house, open to the sky, wrapped in the arms of a tall American boy called Josh who hailed from Cincinnati. When he returned to America, another boy, David, took his place. Getting bored with skinny yellow dogs that panted in the sun and pot-bellied men who tried to press against her on the streets while calling her 'bitch', and friends who smoked too much hash and cared about nothing too much, she said goodbye to Leilah, packed up her wire-cutters and pliers and lino cutter and bags of blue-tinted beads, and headed for Spain.

Habit brought her to the hippie market in the old town of Ibiza, where the Germans and Danes admired her handiwork, paying with pesetas and Deutschmarks for their trinkets. Over a summer she amassed enough to open a bank account and put money by for when times were tight.

One evening she was sitting on a stool, concentrating on the wave-shaped earring she was making for a Viking from Copenhagen, when she heard a familiar voice.

'Romy? It is you, isn't it?'

Startled, she looked up, recognizing the strong Irish accent. It was her sister's friend, Minnie Doyle.

'Romy, how are you?'

'I'm fine.' She smiled, laying down her work, her mind racing.

'Did you make all this jewellery?'

'Well, most of it.'

Minnie fingered a fine necklace with glass and turquoise on silver. 'God it's gorgeous! It's so unusual!'

Romy smiled. Most of the bracelets and necklaces she made were very similar, things the tourists liked, but there were always pieces that stimulated her and gave a creative edge to her work.

'You look so different, your hair's so long and you've gone so fair I'd have hardly recognized you.'

Romy thought Kate's friend hadn't changed a bit. Her dark hair and dark eyes twinkled like they always did.

'How's Kate?' she asked, nervous. 'Is she with you?'

'God no! You know Kate, I couldn't get her to take a break. She's the same as ever, working too bloody hard. No, I'm with two other friends, we just came out for the week to have a bit of fun in the sun, as they say.'

'Will you tell Kate I said hello when you get back?'

'Hold on, Romy, why don't you come and

meet myself and the girls for a drink later?'

'I'm not sure...'

'No pressure, just a drink,' coaxed Minnie.

Curious, she agreed to meet them at the Flamingo Bar, down near the harbour, later that night. Sitting in huge cane chairs, Minnie filled in Romy with all the news from home.

'Do you keep in touch at all?' she asked.

'I send them cards and a letter to my mother on her birthday, otherwise not really.'

'They miss you,' said Minnie softly, her eyes serious, 'especially Maeve.'

She could imagine her mother kneeling in the church praying, doing novenas for her, while her father sat up at the bar in McHugh's priding himself on getting the family out of an embarrassing situation, believing the thousand pounds he'd sent her money well spent. She hated him for it! For his hypocrisy, for letting her down when she needed him most!

'I know Kate and Moya miss you. Did you hear that Moya and Patrick have a baby girl, Fiona?'

'So I'm an auntie now!' laughed Romy, suddenly jealous of her older sister and her nice safe life. A baby! Moya was bound to be the perfect mother.

'Romy, why don't you come home for a holiday?' coaxed Minnie over a Bacardi and Coke. 'See them for a few days. Your folks are getting older.'

'I know, it's just that right now is not a good time for me,' she apologized. 'You wouldn't understand, Minnie, but I just can't.'

'OK, OK, I'll keep my big fat mouth shut and my nose out of it.' Minnie grinned, squeezing her hand.

She had a laugh with them as they filled her in on the Dublin scene, which seemed a million miles from the balmy heat and tranquillity of sitting under a starry Ibizan sky with a glass of ice cold rum and fresh lemon juice in your hand.

By the weekend Romy had packed up what was left of her stock and a few possessions, selling the remaining lease on her stall to an English potter and his wife Carrie as she headed for the mainland. She wasn't taking the risk of having her mother or Kate coming out to find her. It was time to move on.

Chapter Twenty

In Barcelona, the city of Gaudi, she'd spent six months teaching English to wealthy Spanish teenagers who wanted to know how to curse and to make love in her native language. Tongue in cheek, she had taught them words like 'feck' and 'shite', wishing she could be there to see the reactions of British hosts or visitors to the Irishification of their swear words. Restless and feeling the urge to travel further she considered the map she'd spread out on the bed, trying to work out distances to Lisbon, Rome or Milan. She wanted a change and in the end decided to toss a coin in the air about deciding to stay in Europe or not. She tossed again, torn between New York and Sydney. Australia won.

The far side of the world was as far away as she could go and she phoned her parents and sisters briefly to tell them of her planned change of continent.

'Please, Romy!' her mother had pleaded. 'Come home for a few days before you go off. I promise there will be no questions or upsets. We just want to see you.' She had hardened her heart, reluctant to put her travel plans in jeopardy, and had instead flown to Sydney via Bangkok and London.

Australia suited her and in Sydney, the magnificent city on the sea, she found work in Molloy's, an Irish bar, serving pints of dark Guinness and traditional brown bread and fresh prawns to city businessmen and tourists and freckle-faced Irish students missing home. Living only a block from the beach at Coogee, life was almost perfect. Then after twenty months she'd been hit by wanderlust and had once again packed up her bags. Aunt Vonnie had been right about her when she was a kid, saying she was like a tinker that could settle no place and wanted to be on the road the whole time. Bussing it up to Brisbane she had discovered paradise in Byron Bay. Bypassing the temptation to join the hippie trail in Nimbi she had instead rented a one-bedroomed beach-front apartment overlooking the ocean. The place was packed with surfers and those searching for something more to life than wealth or position: writers, artists and researchers. Romy immediately fitted in. Bar work was plentiful and in a few weeks she had mastered the art of mixing cocktails and surf-speak and cleaning sand off the wooden floorboards and making tuna melts for the masses.

Rob Kane came into her life not long after.

She had watched him often from a distance on the beach early in the morning, chasing the waves, envying his ability on a surfboard, and was surprised as hell when he had come over to watch her feeble attempts to barely stand on the second-hand board she'd borrowed off Marti, one of the girls she worked with.

'You're doing it all wrong,' he chastised her, standing on the sand watching her. 'The board knows you're afraid of it and it's just tossing you.'

'The board knows I'm afraid?'

'Have you ever ridden a horse?' he insisted.

'Yeah of course, back in Ireland.'

'Well did you let the horse know you were afraid?'

'No, Paddy Ryan told us that the rider is always boss.'

'Well the same goes for boards! You walk out a bit further. You're playing it too safe here, making it easy to fall off where it's shallow.'

She waded out further and further.

'Good girl, climb on now!'

She looked like an ungainly seal trying to climb onto the slippy board, Rob suddenly holding it steady for her as she managed to right herself and, trying not to wobble, almost stood up.

'Don't look down, only look up!'

Unbelieving, she had caught a gentle wave and actually stayed on the board for a few seconds before tumbling off again.

'Not bad,' he praised, as dripping she stood up out of the water, her hair and face covered in sand. Mortified, Romy introduced herself.

Rob must have been a glutton for punishment as over the next week he seemed to miraculously appear just when she needed him, ignoring her pleas to just leave her be and 'Go off and surf!'

One Saturday night he'd turned up in the bar with a crowd of friends. Romy waved to him and gave him a free beer in return for her lessons and was amazed when at the end of the shift he was waiting out on the veranda for her and insisted on walking her home. They sat on the cold sand in the moonlight talking for hours, Romy hugging her knees as she told him about leaving home and all the places she'd been, Rob telling her about his Melbourne childhood, confessing his sole obsession was with the waves and where they ran. As the morning sun came up, she led him towards her lonely bed and they made love till they were both sweat-soaked and exhausted and Romy fell asleep in his arms. The next day he'd packed up his things – a computer and three boards – and moved in with her.

He worked designing websites – surf sites

for boardies, mostly: places, resorts, best boards, surf gear, competitions. His dream, he confessed, was to create a surf game for non-surfers to enjoy.

He was easygoing and fun and very loving, working at night and the evening mostly on his own projects or as a programmer for the bank while she was busy in the bar, the days kept for the water. He had a huge group of friends, all sharing the same obsession, a gaggle of beach-babe girlfriends in attendance as they polished their boards and worked out a strategy for tackling each day's waves.

Month after month passed and Romy had never felt so relaxed and comfortable with her surroundings. Using her tools she had bought some silver and designed a few pieces based on surf and the crashing crescendo of waves on the rock and beach. She showed them to Tilda Gray, who ran a high-class jeweller's and gift shop on the Shore Road, and was pleased beyond belief when Tilda put on her glasses and studied them, immediately ordering more.

'Wow that's great!' shouted Rob, scooping her up in his tanned arms. 'Now you've got your own business too.'

'It's just a bit of silver work, that's all.' She didn't want to make too much of it or take on more work than she could handle.

'If you want I can set you up with a website to sell your designs.'

'What do you mean?'

'Well, maybe people who can't come to Byron Bay or to Tilda's might be interested in your designs and want to buy them?'

She hadn't even thought about it. It was too soon to think that way.

'You don't have to do anything, Romy. I'll set it up for you and you can expand it and operate it any way you want in the future.'

On Christmas Day she had sat at a massive barbecue on the beach eating shrimp and steak, drinking chilled sparkling Australian champagne and thinking of Moya and Kate gathered around the Christmas tree down home, her mother fixing the stuffing and cranberry sauce for the turkey, her father throwing logs on the fire and making sure the booze cupboard was adequately stocked for the arrival of their cousins and friends. The scent of her mother's hot mulled wine would be filling the Stone House.

Overwhelmed with loneliness and home-sickness she stared at the sun dancing on the waves as crowds of holidaymakers took to the water, swimming and surfing and splashing around. This was such an alien landscape.

'Happy Christmas!' yelled Carl, one of Rob's friends, wearing red Santa swimming trunks and a silly red hat.

Romy, trying not to cry, told him to 'Feck off!'

In the New Year Rob and some pals wanted to go up north to Cairns and the Reef for a few days. Romy took holidays and joined the surf pack on the move. The Reef blew her mind, the colours, the shapes and the azure blue sky and tropical landscape like nothing she had seen before. She didn't need much persuading from Rob to don goggles and a mask and do some diving. After two weeks she had returned to her job and her commissions from Tilda's, unwilling to throw away her work to up sticks and move with Rob and his cronies to follow the surf further north.

The business grew and grew, Tilda taking almost as much as Romy could make, the rest orders from those who had seen her designs on the internet. She cut back her hours in the bar to concentrate on creating handcrafted pieces of silver and bronze. With ferocious intensity she had written a cheque to her father for the sum of one thousand pounds, returning his blood money with no note or letter.

Weeks turned to months and eventually Rob reappeared with a broken collarbone. Temporarily out of action, he was planning his next campaign. It was good to have him back in her life again and Romy promised herself that the next time, wherever he travelled she'd go too.

Chapter Twenty-one

Moya had an appreciation of things that were beautiful and balanced and as she and Patrick moved into their first home she endeavoured to surround herself with such things. Simple heavy glassware bought from the factory in Jerpoint, Stephen Pearce pottery and a classic Wedgwood dinner service. A Brian Bourke painting and a Bobby Ballagh print – small pieces but items that made her feel that the three-bedroomed home they'd purchased in Dundrum's leafy suburbs, a house like a hundred others, the garden a mass of builder's rubble waiting to be cleared, was something special.

Stretched across their enormous bed Moya pored over her brand-new recipe books to find interesting dishes to entertain their family and friends with, while Patrick tried his best to distract her.

Each weekday morning, Patrick dropped her off at Stephen's Green close to Taylors, the big art auction house where she now worked, typing up catalogues, talking to owners and checking details on paintings and sculptures and artefacts that they handled. Insurance, delivery, security, as works of Yeats and Orpen and Louis le Brocquy – all the Irish and international art beloved by collectors – passed through their rooms. She loved to listen to the experts detail the brushwork, the influences, the studios where paintings originated as she dealt with the nitty-gritty mundane details essential in looking after such valuable works. Growing up, she had attempted to paint, to capture the beauty seen with the eye and transfer it to the canvas, but the results were disappointingly dead and flat and soon Moya realized that, despite Sister Angela's encouragement during art class, she would never be an artist. However, she had an ability to recognize and appreciate the work of others even if she could not emulate it and painters and their work continued to fascinate her.

At lunchtime she ran around to the shops buying steak or pork chops and selecting fresh vegetables from the greengrocer's in South Anne Street for their evening meal or, if she had time, browsed around the latest fashions in Brown Thomas. Otherwise she had lunch with a colleague or some girl-friends. Marriage was bliss. Night after night lying in bed with Patrick exhausted from lovemaking as they tried to conjure up new ways to pleasure each other, she realized that she had never been so happy and that being married suited her.

Within a year and a half Fiona Mary Redmond was delivered without any complications or fuss in Mount Carmel, a private hospital. Both sets of parents were overjoyed and had made the pilgrimage to see their first granddaughter.

'She's absolutely beautiful,' declared her mother, 'the very spit of you when you were a baby.'

Moya had to admit that Fiona was the prettiest baby by far in the nursery. Patrick and herself were mad about her and dying to get her home. Minding the baby and keeping the house running smoothly took up most of her time. Returning to work at the end of her maternity leave she found herself stretched trying to manage it all. Patrick was promoted and needed to work longer hours as he dealt with a portfolio of new clients and their investments, trying to stay on top of deal after deal, throwing a fit almost at the suggestion that he give her more of a hand.

'For Christ's sake, do you want me to tell the senior partner I have to go home to mind a baby!'

Moya had to give up attending art exhibitions and lectures in the evening unless they were essential, not wanting to ask her childminder Denise to spend even more time with the baby. Friday nights meeting Patrick for a drink after work also went by the board as she rushed home to their daughter.

Patrick's parents led a busy social life and were unavailable to babysit but once every three weeks they invited them to Sunday lunch, where Annabel praised Fiona's progress and remarked what an intelligent and bright child she was. Kate helped out if she was really stuck but Moya knew her sister was uncomfortable in the house and preferred to avoid being around Patrick. Moya often wished for a return of the old closeness and fun that they'd shared, but suspected she'd hurt Kate too deeply for it to happen.

Fiona was just starting to walk and take her first steps when she discovered she was pregnant again, and nine months later their son Gavin was born. A long lanky baby with his father's features, he was almost as good as his sister.

'Maybe you should think about staying home,' suggested Patrick. 'The child-minding is costing a fortune and the two of them are such a handful, maybe it would be better if you concentrated on looking after them.'

His career had taken off and he was now travelling away at least once a month and couldn't even be relied on to be home.

Looking at the big eyes and baby faces of her two small children, it was an easy decision for Moya to make and with few qualms she gave in her notice and stayed home with Gavin and Fiona.

She enjoyed motherhood and the freedom to do what she wanted once she didn't mind having two small people in tow. She met other young mothers in the same situation, as they mapped out meetings and lunches and play sessions and shared walks and trips to the park.

The growing family moved to an old house in Sandymount.

'But it needs so much work!' she worried, looking at the builder's quote.

'Listen, it's got Regency charm and is a lot closer to my office. Besides, even your father agrees we should double our money on it in a few years' time.'

Patrick was still working night and day and was rarely home, barking at the children and shouting at her when he did appear.

Hurt, she decided to surprise him. One night she arranged a babysitter and dressed up in an expensive black Joseph top and skirt and knee-high boots, joining the throng inside the Shelbourne and searching for him in his regular spot, the Horseshoe Bar. She was talking to Gerry Gorman, a tax specialist, when she spotted Patrick up at the counter. Excusing herself to go and say hi, she had to almost push a pretty young woman in a grey suit who was flirting with him and hanging on his every word out of the way. Patrick, embarrassed by her arrival, introduced her to Jenny, one of the new graduate trainee accountants.

Moya pasted her biggest, widest smile on her lips and slipped in beside him as he ordered her a drink.

That night when they got home they had the biggest row they'd ever had since they got married, Moya accusing him of going off with other girls.

'I swear to God, nothing has ever happened between us. It's just a few drinks and a laugh. It means nothing,' he insisted. 'Moya, you know that you're the only one I care about.'

Relieved, she had believed him, deciding they loved each other too much to be unfaithful. However, she wasn't stupid and now began to join him for dinners with clients, attend functions with the senior partners and their wives, and host drinks and small dinner parties in their home.

She missed working, and once Fiona started school and Gavin was able to go to playgroup was thrilled to get a part-time job in a small local gallery, the Martello. They specialized in limited edition prints and etchings and two or three times a year held an exhibition. Moya took on the task of organizing these events and built up a collectors list to target for future sales.

Sylvia Toner, the owner, had a good eye and instinct for what would work or not work, and the two of them worked well together, with Sylvia saying little if Moya had to make the odd dash to the school or the doctor.

'Kids are kids,' she'd sigh, looking at a photo of her own brood of four when they were younger.

Fiona was making her first Holy Communion the year Patrick told her of the job offer in the London office.

'It's too good an opportunity to refuse.'

'But what about the kids, and school?'

'Moya, they've got great schools over there. Fiona and Gavin will love it. We'll be able to get a big house, make money, invest! It's just the opportunity that I've been waiting for.'

She could see the excitement in his face, the challenge, the hope of better times. Putting aside her own reservations she flung her arms around his neck, congratulating him, breaking open the bottle of champagne she stored in the fridge for such an occasion.

'London's a big city, way bigger than Dublin,' cautioned Sylvia. 'Are you sure it's the right move?'

'It's the right move for Patrick.'

'But all your family are in Ireland.'

'Except for Romy, and God knows where she is!'

'That's what I mean.'

'Friends and family can visit. It's not the end of the world! We'll be back and forth the whole time and we've decided to rent out the house for a year at least to see how things go.'

'What about work?'

She shrugged. 'I haven't thought that far ahead, Sylvia, to be honest.'

'Well I have,' Sylvia said, opening the drawer in her desk, 'and I've prepared a reference for you, a recommendation as such. You know I worked in London for ten years. Maybe it will count for something.'

Looking at Sylvia with her blond hair trailing all over the place, her plump wrists and fingers covered in silver jewellery commissioned from impoverished art students and the striking array of canvases and work around the small gallery, Moya knew she would really miss the place.

The company had paid their relocation costs, removals, air fares, and first three months' rent as they packed up and moved across the water to a new life in London. The children had acted up terribly, from the minute they arrived in St Albans. They missed going out to play and Moya found the neighbours, although welcoming, more reserved than she'd expected. Fiona and Gavin watched out of the huge living-room window at the empty green and open space devoid of children.

'I want to go back home and play with Aoife and Rachel and Lucy,' sobbed Fiona, missing her best friends from St Brigid's School. Moya patiently tried to explain to her that in the new school in St Albans she would soon make new friends.

'You'll still see Aoife and Rachel and Lu when we go home on holidays.'

'But I want to see them now!' her eight-year-old had bawled, inconsolable.

Gavin's teacher had called her in to say she was worried about him and that he was withdrawn and somewhat hostile to the other children in his class.

'Hostile?' she'd screamed at Patrick when he'd come home on the train from work. She was exhausted trying to unpack and sort out the red-bricked four-bedroomed house they'd rented, with an option to buy, trying to make it homely and put away the chintz and swagged curtains from the previous owners and paint the walls in colours to her taste.

Living far from the city centre, she rarely went into London to join Patrick and his new colleagues after work, for the kids were too unsettled to be left with a variety of strange babysitters.

Her mother and father made the effort to come over to London for a long weekend, Patrick putting on the charm and booking theatre tickets for the four of them to go to *The Phantom of the Opera* one night, and dinner in the Savoy another. Fiona and Gavin were so overjoyed to see their grand-parents, they made no fuss about being left with Amy, one of their neighbour's eighteen-year-old daughters.

'Granny, promise you'll wake us up and tell us all about it the minute you come in,' insisted Fiona, sitting on the couch in her pink kitten pyjamas and slippers.

'I promise, pet,' said Maeve Dillon, wishing the children had more friends to play with like at home.

Moya wept the day she drove them back to Heathrow.

'Are you sure you're all right, Moya girl?' her father asked concerned, his face close to her, anxious as he hugged her goodbye.

Moya blinked back the tears, homesick as the shamrock-painted plane took them away from her.

Six weeks later she discovered she was pregnant again. Disbelieving, she asked the doctor in the clinic to re-check the results. Patrick was so delighted with the news he'd taken her to the Ivy to celebrate.

This time she was tired, irritable, not able to sleep. Her pleas to return to Dublin for the birth were ignored.

'Are you mad? I can't take time off work,' argued Patrick. 'And how would I get to Dublin in time if I was stuck in the London office? It makes no sense, Moya!'

She knew it made absolutely no sense but it was just pure animal instinct that made her want to be home.

Liz and Ruth, two English friends, reassured her that her English hospital care would be second to none and she had nothing to worry about. Her obstetrician, a serious fifty-year-old, also did his best to allay her worries.

'Mrs Redmond, you have had two previous deliveries that were perfectly normal, and there is nothing to indicate any difference this time. Relax and enjoy the next few weeks,' he advised, patting her bump.

She had tried to relax, buying a pile of Jilly Cooper and Maeve Binchy books to read, and a tape of soothing sea sounds to listen to at night. When she was shopping in her local Sainsbury's, much to her embarrassment her waters had burst: the baby was not due for another four weeks.

Patrick had come immediately from the office and held her hand as their second son was delivered: Daniel Patrick, a small four-pound-two-ounce baby with a pinched face, who was whisked off to the confines of an incubator on the fourth floor.

'He's so small,' she kept saying, beside herself with worry.

'He'll grow,' promised Patrick, massaging her shoulders as she sat in the high hospital bed. 'You'll see he'll be taller than me, yet.'

Late at night, alone in the fluorescent-lit nursery staring into the Perspex glass cot, Moya, afraid, knew who he reminded her of. It was Sean, her little brother.

Chapter Twenty-two

Coming home from St Thomas's Hospital without her baby felt strange and unnatural, for Daniel was still in an incubator in unit 5, the premature baby unit. Moya went back and forth to the hospital twice a day to feed him, her tiny son reminding her of a small battered bird in the glass cage, eyes shut firmly against the world. Patrick had to return to the office and she was hugely relieved when her mother arrived over from Ireland immediately to help with the children.

'Mammy, I don't know what I'll do if

anything happens to him.' Her mother held her as Moya broke down and wept for her newborn son.

'Hush, pet, the doctor says he's a strong little fellow.'

If standing in the special care baby unit Maeve Dillon noticed any familiarity between her grandson and her own deceased child she made absolutely no mention of it.

Fiona and Gavin were thrilled to have their granny in residence and pestered her to tell them stories and do things with them. She brought them to Randall's Lane to collect conkers and to the park to feed the ducks and play on the swings, making Rice Krispie buns and teacakes with them when they got home. Covered in chocolate and cake mix they declared her 'the best granny in the world'.

In between hospital visits her mother made Moya rest and sleep and try and get her energy back.

'Danny will be home any day now, Moya,' she reminded her. 'And if you don't rest and sleep you'll be too exhausted to cope with him.'

After an almost endless three weeks, baby Danny was declared fit enough to be brought home, Moya almost collapsing with relief as they got into Patrick's new silver Mercedes and drove home to the house in

Randall Crescent.

The children had done drawings and put up balloons to welcome their new brother home, and Patrick insisted on opening some champagne.

'We did it for the other two, and God knows this little guy deserves it just as much!'

Sipping the sparkling champagne, Moya tried to banish her concerns for her new son as she held him in her arms.

Danny was a tetchy baby and a poor feeder. Moya had to devote hours every day to looking after him, not sure what she'd have done if her mother hadn't insisted on staying on for a few more weeks to help out.

'Mammy, are you sure you don't mind staying on?'

Maeve Dillon looked at Moya's exhausted face and scrawny shoulders, and her two grandchildren who were acting up and a bit jealous now that their little brother had finally appeared home, and knew exactly where she was needed.

'Your father will manage fine on his own,' she laughed. 'You know how he likes any excuse to go and have a pint and eat in McHugh's or the Harbour Inn, and Vonnie and Joe will invite him over on Sunday for lunch and keep an eye on him.'

Patrick, once the baby was home, seemed

to be able to magically forget that their second son was smaller and weaker than their other two had been.

'For God's sake, Moya, leave him be. He'll be fine.'

Moya understood her mother's fierce devotion and care of Sean for those nine months of his life, now that her own instincts were driving her to protect and constantly watch her own small son.

Maeve Dillon bit her tongue and held her peace as her son-in-law ignored the family crisis and refused to even do so much as lift a cup, prepare a meal or bath one of the children, complaining only of himself and how much work he had to do.

'Moya, you must say it to him,' she urged, aware of the cracks in her daughter's marriage. 'You are a family and these are his children.'

'Leave it, Mammy. Patrick works very hard to support us all. The house and the children are my responsibility.'

Call her old-fashioned, but Maeve Dillon didn't agree. She and Frank may have had their fair share of ups and downs over the years but she had always felt that somehow they were a team. She stayed on one more week and then, looking at her small grandson fed and content dozing in his cot, she realized that the time had come for her to go home.

'Danny will be fine,' she assured Moya, as she packed her bags. 'He's starting to thrive, you can see it in his face, and didn't the nurse tell you he's put on almost half a pound since her last visit.'

'I know, Mammy. I know but I can't help myself.'

Maeve Dillon suspected that her daughter had a picture in her head from years ago that would not be shaken, a picture that she herself still replayed again and again. 'Moya,' she said gently. 'Remember, he's not Sean!'

Moya watched Danny all the time, when he was awake, when he slept. A baby alarm was fitted beside his cot, even though he slept in the room with Patrick and herself. 'Christ, how am I meant to get a good night's sleep and do a day's work!' he complained, eventually moving into the spare room.

Fiona and Gavin were confused that she was so devoted to their small brother and so reluctant to leave him.

'Mum, you promised you'd come and watch me swimming!' complained Fiona. 'Why can't Daddy mind Danny for the afternoon?'

'Listen, pet, Daddy will go with you today and I'll see you the next time, I promise.'

As the time went on she couldn't bring herself to do anything, her life revolving solely around the baby and his needs.

'One of my clients is sponsoring a big horse race in Paris,' Patrick announced, flinging his briefcase on the couch and hugging her. 'All expenses paid by the company. Junior partners and their wives invited along for a luxury weekend.'

Moya could sense the panicky feeling deep in her stomach.

'You'll have to tell them I can't go,' she said simply.

'Why? We can get someone to mind the kids. It's only a bloody weekend, Moya. Just think – all those designer shops and you with a Visa card to hand, not to mention rambling around the Louvre.'

'Patrick, I'm sorry. I can't leave Danny, you know that!'

'He's a baby, he'll be fine at home with his sister and brother. I'm sure we can get a babysitter. The kids like Amy, or even if you feel she can't manage, we'll get one of those nanny services. Tony and Beth use them all the time for the twins.'

'Patrick, I'm not going!' she insisted. 'You go and enjoy yourself. I'll stay home with the kids.'

'I don't fucking want you to stay home,' he shouted, like an irate schoolboy. 'I want you to fucking come with me!'

'I can't,' she said, closing the conversation, sending her handsome charming husband to Paris, on his own.

When he returned from Longchamps, Moya knew something between them had changed. Patrick was different. It was barely perceptible, for her husband was as charming and witty and generous as usual, and his bad mood lifted as he presented her with Yves Saint-Laurent perfume, a gold bangle, and a book about Monet's garden. There was a cute 'Hello Kitty' backpack for Fiona, as well as a GI Joe and a rugby shirt for Gavin and an expensive Baby Mini outfit for Danny and a complete set of Babar the elephant books for the family. Gifts that proclaimed what a wonderful husband and father he was, and helped disguise the guilt she saw reflected in his eyes.

Moya felt sick to her stomach as she recognized the difference in him: adrenalin pumping, the excitement of the new, a certain almost giddy devil-may-care attitude that was most unlike him. He took phone calls in secret, going out to sit in the car or going up to the bedroom, claiming he could hear nothing with the noise of the kids. Moya watched him, tortured by the signs of his distraction. She did not know if she should confront him, demand answers, but sensed that declaring herself a shrew wife who would scream and cry and let fly with unproven allegations might herald the descent into a nightmare

258

from which there would be no escape. Instead she kissed him and thanked him and asked him about the trip.

They moved warily around each other for the next few weeks, both complaining about tiredness and fatigue, avoiding the pretence of lovemaking.

Patrick complained about the office, the long hours needed on this new project, the restructuring of assets, figures that didn't add up and the overtime that was expected of him. She almost felt she was colluding with him when he cursed his boss Ken Mitchell and ranted on about having to work so late and at weekends.

'It will pass,' she'd remind him, 'and then we'll all get back to normal.'

She made no mention of the late-night calls to check up on him and her chats with Jerome Wells the night porter, who assured her that Mr Redmond was definitely not in his office.

Patrick was having an affair. She was sure of it. Other women survived it! If rumour and gossip were to be believed, at least two or three of the senior partners had been embroiled in affairs. She thought of stoic Louisa Firth and Caroline Clifford, good corporate wives who had not rocked the boat and who concentrated on enjoying the fruits of their husbands' labours and raising their kids. Moya sighed. She was different from them. She had never imagined a time when she would not be in love with Patrick, would be detached. Never contemplated a life alone!

The children adored him. They needed a father. She herself had found Patrick charming and irresistible from the minute she set eyes on him – women couldn't help but be attracted to him. She'd known that from the start. What she hadn't known was that Patrick enjoyed it, flirting, arranging the odd discreet rendezvous. Perhaps some had been innocent, but now she could see the dropping of inhibitions and his encouragement of a relationship that was as dangerous as it was romantic.

'Patrick, I know about Paris,' she said one night when she could bear it no more. He'd slumped on the edge of the bed, his head in his hands, wearing the navy Ralph Lauren pyjamas she'd bought him for his birthday.

'You fucking wouldn't come with me to Paris. You didn't want to be near me! She was there, she...'

'Shut up!' Moya screamed at him. 'I don't want to hear about her, to know about her. I just want her out of our life! Out of your life.'

Patrick said nothing.

'Otherwise the children and I are lost to you. Do you hear me? I can't live like this

260

any more!'

'It's over,' he flung back at her. 'I've already ended it.'

Relief washed over her as she composed herself. She was too tired and exhausted to fight and she believed him when he buried his dark head against her breast and promised it would never happen again. She had to believe him, as she wanted her marriage to work.

She felt she was swimming in a deep deep pool and if she stopped moving she would drown. She had gone to talk to her local GP, who had listened and told her she was not depressed, just anaemic and exhausted, and prescribed a tonic and told her to try and be kind to herself.

'These days women try to do too much. You've had to cope with a small premature baby who doesn't sleep much, two children and run a home while your body deals with a bunch of crazy hormones that are dipping like a rollercoaster and tries to recover from childbirth. Is it any wonder you feel like hell?'

She didn't know whether to laugh or cry at the sixty-year-old Glaswegian's candid assessment of her problem.

'But I promise, Moya, within a few weeks you will be feeling much better.'

The doctor was right. She'd gone to the local health shop and bought up a ton of healthy foods and herbal remedies and had started to go swimming with Fiona and Gavin one day a week. She had to stop blaming Patrick for the way she was feeling and take control of her own life. She loved the children, and she supposed she loved Patrick despite everything but she knew she had to start thinking of herself.

Everything changed one day when she was changing Danny's nappy and he kicked out with his right leg and hit her in the ribs.

'Ow! Hey, buster! Don't treat your mum like that!' she warned. She stopped, realizing for one bliss-filled minute what she had said. She looked at his naked body stretching and moving, his arms trying to catch his toes. Her son was a bruiser. A small bruiser, but none the less a bruiser! Overwhelmed with gratitude she blew a raspberry on his skin, which sent him into peals of laughter.

'Danny boy, you are a normal baby.' She laughed, feeling the constant pressure and weight of fearful anxiety slide off her, as she enjoyed motherhood again.

With Patrick it was harder to reclaim their relationship and return to the couple they'd been before, as they were still mistrustful of each other, but Moya was determined to hold her marriage together and keep her husband.

It was not the perfect life she had imagined for herself!

Reading about the collection of Irish women painters on show at the Hamilton Gallery for two weeks, she decided to go to town for the day. She couldn't even remember the last time she had visited a gallery or taken the time to sit and study a piece of art, lose herself in it. Mainie Jellett, Evie Hone, Nano Reid – they were certainly images to conjure with, she thought as she arranged for the children to be minded and collected. She'd got her hair cut shorter so it emphasized her eyes and bone structure and had treated herself to facial, nails, pedicure, the works, feeling the despair slough off like old skin.

Two days later she took the ten o'clock tube to Victoria and headed for the gallery in Kensington.

Entranced, she stood looking at the light brushwork, the feathered strokes of women who had captured the landscapes of their own familiar places. She was moved by their originality and individual style and yet haunted by the sense of recognition. Their work, like old friends, comforted her. Red barns, brown hens and the Devil's Glen! Patchwork fields and blue jugs of buttercups! She sucked them in.

'Aren't they wonderful!' smiled the gallery owner, watching her as she studied each picture. 'Have you seen them before?'

'Well, perhaps a few, when I was living back in Dublin. But putting them all together like this makes something different of their work. I suppose it celebrates them.'

'I could have sold most of them a hundred times over,' confessed Brigid Barrington, the gallery owner. 'But they go back home to their rightful owners on Monday week and we go back to our regular exhibitions.'

The gallery was a large rectangular room which overlooked the street, a bright space flooded with light with nothing to distract the eye. One or two visitors came in to enquire about the price of the painting in the window.

'Told you,' mouthed Brigid, as she explained it was not for sale.

Half an hour later Moya found herself sitting on a stool enjoying a coffee and reminiscing about her work for Taylors and for Sylvia in the Martello back in Dublin as it lashed rain outside.

'If you ever are looking for a bit of work, I often need an extra pair of hands for openings and cataloguing,' offered Brigid.

Moya demurred, explaining about her family.

Brigid burst out laughing and pulled a black-and-white photo of three small boys in pirate hats brandishing swords from her desk, declaring, 'These are my three sprogs!

If it wasn't for this place I would have walked the plank years ago.'

Brigid pressed a business card into her hand and made her promise to give her offer some consideration. Moya smiled to herself as the sun came out: she would think about it. Walking up towards Harvey Nichols, she decided it was time to shop. New clothes and lingerie! She was dumping anything that was a reminder of the awful times she'd gone through. Comforted by the fact that Patrick could definitely afford it, she spent a fortune, bumping into Eleanor Palmer in Harrods, who declared she'd never seen Moya look better.

'Will you join me for tea upstairs?'

Moya, who'd forgotten about lunch, was delighted to. It felt almost sinful sitting having Earl Grey and cucumber sandwiches and a slice of Bakewell tart at four o'clock with one of England's great murder mystery writers instead of chasing to collect Fiona from school. Her neighbour Linda had offered to do it as well as manage the boys. She confided in Eleanor how hard the past few months had been.

'You deserve to get out, my dear, now that the baby is well again. Can't beat a little outing to town. Always did me good.'

Moya sat back. Her mother would love to meet Eleanor. The two of them would get on so well together.

'I've a book launch at six,' mused Eleanor. 'Dudley was meant to have come along, but as usual he's let me down and is stuck in that stupid office of his.'

Moya tried not to laugh, for Dudley Palmer was one of the most senior partners in Maxwell, Palmer and Mitchell's where Patrick worked.

'Hates those kind of things! He can't stand publishers or those journalist types. Always rub him up the wrong way. Don't suppose you fancy joining me, my dear? Douglas Carton is an old friend of mine and it should be a bit of fun.'

'I'd love to.' Moya couldn't believe it. She'd just been reading in the hairdresser's that his last book, *Silver River*, was going to be filmed in Ireland.

Picking up her mobile, Moya phoned Patrick, telling him he'd better make sure to be home on time so he could collect the kids from Linda's and to take a pizza out of the freezer for tea.

'Can't you do it?' he began to complain.

'No, I can't,' she said, switching off the mobile and putting it back in her bag.

'Everything all right, my dear?'

'Never better,' she laughed, asking Eleanor to give her the lowdown on Douglas Carton, who wrote thrillers and was always in the bestselling list.

'The two of us have the same editor and of

course you know he won the Golden Dagger Award, the year after me.'

She took a deep breath as Eleanor rambled on. Tonight Patrick would have to go home, feed and change and talk to his children and put them to bed!

Chapter Twenty-three

Summers in Rossmore were sacrosanct. They were Moya's sanity-saver, as she left England behind and returned home for those few precious weeks during July and August. The children on school holiday, bored and restless, were spared the rounds of summer camps as sandals, swimming togs and neatly ironed shorts and T-shirts were all packed in the bag ready for the seven-week-long visit to Ireland.

The Stone House basked in warm sunshine, tall Michaelmas daisies and montbretia trailing up the driveway to welcome them. The children screamed at the sight of their grandparents, jumping up and down with excitement as Patrick and Frank carried in the luggage. Every year it seemed the same, unchanging.

'There's tea in the kitchen,' her mother would announce as like a ravaging horde they descended on the house.

Talk about an understatement! The table was laden down with her mother's baking. A huge cream sponge, melt-in-your-mouth chocolate éclairs, and apple tart, oatmeal flapjacks and iced buns with hundreds and thousands sprinkled on the top. The talk was nineteen to the dozen as the kids fought for attention and tried to fill in for their grandparents all they had accomplished over the past few months.

'I was a butterfly in our school pageant and I had to do a ballet dance with two other butterflies, Granny.'

'She looked beautiful, Mum, I have the photos to show you.'

'I got a new football.'

'My tooth fell out and fell in the garlic bread at Mummy and Daddy's dinner party.'

'Did you find it?' asked Frank, trying to keep a serious face.

'No. Somebody ate it!'

'Oh good God!' murmured Maeve.

'Danny!' reminded Moya, helpless with laughter.

'But the tooth fairy still came though I hadn't a tooth to leave under my pillow.'

'Well that was a good thing then. Decent enough, those fairies,' agreed Frank, pulling his grandson onto his lap to see where the new tooth was cutting through.

Moya could feel the tension seep from her body as the children and herself relaxed and were wrapped in the comfort of her family home and she settled back into her old bedroom, the window looking out on the apple trees and her mother's vegetable patch.

Patrick would only stay for the first week or ten days, depending how busy he was in work. They always stopped off at his parents' home in Dublin for a night or two following the ferry journey. Robert and Annabel would set the big dining table for dinner and make a huge to-do about having guests to stay. Over-excited, the children would eventually go to sleep, leaving the adults to talk until late into the night, Moya making sure to slip away to bed leaving Patrick time on his own with his parents.

Things were different in Rossmore, where they spent much of the time on the beach, playing football and rounders, watching the children swim and splash in the bracing chill of the Irish Sea, trailing up and down to the house with towels and deckchairs and beach balls and lilos. Patrick would organize day trips to local sights and play golf on the course overlooking the sea, the tired look gone from his eyes. At night there were family dinners in the kitchen and, on the patio, Frank Dillon pretending to cook on the barbecue as sausages and steaks sizzled while her mother served big bowls of new potatoes and tossed a salad of lettuce and scallions, freshly pulled from the garden. Uncle Eamonn, home for a few weeks' summer break from Chicago, entertained them with his stories. Aunt Vonnie and Uncle Joe invited them over for Sunday lunch, her cousins and their wives and girlfriends and children all part of the huge family get-together.

Patrick and Moya traditionally went for dinner in Allen's on their own the night before he went back to England.

This year it was awkward. Moya stared across the table at her handsome husband, wondering if she could trust him. A month ago she'd borrowed his Mercedes for the day as her car was in for a service and he was away on business in Gothenburg. Danny had got a nosebleed and she'd yelled at Fiona to quickly open the glove compartment and get some tissues or a cloth.

Fiona, tumbling everything on to the seat, found one of Patrick's expensive hankies for Danny to use. Tidying up the car later, lying beside the service manual and some CDs, Moya discovered a phial of Mitsuo, an Issey Miyake perfume she never used, and a tube of brown Chanel mascara. Her own lashes were jet black and when she did use mascara only black would ever do. She mentally ran through a list of possible females that might have left some makeup in his car, drawing a total blank!

Back in the house she left the kids downstairs watching a video, while she went and did something she had never done before. She checked Patrick's bank and Visa statements. Like all accountants he was organized to a T, and it was easy enough to lay her hands on the indexed files. She started with January and went through the months. Restaurant bills. Most were ones Patrick used regularly for entertaining clients, then she spotted two that were not the corporate type: they were small intimate Italian restaurants. There were tickets for two to a jazz night in a London nightclub, and in March a payment for a small boutique hotel in Bath. She froze. That was the weekend of the Ireland v. England rugby match. Patrick had told her he was taking clients to Lansdowne Road and that it was going to be a boozy stag three days. She'd believed him!

She could still remember the awful feeling in the pit of her stomach as she thought about it. Patrick romancing another woman! Going to bed with her! She had put the files back carefully.

She was calm and composed when he returned from Sweden, nonchalantly presenting him with the evidence from the car.

'Whose are these?'

'I don't know,' he'd bluffed. 'Maybe one of the girls from work.'

'Are you seeing somebody?'

He'd been affronted, shouting at her, 'How dare you suggest such a thing?'

'Patrick, you didn't answer me. Are you having an affair? Yes or no?'

He'd talked and argued and blamed the pressures of work and his career and her lack of understanding. Moya, relentless, kept on, demanding the truth. 'Yes or no?'

'No! No!' he shouted.

'So you didn't have an affair, you can swear that to me.'

He'd put his head in his hands, eventually admitting the truth.

'Do you love her?'

'Don't be crazy! I love you.'

'How long has it been going on?'

'Two months. It's nothing, just a bit of fun, a change. She knows that.'

'I see,' she said bitterly.

'It's you I love, Moya, you know that.'

'Well you sure have a strange way of showing it,' she snapped as she sat on the bedroom floor contemplating what to do. Leave him? Divorce him? She felt like getting a knife from the block down in the kitchen and killing him, he'd hurt her so much.

There was the children, the mortgage on this big new house they'd moved to in Richmond, the years together, the life they had built. She didn't want to throw it all away because Patrick was a stupid shit!

'It will never happen again, I swear,' he promised.

'You utter bastard!' she'd screamed.

'I'm sorry. I'm so fucking sorry. What are you going to do?'

She could sense his nervousness. He had so much to lose. A messy divorce would be disastrous.

'I'll think about it,' she said.

'Jesus, Moya.'

And she had. She had given it huge consideration and thought. She was no doormat but being a single parent with three kids would be hard. She thought of her mother who had always put home and children first and knew that she too was the same kind of person and that Fiona, Gavin and Danny's happiness was paramount. She still loved Patrick and underneath it all, though it seemed pathetic and crazy, believed he still loved her.

By tacit agreement, the mistakes and hurts were once again put behind them, and their marriage for everyone's sake was bandaged back together. Some day they might discover it had become irreparable or she might decide she was better off on her own.

Patrick knew that, but for the moment, sitting across the candlelit table from each other in one of Rossmore's most expensive restaurants, they were together.

'I'll miss you,' he said, pouring more red wine into her glass.

She didn't bother replying.

'You'll be here with the kids and Frank and Maeve and all your old pals. You won't have time to miss me!'

There was a lot of truth in what he said but Moya felt a strange mixture of guilt and mistrust thinking about him back in London commuting to the office, staying in an empty house while she lolled around for another glorious five weeks doing nothing. 'I wish you could take longer holidays,' she sighed.

'Ten days back in the old country is enough for me,' he admitted. 'Golf with Ron and Simon and the rest of the guys in Villamoura in the autumn, that's more my idea of a switch-off holiday.'

'You know I'm not coming back till just before term starts.'

He nodded.

'Danny will be at St Michael's till three o'clock every day then except for Wednesday.'

He looked bored.

'So I'll have a lot more time on my hands. I was talking to Brigid and you know how well we work together. Anyway, she might be prepared to take in a partner.'

'Partner!'

'Don't look so surprised, Patrick. I've always dreamed of opening a gallery of my own, you know that. I mean, we could think of doing up our basement, converting it or look for a suitable piece of property close by.'

'It would cost a fortune,' he protested.

'I know, that's why going in with Brigid would be a good investment. She wants to cut back a bit from the gallery and concentrate on her own painting, visit that house in the Dordogne that Charles bought, but she just can't close up the place. The Hamilton is the ideal place for me to work and build up the business.'

'But where would you get the money?'

Moya looked at him across the table.

'Well I thought you were always on the lookout for good investment opportunities,' she teased.

He realized with a jolt that Moya was flirting with him, noticing the dusting of light freckles across her nose that made her more beautiful than ever. Her beauty had always got to him, somehow made him feel unworthy of her. Sipping his wine he became aware that perhaps his wife was blackmailing him and if he didn't accede to her wishes he was in real danger of losing her.

Once Patrick had gone back to London, the house settled into an even more relaxed routine, with breakfast mid-morning after a swim. Then back to the beach to relax in the sun and read or just close her eyes and daydream, the kids busy building or chasing around.

Cora Costigan had arrived down from Dublin with her two daughters to stay with her mother, and Mary Joyce, another school friend, was ensconced for the whole month in one of the holiday cottages over-looking the harbour with her four kids; her husband, like Patrick, only visited for a week or two.

'It's like old times,' sighed Cora. 'All the gang back down here again.'

'Only this time we have the kids.'

Moya watched Fiona down playing at the water's edge with Cora's daughter Lucy, the two of them engrossed in trying to catch a crab or something, their voices shrieking, laughing, catching on the breeze, Fiona's sallow skin already tanned, Lucy like her mum a mass of pale skin and freckles.

The boys were only a few yards away busy building a sand car, trying to work out the size the seat should be, and everyone was screaming at Mary's little guy Emmet, as he ploughed across it.

'I just love to see them all together,' smiled

Moya, taking her camera from her bag. 'I guess it reminds me of us growing up.'

She watched as Danny dug shovelfuls of sand, scooping it up and then putting it to the back of the car shape, his small face rapt with concentration.

'He's got taller,' smiled Cora. 'I think maybe he looks bigger, stronger.'

Moya was grateful: grateful that Danny was finally managing to catch up with boys his own age and staying healthy.

'Stop worrying, love, he's a normal little boy,' her mother kept saying to her over and over again. Moya was finally able to believe it.

She knew her mother relished those golden days surrounded by her grandchildren, often coaxing her sister Kate to come down home for a few days too. The house was packed with laughter and jokes and mess, the washing machine on full tilt, the line heavy with towels and togs. There was end-less cooking of sausages and chips and pizza and huge plates of toast, along with cleaning and hoovering up sand from the strangest of places. The children would play in the garden till it got dark, only coming in for bed when they had to, Maeve putting on her glasses and reading them stories from favourite books until they fell asleep.

'I wish we could stay here for ever,

Granny,' confided Fiona, curled up in her pink striped pyjamas with her teddy bear Sam in Romy's old room.

'I wish that too, pet,' confessed Maeve, 'but you have a lovely house in Richmond and your school and your friends. You'd miss it all terribly and you'd probably get bored if you were living here all year round and seeing Grandad and myself all the time.'

'I'd never get bored,' she said ferociously, throwing her arms around her.

Moya swallowed hard. All her mother had ever wanted was her children and family around her, yet here she was with one daughter living in England, only seeing her grandchildren twice or three times a year if she was lucky, Kate working too hard, obsessed with her career with absolutely no sign of settling down, and Romy like a tinker moving from place to place. God knows where in the world her sister would end up! She must envy her friends and neighbours whose children had married and stayed in the area, content with their local life. Frank Dillon was the one who had encouraged them all to spread their wings and fly, ensuring they got a good education.

'Now come on! You all have to go to sleep now,' their grandmother threatened. 'Or there'll be no picnic tomorrow.'

Moya smiled to herself as within minutes

all three were curled up under their duvets, eyes closed, mouths open, fast asleep.

They'd driven over to Kilmore Quay, her father pleading an urgent meeting, Moya knowing full well he was trying to avoid Gavin and Danny's constant chatter and pleas for him to do things with them.

'I'm too old to be flying kites and having swim races and cycling to the pier,' he sighed. 'Patrick should do those kind of things with them.'

They had concocted a fabulous picnic, which would feed an army and had spread the tartan rugs on the sand in a good sheltered spot where they could keep an eye on the children and watch the small boats loop in and out of the tiny harbour.

After racing along the strand and swimming the children collapsed on the rugs, demanding to be fed.

'Can I have another slice of ham and a roll please, Granny?'

'Pass the salami ... pleeasse.'

'I'm thirsty.'

Moya watched her mother calmly deal with them. She was devoted to her grandchildren.

'How are things with Patrick?' Maeve asked, once the children disappeared looking for crabs in the rock pools.

'He's really busy at the moment, taken on

more clients and is training in new staff.'
Moya grimaced. 'And he hardly ever gets
home, so what's new!'

'I didn't mean work. I meant things
between the two of you.'

Moya stared out at the sea, watching a
seagull circle above the waves. What was she
going to tell her mother: that she'd discovered Patrick was having an affair? She
didn't trust herself to speak.

'He's hurt you.'

Moya nodded.

'I could kill him for that,' said her mother
softly.

'He's an utter bastard. Did you know
that?'

'Suspected, maybe.'

'Well, it's true. He's been sleeping with
other women, having affairs. He says they
mean nothing and that he still loves me, but
yet he does it again and again. For all I know
he is with someone else as we speak.'

Maeve Dillon shuddered, thinking of her
charming son-in-law and the pain he was
inflicting on her daughter.

'Remember when Danny came home
from the hospital and for months I was too
scared to leave him.' Moya tried to control
her voice. 'Patrick had to go to Paris on
business. I don't know who she was, maybe
somebody from the company or one of the
clients. It went on for weeks. I was worried

sick about our baby while he just couldn't keep his pants on!'

'Oh Moya.'

'I forgave him, blamed myself for not going to bloody Paris, and of course he promised it would never happen again.'

'And?'

'It did!' Moya watched the children paddling in the distance, Fiona lost in concentration as she tried to scoop something from the pool.

'Was this woman important to him?'

'I don't know,' shrugged Moya, 'and I really don't care.'

Maeve didn't know what to say, wondering how it was that time and time again history repeated itself with mothers and daughters.

'Your father and I went through a bad patch.' She hesitated. 'It was a long time ago, and was the roughest time in all our years of marriage.'

'When Sean died.'

'Yes, well you remember what it was like for all of us. I couldn't love him then, couldn't bear to have him near me so he found somebody else. Someone who would give him what I couldn't. It's no excuse but I blamed myself. I was awfully good at that.'

'Daddy had an affair? I can't believe it!'

'It's the truth, Moya. You were all young

and there was no question of me leaving him. So I accepted it. Accepted her. What else could I do?'

'Did anyone else know about it?' Moya asked.

'There was a bit of gossip and rumour-mongering but I just ignored it all.'

Moya was appalled. She had always known that her father was a gambler and a risk-taker but to have an affair in a small town like Rossmore was crazy.

'What did you do?'

'I held my head high. I loved your father and he loved me. I stayed home and raised you girls. I was mad as hell with Frank for what he was doing to us but my home and my family were more important than a hundred women.'

'Things are different nowadays,' sighed Moya. 'More complicated.'

'Not so different,' her mother comforted, patting her hand. 'Though the minute you stop loving him, well, that's a different matter.'

'Granny, Granny, look at the fish I caught. It's a rock breen!' yelled Gavin, running towards them with his net and a slopping bucket of water.

'Come and show it to me,' smiled Maeve, arms open wide, ending the conversation.

Lying in bed that night, listening to the sound of the tide in the distance, Moya remembered all the happy years of her childhood and realized how hard her mother had fought to protect them from everything, just like she was doing with her own children.

Chapter Twenty-four

Kate wasn't surprised when her mother phoned and asked her to come down home for the weekend for she knew with Moya and the children gone back to London it must be lonely for her.

'The house is so quiet your father and I are rattling around like two old codgers, it would be lovely to see you, pet.'

'I've a work function to go to on Friday night, Mum, but I'll come down on Saturday and stay over,' she offered.

'Couldn't you stay longer, pet? Maybe take a few days off work.'

Kate's holiday days were precious, her mother knew that! She might be earning a high-flying figure and paying off the mortgage on the new apartment that she'd bought in Monkstown – which hopefully had already doubled in value – and had made two small investments in start-up companies she'd advised, but the one thing she wasn't rich in was time!

Take a few days off! 'Are you all right, Mammy?' she asked, suddenly worried.

'Yes, love, I'm fine. It's your dad I'm concerned about.'

'Is he sick?'

'No, it's not that,' she said secretively, 'it's something else. I don't want to discuss it on the phone, but he might need your help in the office to sort out a few things.'

Kate was aghast. In all her life her father had never once asked her for a bit of professional advice or even properly discussed the number of business investments he was involved in. He was a wheeler-dealer type, full of bravado and show, turning money easily one day and making it by the skin of his pants another, but he'd always been able to provide his family with a good living. She suspected he sailed too close to the wind but now, she wondered, had he finally run himself into trouble? 'Listen, Mum, I'll ask Barry for a day or two, OK, but that's all I can manage. I'll see you both on Saturday around lunchtime.'

Her mother had made a thick vegetable soup, which was like a meal it was so filling. Her father, at the other end of the kitchen table, looked embarrassed. He'd lost weight recently, had gone grey.

'Daddy, you'll have to tell me what's going on if you want me to help you. The first thing I usually do with clients is sit them down and get the whole story.'

He dunked a piece of bread in the soup, avoiding her eyes.

'Well, I'm not one of your clients, so I'll thank you to avoid the lecture.'

An antagonistic client was bad enough, but an antagonistic father, that was something she could do without!

She said nothing and watched him spoon the soup slowly into his mouth, fiddling with the slice of bread. Normally he'd be gone from the table by now, in watching the racing or the football on TV. Her mother was right, there was definitely something up with him.

'Dad, I'm down for a nice pleasant weekend and to see the two of you. If while I'm here you want a little bit of legal advice, no problem. Otherwise I'm just happy to relax and go for a few walks. Fergus and Conor invited me to go sailing with them over to Passage tomorrow afternoon, so if you don't want to talk to me about whatever is going on I'll just go with them.'

'He's a stubborn old fool and he does need your help,' her mother pleaded. 'For God's sake, Frank, tell Kate all that's happened since Martin retired from the business, please!'

Kate knew it was hard for him to suddenly have to confide in one of his daughters, to step down from his pedestal as head of the family and admit perhaps that he had not been as clever or cute as he should have been.

'I'm ruined,' he said slowly, dropping the spoon, despair etched on his lined face. 'The council are being investigated with regard to planning irregularities.'

'And what's that got to do with you?'

'Well, Martin and I always believed in oiling the wheels, so to speak.'

'Bribes?' Don't say her father was stupid enough to be involved in bribing local councillors, buying his planning permissions!

'It's how things work,' he explained. 'How else do projects get off the ground and everyone gets to make a bit of money so everyone is happy.'

'Dad, tell me, you didn't pay or take any bribes?'

'Kate, it was just dinners here, a few drinks, donations for this and that, weekends away and the odd little holiday, money to good causes, bits of important knowledge passed on to the right people, advice to a friend or two. There was no harm in it!'

'Are there records?'

'I'm not sure. Martin kept the books, dealt with the accounts. My end was buying and selling land and property, turning things around to make a profit or deciding to make an investment or not.'

'Is there anything else?' she asked, suspicious.

'I've had a letter from the bloody Revenue and they're talking about an investigation.'

Kate swallowed hard. It was worse than she'd imagined. She caught her mother's eye: she'd been right to get her involved. Her father was going to need all the advice and help he could get.

Frank opened up the office in town on Saturday afternoon and Sunday, the two of them trying to go through more than twenty years of files and payments and bank lodgements and withdrawals. Even at a quick glance Kate could see where her father and Martin Duffy had turned a quick profit on a huge part of land sales they'd acted on. Kate noted down cases where there were gaps in the registration, sometimes the partnership buying the piece of property and then selling it on to another vendor later, their ownership never legally declared.

'Christ, Dad, some of this is illegal!'

'There was no harm done,' he said defensively.

'What about the mill?' She turned her attention to the old mill at the edge of town; she remembered how proud she'd felt when her father had purchased it. Obviously it had protected status because of its age and historical importance. Kate was flabbergasted to see in the documents the council's permission for its redevelopment as exclusive holiday apartments and a restaurant five months later with absolutely no mention of its status or the protection of its original features. She pulled out the file, determined to go through it later that night with a fine-tooth comb if need be to see if her father had incriminated himself or there was any direct link to the council or its officers at the time. She yawned, exhausted: this was going to take for ever. There were boxes of stuff to go through!

They worked through till late that night, Maeve Dillon producing a slow simmered beef casserole when they eventually got home. Her father excused himself saying he needed a drink as he slipped on his raincoat and disappeared down to McHugh's.

'Leave him go,' urged her mother. 'A pint will do him good.'

Kate lifted in a box of files from the hall and curled up on the couch barefoot to read them, tossing some to her mother trying to explain what exactly they were searching for.

'Is it bad, Kate?'

There was no use lying to her mother. At least she'd had the good sense to get her involved.

'It's complicated, put it that way.' She

sighed to herself, wishing she could spare her mother. 'Dad and Martin have sailed really close to the wind, and with this council investigation and also the Revenue likely to turn their attention to him, it's not good news.'

'How far will they go?'

'As far as it takes.'

Sunday and Monday and most of Tuesday were spent in the same fashion, Kate managing to get two long walks in the fresh air to clear her head. Her father's business affairs were in a worse mess than she'd imagined.

'Dad, we need to get an accountant to look at this and assess the liabilities involved.'

'Larry Flood used to do our audit.'

'Dad, he's about seventy, for God's sake. We need to get a fresh eye on this. I'm not a financial expert. What about Patrick?' she suggested.

'Under no circumstances are you to tell Moya and Patrick about this, do you hear, Kate?'

'Dad, they're probably going to hear, no matter what you do. Patrick's used to this kind of stuff. OK, maybe not normally as messy as this but he's an accountant.'

'Didn't you hear me?' he shouted. 'I'm not having Patrick go through my business affairs!'

Not wanting to upset him any more, Kate let the matter drop. Maybe one of her colleagues could recommend someone.

'What about Martin? You were partners. What does he say?'

'I told you Martin's retired. He's an old man now. He left the business in my hands and this, all of this, is down to me,' he said despairingly. 'We still have some investments together but otherwise he's not involved. I'm not having him dragged into this.'

'Dad, some of this goes back years and no matter what you do or say now, most of it is going to be public. You've broken the law, and there are no two ways around it. Look, you bought two of the fishermen's cottages down on the Harbour Road off poor old Jem Crowley for a song and then five weeks later sold them on to O'Malley construction for a fortune, and looking at the records you failed to register as the owner and never paid tax. The fact that you are also a shareholder in O'Malley's is going to be seen as very suspicious.'

'Jem was delighted with the money we paid him. He was only storing lobster pots in one of them!'

'Come off it, Dad, the other was his home and he'd have been far happier to have got a decent price for them.'

Kate sat in her father's large leather office

chair, knowing that probably within the year the office and much of what he had worked for would be gone. She would advise him to settle. Things could be sold off to raise cash if need be. Looking at him standing in his shirtsleeves at the filing cabinet she felt a rush of pity for him. He'd always been so strong and self-assured, always out, busy working, making money, spending it easily, generous to those around him. Sean's death had almost destroyed him, but somehow he had managed to keep going. She could never understand his getting involved with Sheila O'Grady. She'd never excuse it, but she'd kept his secret all these years. Never said a word to the others. Looking at him now, grey haired, tense, bent down over years of files and paperwork, she wondered how many more secrets of his were to be uncovered.

'I got Jem a place in the Harbour.'

'What?'

'I made Tom O'Malley provide him with one of the smaller holiday cottages, 'twas a palace in comparison to his old place.'

'But he doesn't live there,' she said, thinking of the wealthy families who kept yachts down on the marina who booked the houses from one year to the next.

'I know. Jem lives in two old rooms up behind McHugh's, rents the cottage out.'

'Oh Dad!' she said, throwing her arms

around him. Her father was one of those blustering big men who take on the world and she loved him for that. She couldn't stand seeing him brought down, fighting off grey civil servants and fastidious prosecutors who would rake through every penny that came through this office door and try to smear his good name. She'd do everything in her power to help him, fight if need be and settle where called for.

'Listen, Dad, I'll do everything I can to help. Maybe it's not as bad as it looks.'

Chapter Twenty-five

Back in Dublin Kate could not get the quandary her father was in out of her head. The situation was even more serious than either of her parents realized and she needed financial advice from someone used to dealing with the Revenue Commissioners and government departments. Bill had thrown her the name of a guy they'd used before and Kate had set up a lunch meeting with him in the Clarence Hotel as she had no intention of bringing him to the office.

'Hiya, Kate,' he'd greeted her as they took their seats in The Tea Room, Kate making sure they were seated in a part of the restaurant where they couldn't be overheard. They ordered quickly. Kate was relieved that Rory McWilliams had passed on the alcohol, as she wanted him to have a clear head.

'So what is it?' he asked. Kate was taken aback by his directness.

'I have a problem with someone.'

'A client?'

'Yes,' she lied, 'who is perhaps looking at charges of corruption, bribery, I'm not sure yet. Planning deals that were pushed through a local council.'

'Backhanders?'

'More than likely. The files are in a heap, no proper paperwork, a set of accounts not done for almost three years, insider type trading but with regard to property and land acquisition.'

'Fraud?' he said, leaning across the table.

She reddened. She could not believe the bizarre situation she was in. She could strangle her father for what he'd done. 'I'm not sure.'

He buttered a piece of fresh walnut bread, concentrating.

'Any more?'

'The Revenue are talking about investigating.'

He groaned aloud. 'Just when I thought things couldn't get any worse! Are you trying to ruin my lunch?'

She gulped a glass of chilled Ballygowan,

watching the forty-year-old accountant tear into his seared crab cakes and salad starter. Her own appetite was somewhere down in her toes as she sipped at her soup.

'You said things are in a fucking mess, no accounts done or signed off on. Sounds bad but it could be advantageous. Maybe your client didn't quite know how bad the situation was.'

She sat up, paying attention.

'Was there anyone else involved in this?'

'A partner, but he retired a few years ago.'

'A sleeping partner.'

'No he was the main holder of the company originally, he looked after the finances.'

'Maybe what your client needs to do is play cowboys.'

'Play cowboys!' she spluttered.

'Yeah, come out with his hands up! The taxmen like that. Well, sometimes.'

She was intrigued. As the waiter cleared their plates and brought the main courses, she asked, 'But what about the back-handers, the payments?'

'Obviously there would have to be some sort of an assessment of moneys given and the taxes lost. There are two situations here to be considered and dealt with, the likelihood of the council or whoever is involved being able to prove bribery – not an easy thing to get people to confess or admit to, and an in-depth investigation by the taxmen would likely take an age. For me to ascertain the likely damage to your client and the settlement offer should one be made I'd need to have time to study the files, bank recs, deposit accounts, current property valuations, etc.'

'It sounds very complicated, Rory.'

'I suppose it's sort of forensic accounting, if you want to call it that in laymen's terms.'

'Do you think you'd be able to help us?'

'Should do. Do you want me to go to your client's premises?'

'No, I'll get the information to you, it will take a few days to get it sorted and packed up.'

'That'll be fine.'

'Rory, I'd appreciate it if you kept this under your hat.'

'There is always client confidentiality,' he said seriously.

'It's just that Bill and the other partners aren't involved. This one's mine.'

'I get it,' he said, ordering a milky cappuccino. 'Send the stuff over and I'll get back to you.'

Relieved, she tried to relax and enjoy the end of the meal with Rory, the two of them talking about mutual acquaintances and favourite Dublin haunts. Sitting across the table from him she realized how both physically and mentally she was attracted to him, sighing to herself when she noticed the big gold wedding ring on his finger and wondering why it was that all the guys she fancied lately seemed to be married.

She phoned her mother and father when she got back to the office to tell them the latest progress.

'He's gone into Waterford to meet someone. He should be back for dinner.'

'How is Dad anyway?'

'He's still not eating or sleeping properly, the worry of this is really getting to him. The sooner all this business is over the better and we can get back to normal.'

Kate sighed. The likelihood of things returning to normal were slim, and they'd probably have to sell off some of their assets to clear money her father owed.

'Listen, Mum, I'll be down again this weekend, tell Dad we've a lot to go through.'

What a crap life! Killing herself all week in the office and then the whole weekend given up to sorting out her father's mess, trying to put some kind of order on things before she carted it back to Dublin to Rory.

'What about this one, Kate, it refers to Kirwan's land deal and this one the O'Reilly and the Clears.'

'I'll look at it in a second. Dad, didn't you ever think of getting a computer and putting everything up properly on it? It would cut down hugely on the paperwork and mess. You wouldn't know yourself.'

'Martin wouldn't have it. Kicked up a huge fuss any time I mentioned it.'

'Dad! You told us you had a racehorse. *One* horse!'

'Aye Lovely Lass! She's a grand little filly, heart as big as a tiger.'

'Well it looks like you were being charged for the keep and training of three other horses too by Tommy Brennan.'

'She did well, so it made sense to add to the stable. Sligo Girl, Kilkenny Kate after yourself and Moyaromy.'

'Jesus. Dad, I don't believe you!'

'They've run a few good races, Tommy feels they have potential.'

'Dad, are you gone stark staring mad? These racehorses are costing you a fortune!'

Kate riffled through a heavy black ledger, running her fingers down the columns. Money paid out. Payment for Milo Richardson's farm holding, payment for Mulcahy's outbuildings and four acres... Her finger stopping suddenly. Payment to Hazel Lavelle? That couldn't be...

'Dad, did you pay out money to the Lavelles?' she asked, puzzled.

Her father stopped what he was doing, but didn't turn around.

'I invested in it a few years ago. Hazel

297

wanted to retire, give up the café and was looking for a buyer. We did the usual trawl but no takers, then we realized there was a buyer right under our noses.'

'Sheila O'Grady,' she whispered.

'Aye, the trouble was none of the banks in the county would lend a widow with five children a bob, so she came to me.'

'You financed her!'

'I made a business investment.'

Kate couldn't believe it! She could still remember the winter when Lavelle's small bakery and teashop had closed down for a few months, the whole town curious as to what was going on behind the hoardings, then with huge fanfare it had reopened as a large bright restaurant that overlooked the seafront, with a small paved courtyard to the back. The best of food served from lunch-time right through to dinner in the evening, patrons advised to book a table, especially at the busy weekends. In the separate tall glass-fronted annexe beside the restaurant door a sign proclaimed 'Lavelle's Fine Foods', a totally separate enterprise where fresh breads, cakes, desserts and biscuits and pre-pared meals were sold.

'Sheila was a good investment. She knew the business inside out, was a good worker and in Hazel's eyes was totally trustworthy and a suitable person to take over and run the business.'

'Was this before or after I caught you two together?' she snapped.

'That's none of your business,' he replied slowly. 'Sheila O'Grady is a good woman who has worked damned hard to build up a rock-solid business and I was glad at that time to be able to help her!'

Her father was defending and standing up for the woman he'd had an affair with!

'But what about you and Mammy?'

'Your mother and I were going through a terrible time after Sean died, that's all I'll say. It's not an excuse but it's the truth. Sheila O'Grady understood. She'd lost her husband and was on her own raising a family. I suppose we were both in our own way lonely.'

Kate still remembered it, the awful time when her parents barely spoke and grief had filled the house.

'I don't know what I'd have done without Sheila, probably ended up in St Pat's.' He spoke of the other woman with more than affectionate kindness and Kate suddenly realized that her father actually loved Sheila, and held her in high regard. She hadn't the courage to ask him if the relationship was still going on.

Hunkering down on the floor she riffled through more paperwork, old bank statements.

'Dad, I don't believe it! There's a cheque

here from one of your clients and you didn't even bother lodging it.'

'Give it to me!' he insisted, pulling it out of her hand and immediately tearing it up.'

'What the hell did you do that for?' she demanded.

'I was only holding it for someone. Anyway, it was long out of date.'

No wonder his affairs were in such a state of calamity, thought Kate as she studied a massive red folder, her heart sinking as she perused the contents.

Cove Cottages. She remembered the time her father and Martin had built the sixteen summer homes; a journalist from the Dublin papers had come down to photograph them and everyone was amazed when they were all sold thirty-six hours later. Looking through the folder she discovered a copy of the deed of sale of the late Maggie Roche's three-bedroomed cottage and stables and acre of land to Cove Holdings. Dillon and Duffy had acted as auctioneer for the executor who was Maggie's only living relative, a nephew in New Jersey. A private treaty sale, the old woman's house and land, looking at it now, seemed to have gone for a lot less than the market value. A copy of her father's letter to Dwight Roche advising him to accept the offer as the dwelling was almost uninhabitable and the land not worth much was still on file.

Kate could remember the old woman out lovingly tending her garden and vegetable patch and the two ageing donkeys she kept. The nephew had approved the sale and Dillon Duffy had passed the parcel of land to Cove Holdings, one of their own privately held companies. Planning permission had been granted almost immediately. Kate groaned. What would happen if this nephew surfaced or could ever be found? 'Dad why did you do this?' she said.

'Not a sinner ever came to see that poor soul! Not a visitor from across the way ever, not even a postcard from America – ask Larry Murphy the postman. He'll tell you. Maggie hadn't even made a will. It would have stuck in my craw to send a big cheque off to some high-flying young buck in America! Martin and I did give a big donation afterwards to the Donkey Sanctuary place on Maggie's behalf. She'd have liked that.'

'Jesus, Dad, donkeys or not, it wasn't your decision to make.' She laughed. 'And you'd no right to manipulate the sale. You are legally up the fucking creek!'

'Kate, I know I've let you all down,' he admitted despairingly, slumping across his office desk. 'As God is my judge, I didn't mean for any of this to happen.'

Kate knew from dealing with cases over the years that what he really meant was that he hadn't intended being caught. She'd pack up the rest of the stuff tonight and hopefully get it to Rory over the next day or two. Her father was in a whole heap of trouble and she would have to do her utmost to bail him out.

'I always knew some day having a lawyer in the family might be a good thing,' he said half jokingly as he passed her a box.

'You and your bloody Donkey Sanctuary! The Revenue Commissioners will go crazy!'

Chapter Twenty-six

'Kate, you know something, you're getting to be a boring old fart.'

'Thanks,' she said, taking a sip of her beer. If it had come from anyone else, she would have ranted and raved and retaliated in some smart Alec fashion but since the speaker was her cousin Conor Quinn and he was only saying it in her best interest she had no option but to humbly agree with his rather insulting opinion.

They were in McDaid's in Harry Street drinking pints of cool Miller.

'You bloody well work too hard and don't go out and enjoy yourself enough.'

Sitting in her black pinstripe suit she

stared into the golden bubble of liquid and knew that much of what he was saying was true.

'I have a very demanding job,' she tried to explain, 'and...'

'We all have jobs! Everyone works hard to get the money to go out and give it a lash during the weekends or after work.'

'But my day isn't nine to five. At my level the company expects more as I'm dealing with big corporates.'

'Expects too bloody much if you ask me. Do you want to waste your life away on some big fat ass company when you've no life of your own?'

'Conor, that's a bit harsh,' she argued.

'You hardly ever get home for the weekend. You work overtime so you've no chance to go out with your friends and have a bit of crack.'

There was no point telling him she'd actually spent more time down home in Rossmore the past few weeks than she'd done for months. 'I still see Minnie and Dee sometimes,' she protested.

'Yeah for a quick lunch or to go to the cinema, I bet.'

She slumped against the bar counter. Everything he was saying was true.

'My life is shit,' she admitted, catching the barman's eye and ordering another pint. 'Correction, I enjoy my work but my personal life is shit.'

'Then we need to remedy it.'

'Do what, though?' She felt totally deflated, wondering how she was ever going to rescue herself from the boring structure she had created. Another pint and she'd be weeping on Conor's shoulder.

'Listen, you've got to make sure your free time is your own and that you don't spend it banjaxed lying in bed on a Saturday or Sunday trying to sleep off the exhaustion of a week in work.'

Did Conor have a secret camera hidden in her new apartment or was he just able to read her that well?

'You need rescuing.' He grinned, stuffing his face with peanuts from the bowl near them.

'What did you have in mind?' she laughed.

'Fresh air and sails and life on the ocean wave!' he coaxed.

'Sailing?'

'Yeah I need to crew a boat down to West Cork and I'm short a hand. It's only for a few days.'

'I'm up to my tonsils with work,' she began to explain.

'I'm not asking you about work. I'm asking you to take a few days off work and spend some time on the boat with me. It'll be fun, if you remember that word.'

Fun. That was the something she was

definitely lacking. Between the office and her father's problems she'd been stressed out lately. She didn't even have to think about it any more. She'd always loved sailing and crewing with her cousins, and it was ages since they'd sailed together. A few days of uncomplicated simple living would be great.

'I'll do it. I'll sail to West Cork with you.' She laughed, elated to have made a decision with regard to herself.

Minnie had given a big cheer when she'd phoned her to tell her she would be off sailing for a few days and unavailable for their weekly lunch.

'For Christ's sake have a bit of fun and give Conor a big hug from me.'

Bill O'Hara her boss had huffed and puffed a bit when she asked him for the few days off.

'It's just it's all a bit sudden, Kate. You know how busy we are at the moment. You should have put your holiday request in months ago.'

'I didn't know that I was going to be going away then.'

She knew that Bill was reluctant to deal with Alan MacCarthy on his own, having rowed with him two years ago about the privatization of his company, and now relied on her to smooth the waters.

'You'll just have to deal with MacCarthy yourself,' she said.

'Perhaps we should leave it till you get back?'

'Bill, it can't be left, you know that! Everything is on a tight deadline in terms of the company and announcements. You'll just have to do it.'

Inwardly she cursed the lazy so-and-so who regularly didn't turn in for work and took off for rugby breaks to matches in Paris and Rome and London and golf outings to Scotland and Augusta, and Valderrama while she covered for him. For once she was asking him to cover for her and he was making a big deal out of it.

'Alan's a nice guy, just go easy and give him what he wants and he's like a pussycat. Fighting with him only riles him and brings out the tiger.'

Getting away from the office and Dublin was exactly what she needed and throwing her kitbag on deck of the brand-new forty-footer moored in Howth harbour she banished all thoughts of the office from her mind. The galley was a delight with a huge microwave and fancy gas hob, the fridge stocked with beer and wine and fat juicy steaks, rashers and eggs and tomatoes and salad.

'Hey Conor, this is great.'

'Yeah your man who owns her is a chef. Shay has two or three fancy restaurants in Cork. I suppose you can take the cook out of the kitchen,' he joked, 'but you can't take the kitchen out of the cook.'

'Well at least we'll eat well.'

Kate grabbed one of the small bunk-cabins, plomping her mini-disc player and some reading material on the cosy bed before going up on deck and helping her cousin to cast off. She watched the pier and Howth harbour disappear as they slipped out into the open Irish Sea, the gusting wind catching the sails as she raced from aft to fore, Conor shouting instructions to her.

Later she cooked up steak and onions and mushrooms with big floury potatoes and the two of them listened to the radio and chatted companionably as they washed down a bottle of red wine. They took turns on watch and for her few hours Kate slept like a top, blinking when Conor shook her awake. Up on deck she stretched her limbs, enjoying the peace and solitude of the darkness and the constant lapping water against the hull. Two and half hours later she watched the sun slowly begin to rise from out beyond the line of the water and the light creep across the sky as dawn came. Tears running down her face with awe, she was glad that her cousin was snoring below in the bunk and not seeing what an emotional eejit she'd become.

The day grew cold and wet and windy, and Conor and herself worked well to use the elements to speed them on their way, passing down by Wexford's coast and deserted beaches. Her cousin seemed to know the coastline well, and was like a guide mapping out their position hourly. Hours slipped by and although her arms and shoulders ached she realized that the tension and stress she normally carried had somehow disappeared. Conor made hot soup and brought it up on deck so they could watch a group of seals.

'Look at that fat fellow there!' he joked. 'He reminds me of my old boss.'

Kate looked around to see if she could spot one that resembled any of the senior partners she worked with, but decided that the seals were far too nice.

That night it was dark by the time they reached Cork, Conor mooring the boat in Kinsale so Shay O'Driscoll, the owner, could drive over to see it. After a quick look around his new purchase he insisted they join him for a meal in the Spinnaker.

'I've two huge parties booked in to the restaurants over the weekend, so there's no way I'll get down to our house in Baltimore till Monday. Will you stay on? I'll need you to run through how she works, the spec etc.

with me then.'

'Sure.'

'Then I intend spending the next two weeks with Tina and the kids sailing around Sherkin and Castletownshend and over to Crookhaven and Schull just getting to know her.'

'They'll love it.' Kate smiled, almost envying the O'Driscoll family their boat.

The next morning they set sail again, Kate enjoying a freedom she had forgotten. As they cast off and slipped out into the Atlantic, heavy waves pushed against the boat as strong winds caught the sails. Up on deck she could hardly get her breath as her hair whipped across her face, stinging her eyes; and she felt the sheer exhilaration of struggling with the elements while Conor shouted orders at her. Her body ached with effort but she had never felt better as they passed Cape Clear and Sherkin, the heavy fishing trawlers and the island ferry and finally dropped anchor in the port of Baltimore.

She was tired and hungry and readily fell in with Conor's plan for a huge plate of pizza and fries at La Jolie Brise's restaurant on the harbour, which was packed with sailors and a few tourists and visitors. The young Breton owner discussed the new boat with Conor and promised to go down and take a look at it in the morning.

After wolfing down their food and a carafe of wine, Conor insisted on joining the throng in the pub next door.

'I'm so tired, I'll fall asleep,' she yawned.

'It's just all the fresh air. You're not used to it,' he said.

She would have loved to have curled up in a corner of Bushes, and fallen asleep but Conor ran into an old friend who was down staying in one of the hotels and she was dispatched to the bar to buy a few pints for them. Trying to balance the two pints of Guinness and her own glass of beer as well was difficult enough. Negotiating the crowd around the counter she almost fell, pushing against a wall of navy ribbed wool.

'Hey it wouldn't do to be throwing good pints on the floor,' he teased.

Looking at the big wet stain on his jumper, Kate wanted to die with embarrassment. 'I'm sorry. I nearly fell.'

'No harm done.'

'What about your jumper?'

The words were hardly out of her mouth when he had peeled it off to reveal a pale blue denim shirt the exact colour of his eyes.

'It will dry.'

She stood there feeling like a clumsy oaf with her wind-burnt skin and crazy wild hair as she felt his eyes run over her.

'Here, let me give you a hand with those before you spill any more,' he offered, taking a pint glass from her.

Conor raised his eyebrow when he saw her approaching.

'I'll pass this one to your boyfriend,' the man offered.

'I'm her cousin,' protested Conor, introducing himself and his friend Tom who in a roundabout fashion introduced Kate to Derry Donovan.

Next thing she knew, two more stools had been brought over and Derry and his friend Erik had joined them, Derry's denim-clad leg pressing against hers.

The talk turned to boats and yachts and Conor was incredulous when Derry told them, 'I design boats for my living. That's my profession. Erik here and his family have a big boat yard in Galway where they help me to build them.'

Kate sighed. A boat-builder. She should have guessed. He was broad and strong and obviously worked with his hands; his blue eyes stood out in his tanned face.

Conor told them about the boat they had sailed from Dublin.

'The market is tight at the moment. People are cutting back on their luxuries but I suppose the past few years have been good, and there will always be people who want to sail,' Derry told them.

'I'll drink to that,' joked Conor, as they decided to order another round.

Kate relaxed as the conversation wheeled around her, sipping her beer, watching the beam from the lighthouse through the pub window.

'What do you do, Kate?' asked Derry.

'I'm a lawyer.'

'Defending the poor and downtrodden, I trust.'

'Actually no, it's mostly mergers and acquisitions and compliance, corporate law at this stage. I work in one of the big firms in Dublin.'

'So maybe one day you'll get me to design a yacht for you.'

'I'm only just rediscovering my sea-legs,' she admitted. 'Conor thought it would do me good to come away sailing for a few days.'

'And has it?'

'Has it?'

'Has it done you good?'

Looking into his eyes she could see he was serious.

'Yeah, I guess. I was stressed out, working too hard.'

'So, you will go sailing again?'

'I suppose, when I can get the time.'

'Sometimes we have to make time.'

She watched as he stood up and went for more drinks, Conor and himself laughing

312

and joking already as if they were old friends. She wished she could be at ease and relaxed like that immediately with people, instead of being so fecking uptight.

On his return he once again pushed in beside her. Although everyone laughed and chatted Kate was conscious all the time of Derry, drawn to want to talk to him and have him look at her. As closing time drew nearer she began to dread the time Conor would announce they must be on their way, and was steeling herself to say goodbye.

'Time, folks, time!'

The barmaid began to collect the empty glasses and they all stumbled out of the warmth of the pub onto the roadway, the soft clang of rigging the only sound in the still night air.

Conor and Derry were busy exchanging cards.

'I tell you, Derry, a complete IT package could really simplify your work. That's what I do for small businesses, I give them a state of the art system that makes everything easy.'

'It sounds interesting.'

'Well look me up if you or Erik need any advice. Anyways, Kate and I'd better get back to the boat. I'm whacked.'

Kate stood there with a stupid grin on her face as the moonlight danced on the water.

'It was nice to meet you too,' Derry said,

turning towards her.

'I'm sorry about your sweater.'

He was so close she could feel his warm breath on her neck, and couldn't believe it when he leaned forward and brushed his lips against hers. Kate for one crazy second was tempted to throw her arms about him and kiss him passionately.

'Good-night, Kate,' he said, disappearing off along the front.

The next two days they lazed and read, and Conor had sailed over to Sherkin Island, both of them enjoying the crazy wildness of the place as they picnicked on the beach and swam in the chilly water. She had cooked them fresh fish with greens and baby potatoes, and they'd sat listening to a radio play companionably. She had never felt so relaxed and refreshed. On Sunday night after they'd eaten they'd gone back to the pub, Kate disappointed to see no sign of Derry as they settled into a corner seat.

Conor was good company and soon had her in stitches about Aunt Vonnie and Uncle Joe and his brothers and the harum-scarum things they all got up to when they were younger.

Shay O'Driscoll, the boat's owner, had arrived down to the harbour the next day, all excited to get a proper chance to see his new purchase in broad daylight. Kate skedaddled for a walk as Conor started going through the log book and explaining the yacht's wonderful features and the technical stuff for the forty-footer.

She decided to walk up past the cove and towards the Beacon, the sea on one side, the rough stone garden walls covered in tumbling pink fuchsia, their buds heavy with nectar, on the other. She jumped out of the way as two cars drove by her, the second, a beat-up old Saab, coming to a halt yards away from her. A familiar denim-clad figure stepped out to say hello.

'I thought you were gone,' she blurted out.

'Not till the end of the week! When are you and Conor going back to Dublin?'

'Tonight or tomorrow. Shay said he'd drop us to Skibbereen then we'll get a bus or a train.'

She stood there awkwardly, not wanting to leave him.

'What are you up to?'

'Just going for a walk, kill a bit of time. Shay is down on the boat with Conor and then after lunch he's taking Tina and the whole O'Driscoll family over to Cape Clear for a sail and showing Shay the ropes. There won't be space for me.'

'So you are at a loose end?'

'I guess.'

'You could join me. I'm driving to Schull

315

to collect something. We could even get lunch there.'

She nodded dumbly, trying to control the underlying excitement she felt as she sat in beside him, not believing she was acting so impulsively and getting into a car with a virtual stranger.

The air was electric between them and he put on the CD player. In Schull he drove down by the harbour and fishery ice plant, where he disappeared into a small office.

'Got to collect a cheque for some work I did. I won't be long.'

Afterwards they walked along the main street which was filled with craft and art shops and quaint home bakeries and design studios. Derry insisted on treating her to lunch in a small open-air courtyard restaurant, the two of them opting for fat garlicky prawns swimming in butter and brown bread. When they'd finished he drove along the Colla Road, stopping where a group of curving islands rose up from the sea.

'That's Long Island and Goat Island,' he explained, as he reached forward to kiss her slowly. Kate responded warmly, wanting his kiss to last for ever.

'I've been wanting to do this ever since you threw that pint over me,' he teased.

'It was an accident.' She giggled as she began to kiss his neck and run her tongue along the edge of his ear.

'Hey, we both stink of garlic and if we stay here much longer we risk being arrested for what I want to do to you.'

Kate burst out laughing, not believing his honesty.

'So what about we head back to Baltimore and–'

'Conor won't be back for hours!'

'Then you'll just have to come back to my place.'

An hour later she was lying in bed with him, his arm around her, drenched with sweat as her body rocked with his in total climax, Derry pulling her closer and closer as Kate let herself get swept away by the sheer physical pleasure of being with him.

Later that evening she declined Conor's offer to join him for a farewell dinner in Shay and Tina's home up on the hill, content to be with Derry and gorge herself on takeaway pizza and chips.

'Don't go back tomorrow,' he urged. 'Stay on here with me.'

'I've got to get back, the office are expecting me.'

'Fuck them. Phone your boss and tell him you got delayed or something.'

Kate considered the temptation of being with Derry and staying on for another glorious four days in the revamped coastguard house he was renting. She had never done anything so reckless or abandoned in her life.

'Give me four days,' he pleaded. 'Beautiful Kate, listen to me, just stay.'

Throwing caution to the winds she phoned the office, telling Barry's secretary Pamela that due to unforeseen circumstances she wouldn't be back in the office till Monday. Pamela told her that Barry would go crazy and that he'd set up meetings for Thursday and Friday for her.

'Tell him to cancel them and that I'll talk to him on Monday,' she said firmly, switching off her mobile.

'Shameless hussy,' Derry teased, nibbling her ear.

Retrieving her bag from the boat Conor had a big grin all over his face when she told him he'd be travelling back to Dublin on his own.

'Don't say a word, Conor,' she pleaded, 'or I'll throw you overboard.'

Chapter Twenty-seven

Back in Patterson's Kate was disappointed not to have heard from Derry Donovan. Perhaps she had misjudged him, and their few days together had been just that – a few days, nothing more than a fling. A brief, passionate and mutually sexually satisfying fling!

A fling. Well she sure had flung! Fuck him! Likely he was one of the gold ring brigade, already married, and had hidden it from her or was already involved in a relationship. Funny, she hadn't taken him for one of those slimeball types that she usually ran a mile from in Leeson Street. There was no point beating herself up about it, a good time had been had by all!

She had other things to think of anyway as her father had been summoned before a council committee for an oral hearing to explain various planning applications and appeals over a period of ten years.

'All I can do is tell what happened. If they want to cast Martin and myself as villains then that's what they'll do. We were and are no different from every other builder or businessman in the country. Buy low and sell high, that's always been our motto and there's no crime in that!'

'Daddy, please get someone to represent you,' begged Kate. 'I can come along but I'm not technically qualified in the planning area. You need to have someone advise you before the hearing.'

After some deliberation Jack Hartigan, an old college friend of Barry's, had been appointed.

'I'll come up to Dublin to see him,' Frank promised.

Kate was relieved. She had passed a lot of the accounts and ledgers to Rory, coming clean about her father's involvement.

'Don't worry, we'll do our best to get as discreet a settlement as possible,' he reassured her.

Her father was in ebullient form after the meeting with the solicitor in Fitzwilliam Square...

'There's nothing they can do to me at this stage of the game. All those sites have been rebuilt, there are families and businesses and offices on them now, and there'd be huge controversy if the council tried to reverse legitimate decisions made by their own members. Jack feels they'd be in an impossible position if they tried to backtrack.'

'But, Dad, they could fine you, assess the

profits you made.'

'Aye, they could,' he admitted grudgingly.

Her parents were staying in Dublin over-night with her, sleeping in her bed, while she took the new blue Habitat couch.

'This place is the size of a fart box,' complained her father, examining the modern one-bedroomed apartment overlooking the seafront at Monkstown from top to bottom. 'Though I'll give you it's airy and bright!'

'Frank, the view is magnificent from the front window and balcony and when Kate gets a few pots growing here on the balcony it will be a nice retreat for her after a long day at work.'

Kate couldn't imagine herself in a month of Sundays lugging plant pots and compost and stuff from a garden centre up in the lift and then having to tend them and water and mind them.

'I'll bring you a few clippings and bits and pieces in a pot the next time we're coming up,' promised her mother, as if reading her mind.

Kate loved the new apartment and ever since Minnie had fallen madly head over heels in love with architect Colm O'Halloran and married him, she actually liked being on her own. She liked not having to share, able to collapse into bed after working late with a bowl of Cornflakes and milk instead of making chit-chat with a new flatmate. She was only a few minutes from the DART station, which brought her right into town, and the village had a host of eclectic shops and restaurants, which were perfect for her needs. Being single was something she had to accept and gear herself accordingly.

'Will I cook?' she offered.

'No,' said her father, scanning the small galley kitchen and eating area. 'It'd be nicer for your mother to get to eat out.'

She got a table in FXB's, the steakhouse on the Crescent, knowing her father would approve of the rib-eye, fillet, sirloin and strip loins on the menu.

'Nothing like good Irish beef,' he murmured as the waitress brought their food to the table. Watching him eat, she realized he had got older, shrunk a little; the skin around his eyes was lined with wrinkles and his hair was receding. The past few weeks were bound to have put a strain on him, on both of them. She didn't know how her mother remained so calm and didn't end up screaming and roaring at him. Maeve Dillon looked the same as always, perhaps a little trace of grey in her hair, her skin flawless, her bright brown eyes sparkling under her dark eyebrows, a pretty woman who'd managed to retain her looks.

'We don't know what we'd have done without you, Kate,' she said. 'You've been a tower of strength, what with your good advice and legal connections and getting that accountant friend of yours to look over the books.'

'It's all right.' She smiled.

'What with Moya and Patrick away in London and Romy in Australia...'

'I'm not having bloody Patrick shove his nose into my business, do you hear?' Her father gesticulated, waving his fork at them.

She wondered what her brother-in-law had said or done to annoy her father.

'Kate, we'd be lost without you,' said her mother, reaching for her hand. 'You are such a good daughter!'

Kate sighed. It must be hard on them, growing old together now she and her sisters had all grown up and moved away. Her father unfaithful and at risk of financial ruin, her mother's honesty compromised, her head buried in the sand unwilling to face up to all that had happened. But yet looking across the table at the two of them it was clear that they still loved and cared for each other deeply.

'Your father knows he has to change his ways,' smiled her mother. 'That things in future have to be done correctly – people expect it!'

'Aye paperwork and forms filled in and certificates to beat the band! I'll get Jackie a bloody computer to put up our files on and do the correspondence. She's a bright girl, she'll have it set up in no time. Maybe even take in a junior partner, train him in.'

'That's good.'

'Once this business with the council is settled and I know where I am with the taxman, it'll be a clean slate. I promise you!'

Kate tried to convince herself that he really meant it.

The next morning she left them having breakfast in the apartment, arguing good-naturedly over a pot of marmalade as she ran for work.

Ten days later her mother phoned to say her father had suffered a massive heart attack behind the wheel of his silver S Class Mercedes about a mile from home and had died instantly.

She immediately phoned Romy in Australia and broke the awful news to her.

'How long will it take you to organize a flight home?' she asked her sister. 'Flynn's the undertaker's need to know.'

Romy had said nothing. Kate knew how much of a shock it must be to hear such news so far from home.

'Tell Flynn's to go ahead, not to wait for me.'

'I don't understand.'

'I'm not coming home! I won't be at the funeral. I'm sorry he's dead but I'm not coming home. There's no point to it.'

'What am I supposed to say to Mammy?' cried Kate.

'Just tell her the truth.'

'You mean tell her you're an enlightened bitch that hasn't the decency to come home and pay your respects to the father who raised you? What kind of person have you become, Romy? None of us know you any more.'

'I'm sorry.'

'What will people think, what will they say?'

'You can tell them I couldn't get a flight, that you couldn't contact me. I don't give a damn what you say because I'm still not coming home. You don't need me there.'

'Mammy needs you.'

'She's got you and Moya. She'll manage.'

'How can you be so hard, so cold?'

There was no answer and when she tried to ring back there was no reply.

Shocked, the family had come together to bury him. Moya and Patrick and the children, Fiona sick with fright and Danny screaming he wanted Grandad to come back. Maeve Dillon, overcome with grief and hurt even further by Romy's absolute refusal to mourn her father, a final act of cruel defiance.

'Why can't she do the decent thing, if not

for him, for Mammy and the rest of us?' sobbed Moya, furious with her youngest sister.

Kate was clueless as to what to say, for Romy had always been wild and separate from the rest of them, a crazy catalyst for making things happen within the family.

Father Eamonn had flown straight away from Chicago insisting that he be the one to conduct Frank's final funeral mass.

'It's the very least I could do for Frank, who always made me welcome and made me feel part of the family.'

Kate could still not believe it: that the man she thought invincible was actually gone, her father's huge presence and life force so suddenly removed from all their lives.

Rossmore's church was packed with friends and family, locals and a number of her father's business acquaintances, including most of the members of the local county council and their sitting TDs. Gerard O'Malley the local Fianna Fáil representative was fulsome in his praise of her father, Kate wondering would he have been so supportive if faced with a legal hearing in a few months' time. A number of businesses closed out of respect, not just in the town but also in Waterford itself. The blinds were down in Lavelle's as the restaurant and shop had closed for the day as a mark of respect.

Her mother looked in a state of shock. Dressed immaculately in a black suit, she sat small and fragile in the front pew. Moya was gaunt and pale, her eyes red rimmed as she tried to control her own emotion and look after the children, who were collapsed with grief. Kate sat utterly numb through her uncle's mass, refusing to believe that the father she loved, and she did love him despite all his failings, lay in the large coffin in front of the altar.

He was buried in the graveyard only a mile away, laid to rest beside his infant son. Those attending were asked back to the Stone House for drinks and some food. Kate, taken aback, saw Sheila O'Grady and one of her daughters passing around plates and helping to serve the buffet. She'd seen her at the back of the church – but here in the house!

'What are they doing here?' she demanded of Moya.

'Mammy asked them to do the catering. We'd never have managed this big crowd on our own and Sheila was the one suggested the hot buffet.'

'I don't believe it,' moaned Kate, close to tears, not believing the audacity of the woman, standing here in her mother's home.

Out of the corner of her eye she could see her mother and Sheila talking, Sheila squeezing her mother's hand before carrying a tray of vol-au-vents to the other side of the room.

Aunt Vonnie appeared beside them.

'You all right, Kate? Your mother wanted Sheila here, wanted her to be the one to do the food for Frank, to be involved. They are old friends and they have always had a lot in common. You're too young to understand...'

Kate nodded. She didn't understand it! But she had no intention of causing a scene.

'Maeve adored your father and is going to be absolutely lost without him.'

'Frank would have liked that Eamonn was here for the ceremony,' interrupted her Uncle Joe who was nursing a brandy and port, 'and the fact so many people came to pay their respects. He was respected, you know, and despite all the stupid rumours and gossip lately, well liked. He did more for this part of the country than most people know. He was a good man, and you girls remember that!'

Kate nodded. Funerals were bloody awful things, a test to be endured to see if you could still walk and talk and stand and eat while absolutely paralysed with grief. It was late when the last visitor left, Danny sprawled on the couch asleep, Patrick lifting him upstairs to bed. Fiona had spent her time talking to her cousin Billy who was only a few years older than her, the two of them laughing and telling each other stupid jokes and stories. It was the first time she'd smiled in days.

'Mammy. We have to go to bed,' urged Kate.

'Maybe I'll just sit in the armchair for a while yet.'

Maeve often sat up in the chintz armchair beside the fire waiting for their father to come in after a late night out or for one of them to arrive home safe from a party or a disco.

'Not tonight, Mammy, you're exhausted,' pleaded Kate. 'You need to lie down and sleep. We're all here. I'll lock up and turn off the lights.'

Reluctantly Maeve Dillon climbed the stairs, Moya helping her to get ready for bed. Unable to sleep, Kate listened in the silence of the house to the clock ticking in the hall as her mother's sobs gave way to regular breathing and her usual snores. Moya in her old room was comforted in her husband's arms, while she lay alone in the dark.

Chapter Twenty-eight

The Stone House was strangely quiet without her father. Kate hadn't realized how much noise he'd always made, a big man with heavy footsteps on the stairs in the hall, listening to the radio, watching the news constantly and the racing results, making coffee for himself and banging about in the kitchen, or on the phone, raising his voice because he was slightly deaf. His huge presence suddenly gone!

Her mother had slept solidly for sixteen hours without budging, Danny, afraid, asking if his granny was about to die too.

'She's just very tired and sad, pet,' Moya reassured him, hugging her little boy close.

They were all concerned for her. Kate had always imagined her parents growing old and crabby together, her father retired, bossing her mother like he always did, as they went away on weekend trips and holidays. They had never considered their mother alone and vulnerable, nervous for the first time ever in her life of being on her own.

'Mum, would you like to come and stay

with us in Richmond for a while?' offered Moya.

'Or my apartment in Dublin?' asked Kate.

'No, I'd prefer to stay here,' admitted Maeve, honestly. 'This is my home and I don't want to leave it.'

In the house she felt safe, surrounded by familiar things and memories of years of married life, Frank's presence everywhere. She couldn't leave the house!

They all sat in silence when Pat Hayes, the local solicitor, called to the house a few days later with a copy of the will. Maeve had been left almost everything.

'You already own the family home, Maeve, but Frank was keen for you to realize some of his property investments,' he explained carefully as he put on his reading glasses. 'There is a three-storey office building in the centre of Waterford on the quays, a single-storey office building in Rossmore, five apartments in the Old Mill development, four holiday homes on Harbour Road, two shops on Harbour Road, three cottages in the Cove, and an eight-bedroomed con-verted house on Tramore Strand being in use as a bed and breakfast. Four racehorses and a portfolio of shares and a number of small farmland plots.'

'Oh my God,' sighed their mother.

'To Moya, Kate and Romy, each of my

daughters, I leave a half-acre of land in Woodstown overlooking the sea for their own use or the use of their families. My wedding ring with the sapphire stone I leave to my eldest grandson Gavin Redmond, my gold watch to my grandson Daniel Redmond and my gold chain to my granddaughter Fiona Redmond.'

Moya's eyes welled with tears. Her father had adored his grandchildren. Kate and herself held hands as Pat Hayes finished off.

'Thank you, Pat,' said Maeve when he'd finished. 'We appreciate it.'

'There is extensive property but as far as I'm aware there may be some borrowings against them,' he warned.

'Some borrowings!' pressed Patrick. 'What do you mean?'

'Bank loans, heavy mortgages. Frank had mentioned to me recently that he was hoping to offload some of them and pay off the loans.'

'Are you sure?'

'Aye, I spoke to him after he came home from Dublin last week.'

'Perhaps we should talk to his bank manager, then.'

Two days later found them sitting in Rossmore's Bank of Ireland branch close to Frank Dillon's offices as Niall Brady explained the situation to them.

'On paper it all looks very rosy and good, but in reality it's not as healthy as we'd ideally like. Everything is heavily borrowed, with interest payments just being met but no decrease in the actual capital sum from month to month.'

Patrick groaned. Kate stared at the family photos on the bank manager's desk, trying to control herself.

Patrick was like a terrier dog with a bone and although their father was only dead and buried a few days he insisted on putting all the information together. Following a phone call to Rory McWilliams, they drove up to Dublin to meet him.

Everything was itemized and listed. The holiday cottages were part of a designated tax scheme and for the present could not be sold without inviting huge penalties. The B&B in Tramore was in need of extensive refurbishment before the start of the summer season and one of the tenants of the shops was in arrears on his rent and had given notice he intended retiring.

It was all a huge mess and Kate could feel tension gnaw at her jaw and shoulders as she listened. There was only one good thing: the council investigation into her father's affairs was over, as without his evidence it could go no further. The Revenue Commissioners were less forgiving and even with

Rory and Patrick's input, the final sum arrived at seemed an absolute fortune.

Most of what their mother had been left would have to be sold to cover the amount.

'I just want to clear it off, pay them all what they are due,' insisted Maeve Dillon angrily. 'Frank did his best during his lifetime to provide for us all. I couldn't ask for more.'

'We could sell the land Daddy left us too,' suggested Kate.

'Your father wanted you to have it,' Maeve reminded her.

'But Mammy, if you need it more, that's what we'll do. I'm sure Moya would agree.'

'There is no question of any of you selling the piece of property your father gave you!' she exclaimed angrily. 'The money will be found to pay off his debts.'

A discreet valuation of the plots showed that without planning permission the land would only fetch a fraction of what it was worth. Reluctantly, Maeve Dillon gave instructions to one of the large auctioneers in Dublin to realize as much value from her husband's properties as possible. Everything except for the holiday cottages and his old office in Rossmore would have to be sold, not a penny of it benefiting his widow. Her father had not believed in pensions, trusting his investments in land and bricks and mortar to be a sounder proposition.

'How will you manage, Mammy?' Kate asked.

'Don't worry, pet, I'll be fine.'

'Would you think of moving?' she suggested gently. 'Maybe the house will be too big for you with all of us gone and the gardens to manage.'

'I love this house,' she replied, affronted. 'My grandfather built it and Vonnie, Eamonn and I were born and grew up in this house, your father and I raised all of you here. How could I possibly ever leave it!'

'I just meant maybe somewhere smaller, a bungalow or an apartment might be easier.'

'And where would Moya and the children stay when they come home for the summer, or Eamonn have a bit of space for himself when he gets a break from his parish?'

'Mum, I know what you're saying.'

'And what about Romy? Do you think I'm going to have your sister come back to Ireland and find her family home sold? No. I'll manage. There's your father's shares and the rents from the cottages and the office. Don't you worry, Kate pet, I'll get by.'

Kate sighed to herself. She loved the Stone House just as much as her mother but she could see the struggle it might become to maintain it.

Chapter Twenty-nine

When Kate returned to work the week after the funeral, Bill O'Hara surprised her by taking her to lunch in Dobbins and actually being kind.

'There's a massive fucking backlog,' he admitted, 'but I know you'll get through it in your own good time.'

She had thrown herself in at the deep end, working late and scheduling early-morning meetings for the next few weeks as she worked on a number of mergers including the complicated takeover of an Irish publisher by an English rival. She felt tired and drained, her father's death obviously taking its toll.

Derry had phoned her out of the blue, asking her to go for a drink with him later that night.

'I can't,' she explained. 'I have to work.'

The managing director of the UK publisher was flying into Dublin to meet the other principal in her office and discuss terms, before the contract-signing in the morning.

'Don't work too hard then!' he'd said sarcastically, not offering her an alternative.

Too shattered to care, she put him out of her mind.

She was working day and night, crawling home to bed in the apartment. Stressed out, she felt rotten and even got weak while standing at the photocopier. Jilly, one of the secretaries, had to get her a glass of Ballygowan water before she stepped into a meeting. The next day she felt no better and dialled the number of the doctor with an office closest to where she worked for a late appointment.

Two hours later she was shocked to discover that she was pregnant!

Everything logically clicked into place as she thought of herself and Derry not taking the slightest precautions the first time they made love.

Standing up, she thanked the doctor for the good news. She had thought about it, and after all the shitty things that had happened over the past few months it *was* good news. Her biological clock was, she supposed, ticking away as it said in those articles she read in women's magazines so perhaps it was the right time for her to have a baby. It was somehow comforting to know that she was at least fertile and would experience motherhood and have a child of her own. At home making hot chocolate and munching a Goldgrain biscuit she wrapped herself up in the cosy comfort of her duvet and fell asleep dreaming of a stroppy toddler stomping along in wellington boots as she tried frantically to keep hold of its hand.

A few days later, trembling with nerves, she finally had enough courage to phone Derry.

'So are we going for that drink then?' he teased.

'I need to talk to you.'

He mentioned a bar in town.

Telling him of her father's recent death and explaining she was not in form for a raucous night in a crowded bar, she instead invited him to the apartment.

Derry was busy on the Saturday night but agreed to come over on Sunday when she promised to cook pasta for them both.

He arrived with a bottle of Chianti, pouring her a glass as they sat down on the sofa. Kate pushed it aside, trying to find the right moment to tell him as he excitedly talked to her about the large catamaran he'd been commissioned to design.

'That's great.' She smiled, nervous.

'I'll be back and forth to Belfast a bit but it's really good news. The client is an American and he races boats, can you believe it!'

'I've a bit more news,' she said, taking a deep breath.

'Work – you got promoted!'

'No.'

'You got fired!'

'No, different.' She tried to control her voice, all the time watching his face. 'I'm going to have a baby.'

'A baby?' Derry looked puzzled.

'Our baby.'

'What! Jeez I don't believe it. You're pregnant! When did you find out?'

'A week ago.'

She could see his uncertainty.

'It is yours,' she affirmed. 'Definitely.'

Giddy and nauseous, she awaited his reaction.

'Should we get married, then?' he said very slowly. 'It's the right thing to do.'

Kate sat back against the cushion, the breath almost leaving her body. What! Was he mad? Get married when they hardly knew each other. She looked into his eyes. He'd said what he meant, that was the kind of guy Derry was. She'd known that right from the start. He hadn't said 'I am madly in love with you and want to get married' or 'I can't live without you, let's get married'. He had simply faced the obvious: that she was single, unmarried and expectant and getting married might be a solution.

'Did you hear what I said, Kate? You're having my baby and I think we should get married.'

'It's a nice thought,' she said, trying to

remain calm, 'but it's a big decision, one not to be rushed into.'

He sat up, hurt.

'For Christ's sake, you're carrying my child, Kate! There is absolutely no question of me not being involved or being part of it, do you hear me?'

'Of course! But I wasn't sure what way you'd react when you heard about the baby. You could have run a mile, told me to piss off. It's great that we both want the baby. He or she will be totally loved and that's all that matters.'

'What about marriage?' he insisted.

'Maybe we should just see how things go. Not rush into anything until we are sure.'

'Is that what you really want?' he said, taking her hands in his.

She nodded, not trusting herself to speak as he hugged her in his arms. If he had asked her to marry him down in West Cork when their bodies were screaming for each other and she wanted their four days to last for ever she would have said yes. But now this proposal! She had no intention of using the fact that she was pregnant to get him to marry her. This wasn't the 1950s and she was no silly young girl, she had a good job and a career, and was quite capable of raising a child on her own like lots of other single parents.

That night Derry stayed until the early

hours of the morning, both of them talking non-stop, thrashing out their opinions on shared parenthood, and access. Kate felt comforted by Derry's assurances to her that he would be a good father and would help with raising their child.

'I promise to be there for you both, Kate. I'm not some kind of heel who's going to run off and leave you. Honest I'm not.'

She sensed that with little encouragement on her behalf Derry would have stayed the night but knew she had to get things clear in her mind. Her impetuosity had landed her in this situation, but now with a baby to think of she had to take things slower, be more practical and put notions of sexual attraction and lust behind her! Derry gently kissed her at 3 a.m. as he was finally leaving, telling her she looked even more beautiful than ever. She longed for them to make love again and swore at herself for being so prudish as she snuggled up in bed alone.

Minnie had yelled and screamed when she'd heard the news.

'Congratulations! You'll be a great mother!'

Kate hung onto the phone and gave her blow-by-blow details of finding out and Derry's reaction to fatherhood.

'Are you and this Derry guy getting married?'

'Hey Min! Don't you know having a baby doesn't mean you have to get married? I'm fine the way I am.'

'Then I'm delighted for you. What does Maeve think about having another grandchild?'

'I haven't told her yet,' she explained. 'I don't want to upset her, so soon after Dad.'

'Don't be surprised but your mother might be pleased,' hinted her best friend. 'My mother has me demented looking for a grandchild!'

In work she informed the personnel department of her need for maternity leave and for them to organize cover for while she was out. Nesta, the girl from the department, congratulated her warmly and went into raptures about her own year-old baby who was ensconced safely below in the company crèche. But Bill had taken it badly, refusing to believe that it was true.

'How will you manage?' he asked. Kate simply raised her eyebrow at him, reminding him he was stepping on dangerous equality territory.

'I'll work hard as I always do and look after my family, like lots of women do!'

Ignoring the gossip that went around the departments, Kate concentrated on keeping her work up to date.

She had excellent health cover and booked

in with a forty-year-old female obstetrician who had worked right through her own pregnancies and declared her to be very fit but a little anaemic.

'Liver, steak and plenty of spinach and greens and a bottle of these,' she said, prescribing folic acid tablets.

Minnie had gone shopping with her helping her to choose two very expensive work suits in the French maternity shop in South Anne Street and comfy underwear in Dunne's Stores.

'Do you think I'm mad?' Kate asked her.

'Mad having the baby? No. There's Colm and I married a whole year and like two rabbits and not a sign of a bambino and you go and do it one night and bingo!'

'Minnie!'

'This baby is going to be the cutest in the world and Auntie Minnie's going to spoil it rotten.'

'What happens if I can't cope, can't manage work and a new baby and...?'

'Will you stop, Kate. You are one of the most capable, organized people I know on the planet. We are talking about one small baby here, not a frigging elephant.'

Kate burst out laughing.

'And knowing you, you could probably rear an elephant too if you had to.'

Derry and Kate had argued about telling

her mother, Kate deciding to go down home by herself for the weekend.

'I'm not having her think that the father of the child is some fly-by-night guy, who doesn't give a shit,' he protested. 'Let me drive you down.'

'No,' she'd insisted. 'I'm going on my own but don't worry, I'll tell her you're supportive.'

Four days later she'd driven down to Rossmore. As always, she was welcomed with open arms and trailed around admiring the garden and her mother's hard work in the beds and vegetable patch.

Maeve Dillon fussed over her and, stuffing her with pancakes and scones and strawberries and cream, asked her all about the office and her career. Kate for once was lost for words.

'Mum, at this rate I'll burst,' she joked, 'and I can't afford to put on too much weight. Listen sit down, I've something important to tell you.'

Her mother had sat quietly as Kate told her about the new grandchild she was carrying which was due in early March.

'I should gave guessed,' she joked. 'You look all aglow!'

She could see her mother waiting for the next announcement, about a partner, a lover, a boyfriend, a future son-in-law, becoming confused and awkward about the

344

situation when she realized that Kate would be a single parent.

'And what will you do about the baby?'

'Mum. I'm keeping the baby.'

'I'm glad, pet,' she said, relief in her eyes.

'I'm healthy and well and single, earning enough to keep us both. The father will also be supportive and involved.'

'Oh Kate, I'm so delighted for you,' smiled her mother, hugging her. 'And you know I'll do anything I can to help.'

Sitting in the cosy warmth of the kitchen, Maeve confided about the shock of her own first pregnancy.

'I was scared out of my wits! Your grandfather was furious, as in those days he couldn't stand Frank, didn't think he was half good enough for me.'

'Mammy, I don't believe you!'

'Poor old Eamonn had to marry us. I think it was the first marriage ceremony he performed, not long after his ordination. We hadn't a penny then and ended up having to move in here with your grandfather. He looked after us and we ended up taking care of him!'

Kate relaxed listening to her mother, looking forward to the idea of sharing her life with a child.

The weekend passed far too quickly, with her mother insisting on treating her to dinner in the Sandbank. Aunt Vonnie and Uncle Joe decided to join them. Glancing across the table at Kate engrossed in conversation with Vonnie, Maeve Dillon found herself thinking of Frank and how he would have taken Kate's news and of her youngest daughter Romy, lost and afraid, who'd panicked and chosen to run away.

'Congratulations, Kate dear!' Her aunt smiled, toasting her. 'Babies are always to be celebrated. And we all know you will make a wonderful mother.'

Chapter Thirty

As the weeks passed, Kate began to adjust to her condition, to the office porter holding the door for her, the post boy keeping her supplied with fizzy Ballygowan water, and Bill not blowing a gasket when one day she actually dozed off in the middle of a meeting and woke up to find herself covered in a throw and with the blinds drawn.

Derry phoned her once or twice a week and their conversations often went on for hours. They went for healthy walks every few weeks and he had accompanied her to the hospital for her ultrasound scan, which made her feel like a character in a Richard

Curtis film. But otherwise she saw very little of him for he travelled a lot and was busy designing and supervising the building of a catamaran in Belfast. Kate in turn was content to live a quiet life. To read and relax and walk, and enjoy solitary pleasures before the impending upheaval of a child which her friends were warning about.

'Everything will change. Just you wait and see!'

'Come on, Kate. Come out and enjoy yourself now!' pleaded Alison, who was organizing her sister Dee's hen night.

Kate had never considered the raucous behaviour of a group of women, single or married, celebrating the impending nuptials of one of their group by coming together in the shared female spirit of drinking and eating and dancing together till all hours something that needed to be copied. She often sidestepped such gangs as they giggled through the city streets with Manchester and Limerick and Belfast accents. However, now that Dee, one of her college friends, had finally decided to tie the knot with her partner Johnny after five years, a form of ritual female celebration was definitely necessary and she had agreed to join the merry throng.

Minnie's whirlwind romance and marriage to Colm had been celebrated with a glitzy hen weekend in New York with a faithful few. Dee's at least was simpler, less expensive and less exclusive, friends she'd amassed over thirty years all roped in. Kate was really only going along with Minnie and the rest of the girls in a vague attempt to make herself feel young and sexy and available. Dee was determined to give it a lash on one of her last nights of freedom.

There was dinner in Eden, followed by a pub-crawl to two places in Temple Bar and then a nightclub.

'What's the point to me going?' she'd argued with Minnie. 'It's not like I can drink a lot with the baby and all I keep doing at the moment is falling asleep.'

'All the more reason you need to come, Kate! You're not sitting at home knitting bootees, that's for sure.'

She'd pulled on a John Rocha black top and a Guess skirt that didn't cut into her waist and made her feel floaty and feminine. Lots of black eye-liner and a ton of mascara made her eyes huge in her face, which of late seemed to have got rounder and full. She had forced herself to eat half a packet of water crackers and some cheese, washed down with a glass of milk, before she went out. She promised to be good and stay on the straight and narrow and confine herself to wine spritzers for the night.

Minnie was wearing a plunge bra under an

almost see-through pale pink shirt and jeans that looked like they were almost sprayed on.

Kate sighed.

She wasn't even a mother yet, but already she felt like an old fuddy-duddy!

Temple Bar was jammered as they made their way to the Eden restaurant, where the bride was already on her third cocktail. Everyone agreed that food was definitely a priority as they perused the menu.

Kate relaxed, letting herself enjoy the atmosphere of the restaurant, and joined in the joking and reminiscing with Dee's school and college friends and the people from Aracon, the computer company where she worked.

Dee was happier than Kate had ever seen her and hugged them in turn when they each read out a verse of poetry they had written about her. The wine was flowing and the conversation getting more animated and noisy when, deciding to skip desserts – 'We've got to watch our figures for the wedding' – they paid their bill and set off along Eustace Street for the Temple Bar, one of the busiest bars in the area.

The place was heaving and they had to shout at each other. Minnie was fending off a drunken Scot who was on a stag night also.

'We two should get it together,' he tried to

persuade Minnie, tipping a glass of Heineken over her shirt.

'Piss off!' she told him, before she disappeared to the Ladies to try and get the stain out.

'This cost me a fortune!' she moaned as Kate patted at it with some water and Minnie dried it off on the hand drier.

Kate checked to make sure the coast was clear before they went back outside.

Dee was flirting outrageously with another Glaswegian, and for her sake Minnie and her sister Alison decided it was time to leave.

'Come on, Dee, we're moving!'

The reluctant bride had to be reminded of the ring on her finger and Johnny, the man who'd put it there, as she was pushed out the door to safety.

'God, that was a close thing!'

'The Porter House next!'

A huge cheer went up the minute they crossed the threshold as a load of Dee's colleagues were already *in situ*.

Brews and beer, wine and vodka... Kate had to remind herself of her condition as she ordered a sparkling water. The bar was hopping, the girls going crazy as they joined in a singsong version of 'Waterloo', and shouted and screamed to be heard. Kate felt like a spinster aunt. Ally was complaining about her boss and Sorcha, a tall thin girl she barely knew, was telling her the intimate details of her five-month affair with a married colleague. As Minnie passed with a tray of drinks, Kate grabbed a glass of wine. She'd sip it slowly.

The barmen were calling closing time when they finally managed to round everyone up for the trek to Leeson Street, waving like a shower of lunatics as they flagged down a posse of oncoming taxis.

Buck's was still quiet as they marched down the basement stairs, a couple of banker finance types ensconced at the club's bar talking loudly above the music about trades and interest percentage points. Kate stifled a yawn. At the moment they were all busy trying to impress each other. It would be another hour or two before they turned their attention to the ladies. She threw some money into the kitty for champagne, hoping they had orange juice too, and collapsed into the comfort of a red leather couch. This was more like it. The dance floor was empty and a few couples were wrapped up in each other in the small booths. Strange, normally she could keep going, dancing and talking till the wee hours of the morning but at the moment she was like Cinderella, wanting to race home at midnight. Minnie passed her a warning glance and she tried to sit up and appear animated and full of life, banishing her intense longing for the comfort of her own springy mattress and plump pillows. This was awful! She had to pull herself together! Perhaps if she went to the bathroom, threw some cold water on her face, replenished her lipstick and mascara. She slipped out of the seat in the middle of Dee's emotional retelling of the first time she'd had sex with Johnny. That she could definitely do without!

She glanced at her exhausted face in the mirror, using her mascara brush to curl her eyelashes up to make her eyes look more open and alert.

She'd walk around the place slowly on her way back. Another hour and she'd make her excuses. Dee wouldn't mind. As she exited the pink and silver Ladies, she stopped in her tracks. Derry was leaning across the rails opposite. She hadn't seen him for weeks, not since they'd walked along Dun Laoghaire pier and shared a snack in It's a Bagel. He looked over at her.

He smiled and her heart lurched as she went towards him. She would never have imagined him here in Buck's!

'Kate! What are you doing here?'

Her cheeks flamed. It was hardly the place to find an expectant mother.

'I'm with Minnie and a crowd of the girls. It's Dee's hen night. What about you?'

'I'm with a friend.'

He hugged her awkwardly, and the smell of his Hugo Boss cologne and alcohol and sweat made the familiar longing to stay in his arms wash over her.

'How have you been?'

'Never better.' She felt giddy and it wasn't the baby, it was just being around him.

'You look great. Glowing.'

She stood there simpering like an eejit.

'You know if there is anything you need ... anything!'

'Anything...' she repeated slowly, wanting to pull him closer to her.

'For the baby.'

She stood for a second, suddenly conscious of a petite dark-haired girl who had appeared beside them.

'Derry, I told you they had food. There's panini, pasta or fish. The waitress said she'd bring a menu over to us in a few minutes.'

The sallow-skinned vixen pushed in between them, her green eyes teasing. She was about five foot two and was tiny and perfect, wearing a simple cream shirt and a pair of black trousers, her waist emphasized with an expensive silver belt.

'Nadia, this is a friend of mine, Kate. Kate Dillon.'

Wary, they said hello to each other. Kate could feel the other girl's eyes run dismissively over her, deciding she was no threat as she possessively put her arm around Derry's waist. She didn't own him! She should have known that a man like Derry was bound to be involved in an intense relationship. She had been a diversion, a simple diversion, sexy, pleasurable, a few days' fun. Nothing more than that. Who knew what went on in a guy's head, but judging by the lady at his side Derry was most definitely taken.

'I'm starving, Derry,' Nadia complained.

Derry looked uncomfortable and Kate surmised he was only being polite to her. There was no competition between herself and the raven-haired sexy nymphet who was obviously his girlfriend. This was all too bloody awful and embarrassing to be true and she could have happily murdered Minnie for not letting her follow her instincts and stay home. He must think she was pathetic. On the prowl with a rowdy lot of women who were doing their best to disgrace themselves on the dance floor. It had to look bad!

Kate fixed a polite smile on her face. Dee and Lisa and Jane and Minnie were screaming at her to join them. Derry looked amused. 'I'd better go,' she excused herself, 'my friends are waiting for me. Nice to meet you both.'

She felt hurt and humiliated and longed to grab her coat and leave the stupid club immediately, but knew it would be too obvious.

Hell would freeze over before she'd join

354

the girls and give that Nadia the satisfaction of seeing her make a fool of herself. Instead she slipped back to the couch. Sorcha was weepy and was now confessing the fear that her affair was coming to an end. 'What am I meant to do?' she wailed. 'What am I meant to say?'

Kate tried to look interested and ignore the couple wrapped around each other in the back booth. She had to get away, get out of here. It was as if every bit of her was over-aware. Senses heightened, she was conscious of Derry's presence only a few yards away. She thought she had accepted her position with him, but now realized that the idea of him kissing or touching or being intimate with another female was too much to bear.

Minnie and Dee collapsed hot and sweating on the bench beside her. She hated being a killjoy but she had to get away, escape.

'Dee, I'm really sorry but I'm going to have to go.'

'Ah Kate, c'mon! Don't be such a loser!'

'I'm sorry, Dee. I just feel exhausted. I'm not much fun at the moment.'

Minnie glared at her.

'Look I *am* sorry.' She stood up to go, hugging them both. 'Have a great night. I'll ring you both tomorrow.'

'Will you be OK?'

'Yeah, sure.'

Never had anyone got a coat and run up the stairs and into a cab so quickly. Kate was relieved that Derry hadn't even once glanced in her direction or noticed her leave. Tears pricked her eyes and she cursed her own stupidity. She wondered when Derry would get round to telling his beautiful girlfriend of his impending fatherhood!

Chapter Thirty-one

Molly Catherine Dillon Donovan was born two weeks early much to the surprise of her mother, who on her last day in work was standing at the office lift when she went into labour. Kate frantically tried to remember what she had learned in her pre-natal classes as a wave of contractions overcame her on the taxi ride from the IFSC to Holles Street Hospital.

Only minutes from delivery with a nurse holding her hand, Derry arrived in, having driven like a lunatic up from Wicklow when he'd got her phone message.

'Are you sure you want to be here, Derry?'

'I'm sure,' he insisted, sitting down beside her and kissing her sweaty forehead.

Her labour was fast and furious and thirty minutes later she delivered a most perfect baby girl.

She had a fuzz of light fair hair and a rosebud mouth and button of a nose and cried loudly until Kate held her, skin touching skin. Overcome, Derry wrapped them both in his arms.

Exalted and exhausted, Kate was glad of the small private room where Molly greedily sucked on her nipple, as Derry took photos of his beautiful new daughter.

Lying awake in the darkness later that night Kate stared at her sleeping child, realizing that now her world had changed for ever.

Her mother and Aunt Vonnie arrived up to see the new arrival two days later.

'She's such a darling,' laughed her mother, with Molly's fist wrapped around her little finger. 'I just wish your father was here to see her.'

Aunt Vonnie took a turn at holding the baby.

'Kate, she has your eyes but don't you think she's got a great look of Maeve?'

'Will you be all right going home, Kate, or would you like me to stay up for a few days with you?' offered her mother, delighted.

'No, Mum, I'll be fine. Anyways, Molly and I have to get used to each other.'

'You know you're more than welcome to come down home and let me pamper you!' smiled her mother. 'New babies are hard work.'

Moya had sent a huge bouquet of flowers and a card, and Bill her boss had arrived in looking sheepish with a spray of white roses and a big teddy bear for Molly.

Minnie produced a bottle of champagne and a few glasses during visiting time, telling Kate it was high time they drank a toast to her new god-daughter. Two days later, Derry collected them and drove them home.

Her modern apartment suddenly seemed even less roomy as it began to fill with baby paraphernalia, every spare surface covered. Molly, noticing the strangeness of the place, opened her mouth and yelled as Derry and Kate did their utmost to quieten down the baby. So much for a calm homecoming, she thought, as they took turns pacing the floor with the tiny bundle, who loved being walked and held.

Exhausted Kate fell into bed after a sandwich and a glass of milk and was almost unconscious with sleep when Derry woke her to tell her Molly needed feeding again.

They managed to struggle through those first few days, Kate eternally grateful for Derry's calm demeanour as he walked and held and changed the baby, making sure she got time to eat and sleep and get showered.

A few weeks later, walking together along Sandymount Strand with Molly dozing peacefully in the buggy, she realized how impossible her situation would have been without him, and how utterly attached to him both she and Molly had become.

'Marry me, Kate,' he asked, as she stared at the Poolbeg towers and the cranes and towers of the distant docklands. 'Molly needs a father.'

'You are her father,' she replied, surprised.

'She needs to be able to go to school or playgroup and be like all the other kids with a mammy and daddy, Mr and Mrs Donovan, that the teachers can write home notes to.'

'I think it's a bit too soon for that.'

'Please, Kate, think about it.'

She must be mad, she thought. The man she was crazy about was proposing for a second time and she still couldn't say that simple word yes. He didn't have to be besotted and madly in love with her – surely loving Molly would be enough. She swallowed hard, she was expecting far too much, expecting someone like Derry Donovan to swear undying love and devotion for her. She'd read too many soppy romantic novels and watched too many mushy films and now when she was faced with reality was hoping for an orchestra and violin strings and a Tom Hanks ending. Fucking wise up, Kate, she told herself as she promised Derry she'd think about it.

Molly thrived, and her own hormones finally began to get under some control, so she didn't weep when she saw a child and a kite or an old man and his grandson kicking football in the park and was finally able to sit at her kitchen table and eat toast and drink coffee and finish the *Irish Times* crossword.

The christening was held in the Stone House, during the summer, when her Uncle Eamonn was home from the States and Moya and her family were over. Kate knew the Monkstown apartment would never fit the relations and friends and besides neither Derry nor herself had any affinity with any particular parish.

'I do pray,' she protested, 'but in different churches and places.'

Minnie was thrilled at the out of Dublin location for her goddaughter's christening. 'Who'll be the godfather?' she quizzed Derry.

His brother Tom was away working in Saudi and Kate was pleased when he suggested Conor Quinn, her cousin.

'After all, if he hadn't dragged you off sailing, Molly minx might not be here!'

On the first Sunday of the month in July the christening was held. Father Glynn had no problem handing over his altar and baptismal font to Father Eamonn Ryan who at this stage had become an old friend. His predecessor Father Bolger wouldn't have let Kate Dillon and her child across the threshold of the church but thankfully those days of hell and brimstone Catholicism were gone and he was delighted to welcome another Dillon to the parish.

Kate had picked out a simple cream linen dress with a square neck and broad straps to wear and a pair of strappy sandals, determined to enjoy Molly's big day. Moya helped her to dress the baby in the family christening robe that had last been used for Danny's christening.

'She's like an angel,' she declared, covering her little niece in kisses. Derry took photo after photo of his daughter as she gurgled and smiled for him before they left for the church.

'I think she's a "daddy's girl,"' remarked Patrick.

Kate tried to be nice and smile and banish any enmity between them. Now he was more than just her brother-in-law, he was the father of Molly's first cousins, her uncle. Maeve Dillon fussed around, thrilled to have another grandchild to love and pet, and Fiona, Gavin and Danny ran around the church grounds.

Moya dressed in turquoise, though stunning, looked too thin. She had confided in

Kate that the gallery was taking up a bit more time than she'd planned and that Patrick was objecting to her not being around when he needed her.

'We're mounting a big exhibition of illustration at the end of September, you should try and come over for it. There's a lot of work pulling it together but the work is so wonderful!'

Minnie had taken the role of godparent very seriously and had arrived in a subtle soft mauve suit with a skirt that actually came to just above her knee, Conor whistling with appreciation when he saw her.

Molly was as good as gold as Uncle Eamonn anointed her with the baptismal oils and poured the holy water on her forehead. Kate tried to compose herself as she looked around the font at all the people in her life that mattered: her mother, her sister, her niece and nephews, her aunt and uncle, her cousins, her close friends and Derry. She wished that more of his family had been able to make it, but with the exception of his Auntie May and her husband Bill, and their son and daughter, and his friend Erik and his wife Shona he was on his own, his widowed father in early-stage Alzheimer's too elderly to come.

After the ceremony, they made a run in the drizzling rain back to the house where her mother had laid on plates of baked ham and salmon with salad and potatoes and fresh bread; Fiona and Gavin passed around the wine. Aunt Vonnie over in the corner was regaling Derry and his aunt with stories of what a good baby she'd been. Afterwards, there was champagne and an enormous layered sponge christening cake inscribed with Molly's name, which her mother had made, and everyone raised their glasses to Molly Dillon, her granddaughter.

Kate had decided to stay on for a few weeks after the christening as she was still on maternity leave. Derry was heading off on a three-week project to the South of France. Kate, trying to stifle her pangs of jealousy, wondered if Nadia was with him. Her mother was in her element at the thought of having two weeks to get to know her latest grandchild. It felt weird to Kate moving back into her old room with the cot set up at the end of the bed, and a mobile dangling from the overhead light, not something she had ever imagined.

Moya and her brood had taken over the rest of the house, Patrick sloping off to play golf most days while the rest of them relaxed and enjoyed late breakfasts and walks to the beach and a swim. Two or three nights herself and her mother babysat while Patrick and her sister tried out the newest gourmet restaurants in the area. Kate demurred when Moya invited her to join them, because she was breastfeeding. At night she was content to curl up on the couch with the kids and play Snap and Fish in the Pool and make bowls of popcorn to eat while they watched videos of *The Wizard of Oz* and *Mary Poppins*.

'What's going on between you and Derry?' asked her mother as they sat out on the loungers on the patio, the night warm, the children finally gone to bed.

'I don't know.' She sipped her red wine.

'He loves Molly.'

'He adores her! He's a wonderful father, and is always there when she needs him.'

'But what about the two of you?'

'I don't know!' Kate shrugged. 'He has girlfriends, but he asked me to marry him.'

'He did?'

'Yeah, but only because of Molly.'

'Kate, promise me, if he asks you again, if he says he loves you, promise me you'll marry him!'

'Mum,' she laughed, 'that's never going to happen.'

Chapter Thirty-two

From the rented house overlooking the South Pacific ocean, Romy was fascinated by the constant swell and pound of the rolling waves. She'd always loved the sea, the tide rushing in on the beach below their house in Rossmore. But here the ocean was different, the surfers using its power to control and ride it.

The day her father was laid to rest in the damp, cold Irish earth she had pulled the curtains and closed the windows of their duplex in Byron Bay, blocking out the searing Australian sunlight and the sound of the foreign surf as she thought of her father and in her own fashion grieved for the man who had held her hand and bought her ice-cream more than two decades ago.

At night Rob concentrated on his business, excited by a new gaming concept that he was developing.

'I think this will really work,' he said, trying to demonstrate on the computer screen how the magic board could be stimulated and moved, against various elements and the distractions faced by the average surf dude.

'It looks fun!'

'Yeah but could you imagine it with top-quality graphics and digital format? The sea would look so real and wet you could almost feel it, taste it!'

Romy also worked, sketching new designs inspired by the lush pink, red and fuchsia flowers and foliage that grew everywhere and the ripples from the breeze in the shifting sand, trying to work out a way to twist metal and glass to their shapes as she sat on the bleached sand.

Rob was getting some feedback on his game ideas from two interested gaming companies, one in Melbourne and one in San Diego.

'Wow Rob, that's wonderful!' she said, kissing him all over. 'What are you going to do?'

'There's no question. It's got to be America. It's the centre of the universe in terms of media and game development. I should pack up my board and gear and just go see what happens.'

Romy swallowed hard. He made no mention of her.

'Mind if I tag along?'

'No problem, baby.'

She packed up and said goodbye to Mitch and Ronnie and the rest of the gang in Shanhans. Tilda and herself had gone for coffee, Tilda upset when she told her she was leaving.

'You sure you're doing the right thing, Romy? If you stayed here, settled here, Rob might still come back.'

'Nah, it's time to move on,' she admitted. 'I'm not much of a one for staying in one place.'

'You can't keep running for ever. Some time, some place you're going to have to stop. I know what I'm talking about. Some day you will want to put down roots, make a home for yourself and have kids.'

'Well I'm not planning on having any kids!' she retorted.

'Don't say that, Romy. We'll keep in touch, you let me know if you come up with any more of those fancy designs that would suit the shop, we'll work out a good price, OK?'

By the end of the month they were *en route* to California, Rob's precious game secure in his hand luggage.

They checked into a Ramada Inn just off the beach in San Diego.

Romy swanned around the shops and took in a few craft stores and art galleries while Rob had round after round of meetings with the initial games company designers and its R&D department. If they were interested, the designers would do projections on play possibility and the company would talk to investors about the property. At night anxious and agitated, Rob hardly slept thinking of the next day's meeting, Romy doing her utmost to relax him by giving him the kind of loving he liked most.

'Shit, I don't believe it!' he'd shouted when he got back the next day. 'Their fucking head of development told me they are looking at a similar game that is more cost effective to develop and geared towards a broader audience!'

'They are only looking,' she reminded him. 'Maybe they're just bluffing you.'

'I'll kill that bastard if they're just stringing me along!'

For the next few weeks they were in virtual limbo, in gaming hell as the corporation considered their development options. Eventually Rob was forced to settle for a percentage of what he had planned, as only small elements of his design were to be used in the game.

'Come on, at least you've sold part of one of your game ideas to one of the biggest game companies in the world,' she consoled. 'You should be thrilled.'

'Romy, I'm only getting a fraction of what I should be getting. I should have stayed in Australia and developed it from there.'

'Listen, Rob, this is just one of your games. I've seen some of your stuff, it's really good. There must be people out there interested in good ideas!'

Rob listened and thought long and hard about it and instead of heading back home, decided to stay on for the development project, and to put out feelers about which company was open to innovative designers.

Romy loved the Californian landscape but was less sure about the lifestyle. Still, with her height and long rangy figure and red-gold hair she at least fitted in.

She missed the bar and working with Tilda but decided after a few weeks to accept a job offer in a toy store on Columbus Street. The staff were nice and the clientele for the most part ten and under with very definite ideas about what they liked and didn't like.

'They'd sure tell you in the morning what games work and don't work,' she joked to Rob, trying to encourage him to come visit the store. 'It would be great market research.'

Watching young mothers and small toddlers in the babies' area, she tried to ignore the way her heart lurched, as she was reminded of what might have been.

As the weeks went by the realization came that Rob and herself were leading separate lives and that neither of them really cared. She worked all day while he sat in the motel and tried to get meetings with people. It was disheartening, she knew, for him. Two months later it wasn't a huge surprise when he told her that he'd met someone new.

'Where?' she asked.

'Down on the beach,' he shrugged.

Those words creating a strange sense of *déjà vu*, she packed up her things and moved out, discovering afterwards that his new girlfriend worked in the design section of the company he'd signed to.

Kicking the sand from her shoes and out of her hair, Romy decided to fly to New York and thanked God that she was unencumbered and could simply start over.

Chapter Thirty-three

New York – she loved it. She loved its anonymity. Its hotch-potch ethnic mix that spilled out everywhere. Chinatown, Harlem. The districts that went on for miles, the air thick with smells of chilli and spices and neighbourhoods where people prided themselves on being true blue Americans. Romy wasn't sure where she fitted in but she knew at this stage of her life that the city with its big heart was where she had wanted to be.

They loved her red hair and tall catwalk figure and called her an original when she showed them her designs, which she carried in a small velvet wrap in her purse; buyers were impressed when she guided them to the website Rob had created for her. After only two weeks she discovered she was definitely in business and had signed contracts with two exclusive small jewellers. An agency helped in her search for an apartment that would be spacious enough also to act as a studio.

Setting up her tools and workbench in the dining area of the one-bedroomed high-ceilinged fifth floor of the Russell building just between Third and Lexington Avenue, Romy felt a huge sense of adventure.

She enjoyed sleeping on her own and walking the streets of the city, getting to know it and the pace of life that less frantic New Yorkers enjoyed.

Sundays she went to Central Park, buying a newspaper but scarcely bothering to read it as she watched the passers-by. Absorbing the sights and the smells of the city she searched for inspiration for a new collection of work. Donna Taylor, one of the store owners, was very impressed. Donna was the first friendly face and she insisted on bringing her to lunch and to dinners and introducing her around. Most nights Romy was content to stay in and work, soon realizing that she was no Carrie Bradshaw.

She built up a coterie of friends, some from Ireland, others flotsam and jetsam that like herself had ended up in New York. On the day in September when the heart was ripped out of New York she had sat on the pavement crying, not believing that man could inflict such pain on his fellow man. She'd watched the Twin Towers fall over and over again on the TV news and was tempted to pack up her bags and flee. Instead she had stayed as the city mourned. Months later she found herself changed, no longer believing that each man was an island. She had her design work and a job teaching English twice a week but volunteered to help out in the art department of the local high school, showing the kids how to design pieces from recycled trash.

She went on dates, which seemed kind of crazy as she wasn't looking for Mr Right any more. She'd met Greg Anderson in Fitzpatrick's Hotel, the two of them chatting about the coming election primaries at a small fundraiser. He was old-fashioned and conservative and had just split from his wife and was certainly not the kind of guy she needed in her life. He'd asked her out on a date and, encouraged by Donna, she had gone along.

There had been roses and champagne and a candlelit dinner overlooking the Hudson. He told her that he had never been to Europe, never surfed or even owned a surfboard and was more a city boy. They had absolutely nothing in common and she loved him for it! Five days after they first met she'd slept with him. Uncomplicated good sex and wrapped in his arms she felt special.

'You crazy Irish woman,' joked Donna. 'He's never going to marry you.'

'Donna, I can promise you that is the last thing on my mind!'

Greg's life was complicated enough with divorcing his wife, so Romy kept her distance and gave him space and listened when he wanted to talk. Their relationship was different and based on the mutual understanding of sex and companionship, for New York could be a very lonely city. She liked Greg, perhaps even loved him a little, but knew that when the time was right they would both move on. Tilda had been right about putting down roots and belonging: Romy didn't know where she'd end up but suspected this city was not the place. Kate's angry phone call demanding she return home immediately to see her mother was perhaps the catalyst she needed.

Chapter Thirty-four

The three Dillon sisters kept up a twenty-four-hour vigil around their mother's bedside. Romy was content just to hold the hand or touch the bare skin of the person she loved the most in the world. No communication! No way to break the wall of silence! To let her mother know she was there! Why had she left it too fecking late per usual? Her sisters had had a good relationship with her, had stayed close. She listened as they told her about the years missed while she travelled the world, gallivanting, self-centred, wrapped up in useless anger and blaming others for what she'd become. The daughter who'd broken her mother's heart.

The nursing staff slipped in silently around the bed, checking, but there was absolutely no change in their mother's condition.

Romy hated hospitals, the smell and the feel of them. She needed to get some fresh air and asked Moya to take her place as she went downstairs and out to the hospital grounds. She sympathized with all the smokers standing in their dressing gowns in the open air, as she walked past them to sit on a railing and just be calm and breathe. She rummaged in her pocket for a tissue, for although she was home in Ireland she had never felt so alone. Kate was right about her!

Her aunt was sitting beside her mother when she got back up to the unit.

'Have you talked to her, Romy?'

'A bit.'

'Well you just talk to her as much as you can,' insisted Vonnie Quinn. 'I don't care what those doctors say, I believe Maeve senses we are here with her. That she can hear us.'

'I hope so.'

'Talk to her, Romy! You haven't spoken to her for so long, now is the time for you to say all the things you wanted. Tomorrow or the day after might be too late.'

Romy hesitated, unsure.

'Listen, I'll go down and have a bite of lunch in the canteen with the others and leave you in peace.'

Romy didn't know what to say. She hadn't the words for it. She could say sorry a hundred times over and it wouldn't be enough. Sorry for washing the dog! Sorry for being mean to her father! Sorry for getting rid of the tissues and cells that were her baby! She rested her head against the side of the bed and instead began to tell her mother about the great journeys she had made, talking for an hour or two, exhausted, not wanting to stop.

'Go and have a sleep in the day room,' suggested Kate, shaking her. 'We'll wake you if there's any change.'

Jet-lagged, she'd curled up in her clothes on the hospital's narrow couch and fallen asleep immediately. Hours later she was woken by a nurse tapping her on the shoulder.

'Your mother's showing signs of regaining consciousness.'

Twenty hours later Maeve Dillon was off the ventilator and had been moved from the intensive care unit to a normal ward.

'Does this mean she's going to get better?' asked Moya.

The staff were noncommittal.

Romy squeezed her mother's hand, elated that even though Maeve couldn't speak she at least knew she was there.

Her mother would recover. Every day get a little bit better.

There were tests and more tests, her mother now awake, scared, having nightmares, her right side useless, her eye and face slightly twisted. Her breathing heavy, her attempts to speak slow, slurred. There wasn't any huge change from day to day but the three of them were confident she was at least holding her own. They were shaken when Dr Healy the Registrar let slip there would be no improvement. Maeve Dillon was not expected to recover.

Chapter Thirty-five

Dr Carney, the consultant, had called them into his office, a spartan white room with two filing cabinets and a desk with a computer and screen and printer on it. They felt like three bold schoolgirls waiting to be admonished by the elderly medic as he sat back in his swivel chair.

'I've looked at your mother's file. As you know, we have done brain scans and an extensive range of tests, but unfortunately the results show there is evidence of a slight further bleed and indicated weakness of blood vessels in the vicinity.'

'Can you do anything to stop it?' asked Kate.

'There is no question of surgery on someone in your mother's condition. At the moment she is considered stable but I'm afraid there is not much else my colleagues or I can do for her here in the hospital.'

'What do you mean?' they remonstrated.

'What I mean,' he said slowly, 'is that your

mother's prognosis is poor. Maeve is in need of high-dependency nursing care but she does not need for the moment to be in an acute hospital. We need to move her.'

'Move her!' exclaimed Kate.

'Home, perhaps?'

'But Mammy lives alone. I'm working in Dublin, Moya's family are in London and Romy has just flown in from New York.'

'I see, well then, a step–down facility, maybe a nursing home or the Hospice? Beds are difficult to find. I'm sorry but you must know the pressure there is on the hospitals these days with cutbacks and closures and bed shortages.'

'When?' asked Moya, fiddling with the pearls around her neck.

'As soon as we can organize it.'

'Where do you suggest?'

'I can give you the name of two or three places in the county, there's one on the Dublin side of the city, Ardnamone, and one in Tramore. The social worker Clare Maloney will know a few more.'

He stood up to signal that the meeting was over.

'You do realize that your mother is not expected to recover but we do want her to be as comfortable as possible for the short time that's left. I'm sure we are all agreed on that.'

Numb, they had sat in the hospital's small coffee shop, sipping tepid coffee from plastic cups.

'What are we going to do?' sighed Moya. 'What's going to happen to her? If we lived closer I'd willingly have her.'

'You couldn't swing a cat in my place. Molly sleeps in the converted dressing room!'

'Maybe we should go and see the place the doctor mentioned,' suggested Romy.

They drove out to see Ardnamone, a modern purpose-built nursing home three miles from Waterford city. The door was locked so they had to ring and ring for admittance. The matron, in her nurse's uniform, let them in. She offered to show them round. Small single rooms with a nice view of the garden and parking area, a TV positioned on the wall opposite the bed.

The dining area, where the residents came to lunch and tea, was a bright and airy room with a conservatory to one side; the large sitting room, filled with elderly residents sitting in an assortment of couches and armchairs, was dominated by a giant-screen television, which was showing a cookery programme.

They explained to the matron that their mother had had a serious stroke, and loss of function, was classed as highly dependent and would need a lot of nursing.

The middle-aged woman was at least honest with them.

'I have three patients like that at the moment. I'm afraid with my staffing levels I couldn't take on a fourth. Maybe in a few months' time, but for now, I'm afraid no. We couldn't offer your mother a place.'

She walked them to the door, wishing them luck.

Ardrigole, the old Edwardian house overlooking the sea in Tramore, was more like a hotel from the outside than a nursing home. Inside a warren of corridors and high-ceilinged lounges and a dining room with heavy dark furniture and an overpowering smell of cabbage greeted them. The residents seemed ancient, some wheelchair-bound, some strapped in special chairs.

'We have a lot of Alzheimer's patients,' explained the young carer as she gave them a quick tour. The rooms were larger than in the previous home but were filled with a load of oversized shabby pieces, which looked in sore need of dusting. The thought of their mother abandoned and dependent in such a place drove them back to the car.

'I don't want Mammy ending her days in any of those places,' Moya protested, almost in tears.

'We're just not used to seeing them, that's

all,' said Kate. 'I'm sure they look after the old people very well.'

'God, some of the patients looked about ninety!' joked Romy. 'Please shoot me before I end up anywhere like that!'

They sat on the almost empty seafront, in utter silence.

'I think we should bring Mammy home,' said Romy, staring at the waves.

They were all in agreement. It was what their mother would have wanted, what they all wanted. The problem was the mess of their lives and the commitment needed. Moya knew Patrick was already complaining about minding the children in London, and Kate was trying to get Patterson's to give her more time off work.

'It doesn't matter. I'll be here,' volunteered Romy. 'I've no husband or children.'

Moya and Kate looked at each other with relief, knowing that their mother would die in dignity in her own place, her own home. They would organize agency nurses, carers, whatever was needed for Maeve and would help care for her as much as they could.

'Romy, do you know what you'd be getting yourself into? Maybe you should think about it.'

'I don't have to think about it. I'm not putting my mother into one of those fucking places to die. I understand you've both got kids, jobs, whatever, but I'll manage. I told you I'll do it!'

'Romy, are you sure?'

'I'll stay with her,' she promised.

Chapter Thirty-six

The Stone House was unchanged. The paint around the windows weathered from the sea, the front door creaking, sand hidden in the crevices of the red and white tiled floor. Pale roses clambering round the porch and terracotta pots of blazing geraniums around the step. The house was quiet and still as Romy moved from room to room. New couch covers and a fancy reading light, a bluebottle dancing in the living-room window. The dining room hushed and bright. She went through to the kitchen: sunlight streaming in across the patio doors and warming the wooden presses and huge pine table, the teapot still on the table. She rinsed it out under the tap of the Belfast sink. Then along the hall to the glass sun-room – wicker chairs and couches and green plants wilting in the stuffy atmosphere. She opened a window before turning to her father's old study, where the large map of Ireland was still hanging on the wall.

'The only geography you need to know is

your own country.' He'd said it so often, jabbing at a river or the mountains, trying to ascertain where new roads were being built.

Memory hung in the silence as she looked around her. In her mother's absence the tall grandfather clock in the hall had stopped and Romy reached for the silver key on the ledge. Moving the hand to the correct time she gently wound it, waiting for the comforting sound of the timepiece before going upstairs. Her bedroom, small and perfect with a view of the sea, she'd always loved it. Her cork noticeboard was now covered in pictures of dinosaurs and dragons and a painted rainbow. Flip-flops and a baseball cap flung on the bottom of the wardrobe.

She moved from room to room. The library books beside her mother's bed unread and overdue. The Royal Horticultural Society Garden Book, her mother's bible, left where it always was. From the back of the house she could see the orchard at the bottom of the garden was gone, the apple trees cut down, a high wall separating their garden and the tiled roofs of the new infill development. The land sold three years ago, time moving on.

She looked around. They had two days to ready the house for her mother's homecoming.

The ambulance men had been kindness

itself, treating their patient, Maeve Dillon, like she was made of porcelain as they lifted her across the driveway and step, into the hall, Kate directing them into the dining room. They had stripped it of the chairs and big dining table and transformed it into a sunny bedroom with french windows to the garden.

'Isn't it wonderful to be home, Mum, and able to look out into the garden?'

Fergus and Liam had lifted the heavy double bed into position in front of the french windows so her mother had a magnificent view of the herbaceous border and the purple bursting hebes and buddleia in the shrubbery, with the path leading to the vegetable garden only a yard or two away.

'We moved your bed down here so you will be able to see everything instead of being stuck upstairs,' Kate said, pulling back the bed sheets and covers as the ambulance men shifted her mother from the stretcher bed onto the mattress.

'Now you're home,' she said, suddenly overcome with emotion as her mother's head flopped against the pillow. 'Here, let's see if we can make you more comfortable.'

Moya carried her mother's handbag and the small weekend case with her few bits of clothing in her arms, trying to decide where to place them.

'Here's your handbag, Mum,' she said,

placing it on the bed in reach of her mother's fingers, noticing her mother's eye turn in the direction of the precious bag. 'If you want we can look at it later when you feel a bit better.'

Kate fussed around getting towels and pointing out the beautiful John Rocha vase filled with tall blue delphiniums positioned on the sideboard, which now, instead of wine carafes and silver dishes and bowls and plates, held an array of family photos and her mother's favourite ornaments, including a papier mâché pig made by Fiona.

'Do you like the room?' Romy smiled, sitting on the bed beside her. 'We tried to do it the way you would.'

Agitated, Maeve Dillon tried to signal her approval.

'I think you do like it!' Kate smiled, pleased with their efforts. 'You won't be lonely or scared here, Mum, because with the door open we'll be able to see you from the kitchen.'

'We've got a phone there beside your bed and a radio and the TV if you want it, but maybe you should rest quiet for a while.'

Their mother looked exhausted, a smaller, shrunken figure in the bed, forcing herself to keep awake.

'Romy will fix us all something to eat.'

They could hear Romy clatter away in the kitchen singing as she washed and peeled and chopped, banging away at the pots and pans.

'She used to work in a restaurant, waiting tables mostly but sometimes cooking. Can you imagine Romy being a chef!'

'I heard that!' laughed her sister. 'Might I remind you it never does any good to slag off or upset the cook, or God knows what you might find in your food.'

'Temperamental too,' whispered Moya, imagining she could see signs of laughter in her mother's eyes.

They ate off the small side table in the room, potatoes and finely cut strips of chicken tossed with tomato and green beans. Romy had mashed up her mother's potato with milk and cut her meal into tiny pieces, adding a smooth gravy to make it easier for her to eat.

'Nothing like home cooking, compared to hospital food,' she teased.

When they'd finished eating, Kate switched on the news headlines, the three of them sitting in silence watching the flicker of images.

'Mummy, Nurse Reilly, Brigid, is coming tomorrow morning to help wash you and look after you and make sure everything is all right.'

Maeve nodded her acceptance.

'But tonight I'm going to sit up with you and take care of you so Romy can sleep.

Anything you want or need, you know we are all here for you.'

Kate looked around the room: it was warm and cosy, filled with flowers and mementoes of a fulfilled life, pictures of her mother's childhood, and girlhood, her wedding to handsome Frank Dillon and photos of her with her children and grandchildren. So different from the crowded dining room set up for Sunday dinners and entertaining and parties, with the carpets rolled back to dance.

Her twenty-first, her parents' silver wedding anniversary, her father's funeral, Molly's christening. She looked at her watch. Derry was probably getting their daughter ready for bed, putting the toys away, getting a picture book out to read, brushing her hair, making sure she'd gone to the toilet and washed her hands and face and brushed her teeth. She picked up the phone and dialled. Derry answered immediately.

'We're home from the hospital and Mum is tucked up nicely in her own bed,' she said softly, when Derry had filled her in on the day's events. 'Is Molly still up?'

She could hear the giggles and laughter as Derry put her three-year-old on the phone, the shyness in her voice when she first said 'Mummy?'

'It's Mummy, pet. I'm just phoning to say good-night and see how you are.'

Molly took a deep breath and began telling her every detail of the day from the minute Daddy couldn't find any clean pink panties for her to wear, to spilling orange juice on her new cardigan, to the boy who sat beside her being a cry baby because he couldn't match all his shapes on the board, and the new baby ducks she saw in the park after playgroup when Derry collected her.

'There were six, Mummy. Six ducklings and they were so beautiful with their mummy duck.'

Kate swallowed hard – even the mother duck was with her ducklings. She felt guilty for leaving Molly, but relieved that she would soon be going home.

'Granny's here beside me. Would you like to talk to her?'

Molly adored her grandmother and Kate could hear her screaming 'Granny' excitedly as she held the phone to her mother's ear, seeing her lopsided smile as Molly rambled on telling about the baby ducklings.

'Blow a good-night kiss to Granny,' she instructed, and heard Molly making all kinds of noisy efforts to send kisses down the phone line.

Laughing she replaced the line, squeezing her mother's hand, realizing how important the link between generations was to all of them.

Romy had washed up in the kitchen and

put some washing on. She looked tired. 'Why don't you go to bed? You look bunched. We'll be fine down here.'

Romy had shifted the big armchair and pouffe from the sitting room and placed them on the far side of her mother's bed. A pile of magazines, books and photo albums were thoughtfully left on a small square coffee table she'd also brought into the dining room.

'I'll be nice and comfy here for the night.'

Romy came in and flung her arms around their mother, kissing her cheek, her mother's eyes lighting on her face.

'I'll see you in the morning,' she said.

Maeve struggled to try to say the word 'Good-night'.

'Good-night, sleep tight and don't let the bedbugs bite!' grinned her daughter, the same as she'd said it most nights when she was a child.

Chapter Thirty-seven

Maeve Dillon was happy to be home, ensconced in bed, surrounded by her three devoted daughters and the things she loved, with a view of the garden. The nurse had come and washed her and checked her and cheered her up with her easy matter-of-fact way and kindness.

The peace of the afternoon was disturbed by the arrival of Vonnie Quinn to see her sister; she brought a bunch of bright red roses and a light-as-air carrot cake with lemon icing on a big plate.

'This looks good,' admired Romy.

'It's Maeve's favourite. Run in and stick on the kettle and we'll all have a little slice.'

'She's asleep,' whispered Romy.

'There'll be time enough for sleep. I'll go in and wake her.'

Out of the corner of her eye she watched her aunt sit on the side of the bed, gently calling her mother's name and stroking her hand.

'C'mon and wake up, Maeve, I'm here to see you.'

Her mother's eyes slowly opened and her mouth grinned as she said, 'Lo, Vonnie.'

Romy was amazed that over the years the bond between the two sisters had never changed and they still always found some-thing to talk and laugh about. The two of them hugged crazily as her aunt went into a long tirade about the queues in the local Spar shop, the greenfly having a field day with the roses, and the latest twists and turns in her cousin Conor's on-off relation-ship with his girlfriend Anita Murphy. A one-sided conversation, it made no matter, she could see her mother was delighted to be treated normally by Vonnie who'd always been the chatterbox of the family.

'Why don't you girls go out and get a bit of fresh air, have a bit of a walk while I'm here?' suggested her aunt. 'Maeve will be fine with me.'

That sounded good. Romy was in sore need of exercise and oxygen and Moya had been complaining of a headache all day.

It was warm and sunny outside and in a few minutes they were ready, and running down the driveway.

'Where to?' asked Moya.

'The beach!' shouted Kate and Romy, as they crossed the main road and walked down the narrow lane bordered by bracken and tall cow parsley.

Rossmore Strand was all but deserted, and Romy kicked off her trainers and buried her toes in the sand, walking barefoot. Kate tied her sweater round her waist as they followed the shoreline, jumping to avoid the waves, kicking seaweed out of their way as they messed with each other. They walked for half an hour and then sat in a heap on the sand looking out at the waves rolling in. It had been a long time since they had been together like this, on their own.

They talked like they hadn't talked for a very long time and Kate admitted how lonely it got sometimes on her own with just Molly for company and the sacrifices single mothers had to make.

'Though I wouldn't trade her for a billion dollars, I sometimes envy you, Moya, having a husband like Patrick.'

Moya looked strained.

'Whatever you do, Kate, for god's sakes don't ever bother envying my marriage.'

Kate didn't understand.

'All I will say is that Hail glorious St Patrick is not quite as good as he seems,' said Moya bitterly, 'as he has a propensity to chase every bit of skirt that comes his way.'

Kate was appalled.

'How do you stick it?'

'He promises it will never happen again and I put my head in the sand and try to believe him. I've got the three kids so what else can I do?'

'Moya, you don't have to put up with that.'

'Maybe someday I won't!' replied Moya firmly. 'Someday I'll have had enough and I'll throw him out or take the kids and go!'

Kate looked over at her sister, seeing the torture Patrick was inflicting reflected in her eyes. How had she never guessed?

'I'm sorry, Moya, I shouldn't have said anything!'

'It's all right. Patrick and I are trying to work it out. Neither of us wants to end up in the divorce courts. He for obvious reasons and me because of the kids and the fact I'm an old-fashioned catholic girl who still believes in marriage.'

'And what about you, Romy?' ventured Kate.

'No-one gives a shit about me.'

'Come off it!'

'We do give a shit!' said Kate, serious. 'Honest, we do.'

Romy pulled her long legs up under her, not sure where she'd begin.

'Hey this is like confession!' she groaned.

Kate reached for her and hugged her. 'Go on!'

'Kate, you remember the night of Moya's wedding and I went to meet Brian...'

'Yeah, you were mad about him. I remember that.'

'We made love. And I found out I was pregnant when I went back to college.'

She told them the truth about taking the money and going to London, the clinic and the start of the running, of hating herself, of searching for what she'd lost.

'Why didn't you come home?' whispered Moya.

'I couldn't. I couldn't face her knowing what I'd done. I guess I couldn't face myself.'

She told them the rest: sex and sleeping with boys and men whose names she couldn't remember, the towns and cities where she'd stayed, moving and searching, not wanting to be found until she'd met Rob and hoped that he would be the one. Cruel California and saying goodbye to Rob. Being in the wrong place on the day in September when planes crashed and the world burned and men threw themselves from buildings and thousands died in New York.

They let her talk and when she'd finished they lay with the sun beating down on them. Romy stretched out with her eyes shut so they couldn't see her tears.

Afterwards Romy felt drained and looking out at the sea couldn't resist the sparkling blue water, lapping only yards away.

'I'm going for a swim!'

'Don't be mad!'

Romy didn't care and ran to the water's edge peeling off her clothes and flinging them in a pile. She needed to wash it away, feel the water on her. Wading in as far as she could, she gasped as the coldness hit her, then ducked down and floated, bobbing on the waves as they carried her.

'Come on!' she yelled.

Moya looked around.

The nearest person was at least a half-mile away. It was too tempting and in a few seconds herself and Kate had joined Romy, screaming as the freezing water hit their bare skin and they splashed around. They raced and pulled each other along in the water by the toes, ducking and diving like they did when they were kids. Getting out, they fell onto the beach laughing, drying themselves off with Kate's sweater and Romy's T-shirt, pulling on a bit of clothing as they made a hasty retreat to the house.

Laughing and covered in sand, wet hair streeling, they tramped across the kitchen floor. Vonnie and Maeve were equally amused by their dishevelled appearance.

'You girls go and dry off upstairs,' smiled Vonnie, 'and I'll make a big pot of tea.'

Kate felt overwhelmed with guilt leaving her mother the next day but she had to get back to Dublin. Molly was missing her and Derry had to get some of his own work completed or he'd miss contract dates, plus the office had been on repeatedly asking about her return to work. Moya had left earlier that morning in the hire car, as she was on a mid-morning flight to London.

'Romy, are you sure that it won't be too much for you staying here on your own and minding her?' pressed Kate, concerned, standing in the hallway with her bag ready to return to the city.

'I told you. We'll be fine. Anyway, I'm not on my own. There's the nurses and Aunt

Vonnie and Dr Deegan and Mary Costigan across the way plus all Mum's friends.'

'Sure?'

'I'm sure. I wouldn't do it otherwise. And I promise, any change and I'll phone you immediately.'

'You have the numbers.'

'Mobile, office and home. They're on the noticeboard and in Mum's phone number book.'

Kate took a deep breath. Her mother was as comfortable as they could make her, home where she wanted to be.

'Romy, thanks so much. I don't know what Moya and I would have done if you weren't here.'

'Shssh. She's my mother too. Of course I want to be here.'

Romy watched the black car turn in the driveway and disappear on to the Rossmore Road, suddenly feeling the enormous responsibility for caring for her mother during the last days of her life.

Maeve Dillon lay dozing, her tight twisted features now relaxed, curled up amongst the pillows and duvet. She looked younger, her hair brushed off her face, eyes shut, peaceful. Romy picked up some mugs and dirty plates and brought them to the kitchen to wash. For the first time she really felt she was home as she flicked the radio on down low and pushed open the kitchen door, Jinx her mother's cat pushing past her.

'Poor old thing, you're being ignored and you don't like it,' she murmured, stroking the black coat.

Romy had always loved this kitchen, considered it the heart of the house, the place her mother could always be found: washing up, peeling vegetables, baking, stuffing chicken and turkeys and mixing gravy in the big brown jug to pour over the roasts of lamb and beef, sending them to get a snip of parsley or herbs from the garden. The high days of summer her mother lost herself in the garden, out there from early morning till late at night. Picnics on the beach and plates of salad and pots of new potatoes and warm brown bread from the oven were their staple. She still found it hard to believe that her mother would never work in this kitchen again, turn on the gas cooker, pull plates from the racks and forage in the fridge for ingredients to create a meal for her family. It was weird that she was now the mistress of this kitchen and all it contained. Petting the cat, she made herself a cup of tea and slipped back to sit near her mother. Moya and Kate thought they had landed her with the tough job of caring for a dying woman, not realizing she was the one who needed this most, the time to make amends for the mess she'd made in the past and try to make up the years lost by spending this precious time with her mother, the one person who had always unconditionally loved her.

Dr Deegan had looked in briefly on his way home, checking her mother's pulse and blood pressure, looking at the skin on her back and heels and listening to her chest.

'You're doing great, Maeve,' he said, gently pulling her nightdress back down and patting her hand. Her mother had always had a huge regard for the local GP and Romy was relieved that he was looking after her now near the end instead of some junior hospital doctor on shift that her mother didn't know.

'Eating and drinking and sleeping OK?' he enquired.

'Fine.'

'And what about you?'

'I'm fine too.' She smiled.

'Well you know where I am if you need me, and you have my mobile.'

Her mother was tired and content to lie back against the pillows as Romy went through the first of the photo albums she'd found, kissing the top of Maeve's head when she saw the first photo of herself taken a few days after she came home from the hospital, her mother radiant.

'I'm like a monkey wrapped in that pink blanket,' she joked, surprised when her mother touched her shoulder and made an attempt to say 'My monkey.'

God, she'd been so wild as a child, temper tantrums, stroppy, always up to mischief and breaking things. A tomboy, the dog Lucky at her heels, always looking for attention – or was that after Sean had been born? There were reams of photographs: birthdays, Christmas, holidays, on the rides in Tramore, starting school, communion, confirmation, winning the fancy dress competition when she'd dressed up as Humpty Dumpty, playing on the beach in their togs. She hesitated when she came to the one, taken by Moya, of her parents bringing Sean home from hospital. Her father in his suit, her mother's hair curling around her face as she nervously held the small baby in the blue blanket towards the cameras, Sean's eyes tightly shut.

'He was so small,' she said softly, as her mother's finger touched the picture. There were another five or six pictures of her little brother, eyes open staring out at life, smiling with tiny dimples, trying to grab someone's hair in his fist. The very last photo in the album was taken a few days later on her first day at the convent's secondary school, Moya, Kate and herself dressed in their identical uniforms, grinning in the morning sun as her mother captured them on camera, that moment frozen before everything changed.

There were too many memories.

'The night nurse will be here in a few minutes to get you settled, Mammy,' she babbled. Trying to compose herself, she closed the leatherbound album over and put it away.

Chapter Thirty-eight

The Stone House settled into a routine centred around the care of Maeve. Brigid Reilly the nurse arrived about ten o'clock every morning, Romy helping if needed as the nurse washed and changed her mother and administered a range of drugs. Brigid monitored her patient's condition daily, informing Romy over a cup of tea before she left as to how well her mother was doing.

'She's eaten so little for the past three days,' worried Romy. 'Just a bit of scrambled egg or mashed potato or yoghurt.'

'Is she having any difficulty swallowing? Stroke patients often develop a compromised swallow.'

'I don't know.'

'What about drinking? She's still taking a lot of fluids, I presume.'

'Yeah, tea and milk and juice and water.'

'It's very important she drinks enough, especially with all the medication she's on.'

Moya phoned every day around midday to check how things were going and to say hello to her mother. Romy mentioned the nurse's concern about her eating and drinking and the fact that her mother was now sleeping longer and longer. 'Kate's coming down at the weekend so at least she'll be here,' she told her.

During the day many of her mother's friends dropped in, some only staying a few minutes, others sitting quietly beside her.

'Romy's all grown up now,' joked Mrs Grace, one of her old teachers, who played bridge with her mother. 'I'm sure your coming home has made Maeve so happy. She used to tell us about your travels but I know she missed you terribly.'

The ladies from the Garden Club came and with the french windows opened carried pots and planters over to the doorway for her mother to see, admiring her climbing roses and spreading sweet pea.

'Green fingers, you've always had them, Maeve. You put the rest of us to shame. You just had to fling things into the soil and they took!'

Romy knew that even though her mother was weak, these visits pleased her.

Insured to drive her mother's Volkswagen Polo, Romy drove into Rossmore to buy a few groceries while Mrs Grace was there.

The sky was overcast, and it was threatening rain as she pulled into a space outside the supermarket. The small town had changed a lot over the years, with a proliferation of holiday homes and apartments; luckily most were on the outskirts of Rossmore and didn't take away from the quaint charm of the place. The hotels overlooking the front were still the same though some could do with a lick of paint. The newsagent's and the post office were still there, and O'Sullivan's, where she'd worked for two summers, had expanded, the window filled with crystal and silver and pine photo frames, expensive designer pottery and ceramics. The ice-cream machine beside the door had gone.

Further up the street were the bookies and McHugh's pub where her father drank. Lavelle's looked great, the restaurant and bakery painted a buttery cream colour with pine windows and a black awning that flapped in the wind with the signature word Lavelle's. Sheila O'Grady must be proud of the fine business she'd built up over the years. Romy stopped and studied that evening's menu. She'd heard from Moya that the eldest girl Deirdre also worked there, while young Tony was involved in the bakery, which supplied hotels and restaurants all over the South-East.

Romy, embarrassed when she realized that Sheila had spotted her, waved back.

She needed to get some chicken in the butcher's, then bread, pasta, and a few other items in the large Spar. She stopped outside her father's old office: it made her feel sad, a big Closing Down Sale sign in the window. Boxes everywhere. The antique business that had set up there was relocating. She peered in through the dusty window and blind. Smartened up like Lavelle's it could be nice.

Rossmore itself seemed smaller than she remembered, but walking along streets up by the school where she'd chased and raced in her uniform brought back reams of memories.

It had just begun to drizzle, and she pulled up her hood and zipped her jacket, head down. Putting the groceries in the car, she spotted a black Range Rover across the road from her. The tall figure in the black leather jacket was immediately recognizable. Brian O'Grady slowed down to let a woman with a baby in a buggy cross. Shit! She didn't know if he'd seen her or not. Her aunt had mentioned about him being back working in the area. She felt like getting in the car and high-tailing it to the airport but, taking a breath, calmed herself and drove home.

Seeing Brian O'Grady had upset her more than she could ever have imagined, his very presence at such close proximity disturbing her. Romy, upset and restless, knew she couldn't run any more.

She had pulled up the chair beside her mother's bed that night and told her the truth about the abortion.

'It's no excuse but I was scared. Terrified, too young to know what I was doing. Daddy and you and I – we were all upset! We said things, things we didn't mean.'

Her mother tried to say something, agitated, but the words just wouldn't come.

'I lied to you about not knowing who the father was. It was Brian O'Grady. I loved him so much. We were always together. I was so screwed up and sick and scared. Brian had another girlfriend. I wouldn't listen to you about keeping the baby and just went to a clinic in Fulham and had an abortion. I couldn't think straight.'

'It's in the past,' said her mother slowly, the words clear.

'You were right all along. You told me that I would regret it, but I didn't listen to you and I let those doctors there get rid of my baby.'

Her mother's eyes welled with tears.

'I'm a fucking walking disaster. I got rid of my own baby even though you said you'd help me!'

She leaned along the bed beside her mother.

'I was relieved ... the baby was gone. But it was the worst feeling in the world. I don't know how you got through it after Sean, Mammy. I don't know how you did it! I had to get away so I went to France. I kept moving. The further away I went, the harder it was to come back. I kept thinking, I'm seeing the world, but I was just running, running away. It wasn't you or Dad or anything I was getting away from – it was just me ... I couldn't face me!'

Maeve reached for her daughter with her good arm and Romy buried her head on her chest as her mother comforted her like she did when she was small and bold and wild. Romy knew that she was forgiven.

Kate and Molly arrived late on Friday evening. Romy was enchanted to finally get to see her little niece.

'She's a beauty, Kate.'

'Unlike her mother,' teased her sister.

'No,' gulped Romy, mortified. 'Molly's cute and clever and you'd run away with her.'

'I know what you mean. Some days I just can't believe she's mine!'

Romy stifled a pang of jealousy.

'I suppose I envy you,' she said truthfully.

'You've got your career and you have Molly. You are stronger and braver than me and have your beautiful daughter to show for it.'

'Listen, Romy, you were just a scared kid. Time will change things, just wait and see! Some day you'll have another child.'

'I'm not sure that's ever going to happen,' said Romy bitterly. 'Not sure I deserve it!'

Kate squeezed her sister's hand, realizing just how fortunate she really was. She couldn't imagine her life without the curly-haired bundle of mischief hopping up and down in front of them demanding to see Granny.

'Does she understand about Mum?'

'She knows Granny's very sick and tired and she's got to be good for the next two days. That's about as much as most three-year-olds can take in. Derry had to work. He's up in Belfast so I had to bring her.'

'And am I glad you did.' Romy smiled, pulling Molly up on her lap and kissing and hugging her.

'Can I see Granny now?' asked Molly, jumping down.

'Of course.' Her mother smiled as she led her to the dining room.

'Granny's bedroom's upstairs,' Molly reminded her.

'Well since she got sick, we got our cousins to bring Granny's big bed down here so she won't be all alone upstairs.'

Romy had a lump in her throat as she watched Molly march over to her granny's bed and stand there for a minute assessing the situation. Unperturbed by the change in her grandmother's appearance, Molly had simply kicked off her shoes and clambered up in her denim skirt and bright yellow T-shirt onto the bed, pulling back the quilt so she was lying beside her granny. Pulling open her ladybird handbag, she began to take out two drawings to show her.

'Granny, I made this one in play school for you. That's you in the bed and that's Jinx beside you and that's Mummy and me.'

Maeve Dillon nodded as she studied the purple-haired version of herself lying like the princess and the pea on layer after layer of multi-coloured bedding.

'Thank you,' she struggled to say as Molly's dark eyes fixed on hers.

'This one I made at home with all my colours,' Molly boasted proudly.

She slowly unfolded it. It was a garden, but no ordinary garden. It was covered in zany flowers that burst from the ground and the trees and fell from the sky, in the middle of it all stood her grandmother, with her sunhat on, and her sloppy gardening clothes and a huge smile.

'That's you, Granny.'

Kate and Romy looked at each other, both suddenly overcome with emotion as Molly chattered on. Spires of pink lupins and fox-gloves and heavy blue delphiniums and white, sweet-scented nicotiana were bursting with life from their mother's border outside the french windows.

Chapter Thirty-nine

Tired, Romy watched as the nurse's car pulled into the driveway. Deirdre Jennings had been here for the past four nights in a row, bringing a bag of knitting and the latest John Grisham novel to get through the long hours minding her patient.

'She's very drowsy,' Deirdre said.

'I know. She slept most of the day. Aunt Vonnie called in for a while this morning but she kept nodding off.'

'Well maybe she'll be up for a chat later on then!' smiled the middle-aged woman, going into the kitchen to make a cup of tea.

Romy kissed her mother good-night, looking forward to a long soak in the bath before falling into bed. She had a huge respect and deep gratitude for Deirdre and the rota of nurses who cared for her mother night and day, their kindness and profes-sionalism ensuring that Maeve could remain at home.

When she came down to breakfast in her dressing gown in the morning Deirdre told her there was a slight change.

'I changed her nightdress – she's been a bit clammy and sweaty, running a temp. I think it's her chest. She could have an infection. I've left a message with Dr Deegan to look in on her.'

'Is there anything I can do?'

The nurse hesitated.

'Just keep her comfortable. You don't want her getting too hot or cold. I've given her something to try and bring it down. It's hard to tell with these things. Listen, I'm going home for a sleep but I'm on again tonight and I'll see you then.'

Her mother looked wretched and Romy was relieved when Myles Deegan finally appeared.

'The nurse was right. She does have an infection and we need to treat it. There are two ways. I phone an ambulance and get her readmitted to the hospital where she'll be put on a drip and oxygen and monitored carefully, or she stays where she is and I treat her with high-dose antibiotics here at home. If she needs oxygen I'll get it set up here for her. What do you want to do?' he asked gently.

Romy hesitated.

'Will she get better?'

'I can't answer that. She's beginning to fail, her body is under severe pressure. She may have had another slight stroke, who knows. Unless we do a battery of tests, I couldn't say. Pneumonia in this type of situation is relatively common.'

Romy stood, watching her mother, unsure what to do, reluctant to be the decision-maker.

'I know she doesn't want to die in hospital,' she said slowly. 'She wants to be here at home.'

Maeve Dillon, aware of their conversation, had opened her eyes, coughing slightly, raised up on the layers of pillows around her shoulders.

'Maeve,' said the doctor gently. 'I think you might have a chest infection. I can treat it here or otherwise you'll have to go back into the hospital. What do you want?'

Her mother shook her head, her hand firmly patting the bed she was lying on.

'Home, here?'

'I'm taking that as an answer,' murmured Myles Deegan, clasping her mother's palm.

Myles Deegan co-ordinated it all, starting her mother on a course of high-dose anti-biotics and giving her an injection straight away.

'I'll talk to Brigid before she comes over and get her to wait for the oxygen to be delivered. I'll leave her this tray here in case she needs it and I'll call back up before I go home this evening. Don't worry, Maeve will have the best of care, I promise.'

'I know that,' Romy said.

Her mother fell into a deep, heavy sleep once the doctor had gone and Romy took the opportunity to phone Kate and Moya. Both of them agreed to come home immediately.

'I'll be on the first flight I can get,' promised Moya, upset. 'Just don't let anything happen to her before I get there.'

Aunt Vonnie had been philosophical.

'We all knew she wasn't getting any better. God be good to her. I was talking to Eamonn two nights ago and he's coming over.'

'When?'

'His flight gets in early tomorrow morning. Conor said he'd collect him and drive him down here.'

Romy was much relieved that her mother's older brother would be home to see her.

Over the next two days Maeve Dillon slipped further and further from them. They took it in turns to sit with her, as bit by bit she relaxed her grip on life, her lungs heavy, fighting for breath. Moya and Patrick had arrived with Fiona, Gavin and Danny. The three children were curious to meet their

411

Aunt Romy and hear about her travels.

The nurses were discreet as each of them got a chance to be with her, peaceful and quiet, to say what they wanted to say. Fiona, a tall leggy version of her mother, hunched up her skinny knees and legs as she sat beside her grandmother telling her about the play she was doing in school, unembarrassed as she sang the song she performed: 'Scarborough Fair'. Patrick led in the two small boys, who pushed and shoved to get nearer their grandmother as they made their final farewells.

Molly had said little, only that this time she was going to read Granny a story before she fell asleep, half making up the words of 'The Gingerbread Man'.

Father Eamonn had read from his bible, anointed her with precious oils and sat simply holding her hand while Aunt Vonnie gently sponged her face with a wet facecloth.

In those final hours, the three of them decided to sit with their mother for the night. It was what she would have wanted.

'I know you're happy we're all here together,' said Kate slowly. Their mother appeared drowsy, drifting in and out of sleep, sometimes eyes open watching, other times eyes closed listening. 'Back home.'

'Like when we were children.'

'You're such a good mother,' smiled Moya, reaching for her hand, 'loving us all.'

'Putting up with us! We're all so different.'

'Moya, the beauty! No matter what you put on you looked gorgeous and you got all the clothes and the shoes and the guys fancying you. While I was the sensible one, the clever one that got honours in her exams and nobody fancied.'

'And I was the wild one,' sighed Romy. 'Maybe that's what made me crazy, who knows.'

'Romy, you don't know how many times I envied you, wished that I was brave enough or bold enough to take up a backpack and go off round the world, do something daring and different,' said Kate.

'And I wanted to be clever and bright like you, Kate,' confessed Moya. 'I always felt I wasn't intelligent or interesting enough. That people only liked me for my style, my figure, my clothes.'

'Moya you are one of the nicest people I know,' admitted Kate. 'That's why Patrick fell in love with you all those years ago. You must know that!'

'And all I ever wanted was to be like the two of you,' said Romy, ruefully. 'I looked like a stringy boy for most of my childhood and was a disaster at school and college! I guess being bold was my way of getting attention.'

'You were such a tomboy when you were small, Romy. Daddy adored you.'

'Till Sean was born,' she said. 'That changed everything.'

'He still loved you. But the consequences, one thing affects another,' said Kate.

'I blamed myself for not looking after him properly,' whispered Moya. 'It made me nervous when Danny was born.'

Silently they all considered the consequences of their childhood.

'The thing is that despite all the differences, we're here,' insisted Kate, knowing that she had never felt closer to her sisters.

'To think I wasn't going to come home,' sobbed Romy.

'But you did. You've cared for Mammy. You're the one has been here every day with her. Romy, never forget that!'

Maeve Dillon's breathing had got heavier; her lungs sounded as if they were bags of water as she struggled to get air.

'Mammy, don't be scared! We're all here with you.'

'Talking away. We're not going to leave you.'

They sat around, leaning across the bed, watching her, pulling the quilt over them as their mother's eyes closed and she slept, conscious a while later of the change in her breathing as almost with a single heaving sigh her life finally ended.

'It's over,' Kate said, relieved that her

mother was at peace and that the three of them had been together to witness her passing.

'She's gone,' said Moya softly as Romy got off the bed and walked across to the french windows. It was early morning, the sun barely up as she flung the doors open wide to the garden.

Chapter Forty

The funeral was held in Rossmore's parish church. The pews were packed with family and friends and neighbours, the altar decorated with flowers from the garden. Father Glynn the parish priest co-celebrated the mass with Uncle Eamonn, who didn't trust himself not to break down when talking about his sister. Each of the grandchildren had carried up gifts to the altar, Molly bringing her picture of Granny's garden, Derry encouraging her when she got nervous.

Kate sighed. She didn't know what she would have done the past few days without him. He and Patrick had taken charge of all the arrangements, organizing the undertaker and the notices in the paper. Moya's children had cried and cried. Kate was relieved that Molly was too young to understand death and the concept of not seeing her granny again.

Standing outside in the churchyard Romy could not believe how many people welcomed her home when they came up to pay their respects. She was not surprised to discover her mother had been a much loved and valued member of the local community. Her knees nearly buckled from under her when Brian O'Grady came forward to offer his condolences.

'I'm so sorry about your mother, Romy,' he said, taking her hand in his. 'But I'm glad to see you home. Perhaps we might meet up when this is all over.'

She'd nodded like an eejit, trying not to cry, and didn't know what to say. The electricity between them was still obvious and she wished she could be calm and composed like her sisters.

They had walked through the town to the graveyard where Uncle Eamonn led them in the prayers as her mother was finally laid to rest, then back to the Stone House for food and drinks.

It seemed strange to see the house filled with people and her mother not there to greet them. The gathering was subdued at first, but relaxed as drinks were served and people helped themselves to the buffet lunch they had helped Romy prepare.

For Molly it was a long day, and scooping her up in her arms like a monkey Kate held her while she talked to Uncle Pat and his wife, and her cousins who had travelled from Cork. Bill O'Hara and two others from the office came to say farewells before heading back to Dublin.

Those that had to travel began to head for home. Kate was relieved to get a chance to talk to Minnie before she left.

'We're in no rush, so give me Molly,' pleaded her godmother. 'I need to get a bit of practice.'

'Practice?'

'I'm getting one just like her,' beamed Minnie.

'What?'

'Yes, I'm pregnant. Colm's thrilled to bits that he's going to be a dad.'

Kate looked over. Colm O'Halloran was the best thing that had ever happened to her friend. Quiet and thoughtful, he had calmed Minnie down. 'I'm so glad for you both.' Kate hugged Minnie, passing her daughter over. Molly was already making a beeline for Minnie's fancy expensive Lulu Guinness handbag. Uncle Eamonn had aged, put on weight, and his hair was almost white. His sister's death had been a huge blow to him. Kate brought over a glass of wine and sat with him as they reminisced about her mother.

Two hours later only the family remained, Uncle Joe insisting Aunt Vonnie go home and put her feet up.

'She's exhausted after the past few days. She and Maeve were so close I don't even know if it's hit her yet. She needs to sleep.'

'Go home, Vonnie,' pleaded Moya. 'We'll see you tomorrow.'

Kissing them all, their aunt and uncle made their departure.

After clearing away the dirty glasses and ashtrays they all sat around the kitchen table, Romy producing a huge lasagne and a tray of garlic bread. Everyone suddenly found they were hungry. Fiona and the boys tucked into the slices of creamy pasta and crunchy bread, complimenting their aunt on her prowess as a cook.

'I made it a few nights ago and put it in the freezer.'

'What's going to happen to Granny's house now?' asked Gavin.

No-one knew what to say.

'We're not sure yet, pet,' replied his mother. 'We haven't discussed it.'

'Will we still be able to come here on holidays?' he pressed.

'A boy after my own heart,' murmured their uncle. 'I've been coming almost every year since I was ordained.'

'It depends,' interrupted Kate. 'We're presuming the house has been left between the three of us. If so, then we might decide to sell it.'

'Property prices here are still buoyant,' added Patrick. 'A house like this would be very much in demand. Once you had an approximate value it would be easy enough to calculate any taxes payable, and come out with a final figure after dividing it three ways.'

'Patrick, shut up!' retorted Moya. 'There's no point in calculating, because for the moment I have absolutely no intention of selling, unless Kate and Romy make me. Who knows, I might want to come back and live here myself some day!'

Patrick flushed, unsure of Moya's plans.

'I suppose I would have thought of selling,' admitted Kate, 'but now I'm not sure. With Mammy gone it's all we've left of her. It's like a bolt-hole, a place for me and Molly to escape to, but Romy, you might need the money or want to go back to America.'

Romy played with the salad on her plate, considering.

'There's nothing that important for me to go back to,' she admitted honestly. 'I guess everyone that's important to me right now is sitting around this table. I'd be happy to stay right here.'

'Would you move to Dublin?'

'I think I'm finally figuring it out.' She

shrugged. 'I'm a small-town girl. I like visiting cities but give me a place like here any day of the week.'

'You could live here,' urged Moya. 'Make and sell your jewellery and designs.'

'I've no plans, Moya, but I could be persuaded, so we'll just wait and see.'

Derry was sitting quiet, Molly beside him, her eyes closing.

'Hey young lady, it's about time for bed.'

'Can I put her to bed?' pleaded Fiona, hopping up from the table. 'Please!'

Kate laughed. Her niece seemed to be very taken with her little cousin.

'Come on, Molly,' she coaxed. 'I'm going to put you to bed.'

'Daddy and I will come up to kiss you later,' Kate promised.

'We're going to play a game,' suggested Fiona, taking her hand. 'You're a baby and I'm...'

'I'm *not* a baby,' said Molly.

'Oh all right then, you'll be a big girl.'

Kate laughed as she watched them go, helping Romy to clear the plates and pack the dishwasher as the boys said good-night also.

Derry slipped outside, Kate following him. It was a perfect night, and though she should be dead with exhaustion she was wide awake as they walked in the garden.

'I'll head back to Dublin in the morning, Kate, but before I go I need to ask you something,' he said slowly.

Her heart dropped.

'You know how precious Molly is to me,' he began.

'I know,' she said softly.

'Well the truth is there are only two women in my life that I love. One is three years old and the other is her...'

She took a breath. Why today of all days?

'And the other is you. I loved you from the minute you walked into Bushes bar and flung a pint over me, it's the truth. I wanted our few nights to last for ever but I just hadn't the guts to admit it. Being Molly's father is wonderful but it was never enough when it was you I was after.'

Kate stared at him incredulous. She had waited such a long time to hear him say it. 'I love you,' he said, pulling her into his arms.

'You have the worst timing ever,' she said, gulping back the tears, 'the crappest way of saying things.'

He wiped the tears from under her eyes with his thumbs.

'Will you marry me?' he asked.

'The last time you asked me I had just given birth.'

'I know.'

'And now I've just buried my mother.'

'Births, marriages and deaths. It does

make you think, Kate.'

She sighed.

If he loves you, marry him, Kate! Her mother's words came back to her.

'I do love you,' he repeated. 'And besides, I've got you a wedding present already.'

'You what?'

Derry pulled a folded piece of drawing paper from his pocket. It was a sketch. A plan of a yacht.

'They're building her up in Belfast. She's yours and should be ready to sail in about twelve weeks' time.'

'You're mad!'

'I'm mad but...'

'You're mad but I love you and I'm going to marry you!' she screamed, flinging herself at him, kissing him like crazy, knowing for sure and certain that Derry was the only man for her.

Chapter Forty-one

The Stone House began to empty as Moya and Patrick and the children packed up and returned to London, with promises to return during the coming school holidays.

'It's so good to know the house will still be here for us,' confessed Moya, taking a last look around the tiled hall and wide stairway, 'though it won't be the same without Mammy.'

Kate and Derry had driven back to Dublin a few hours earlier. Romy had never seen her sister Kate so happy, making plans to marry Derry as soon as possible. Molly was all excited about being a flower girl at her parents' wedding.

Nervously Romy had asked her sisters if it was all right if she stayed on in Rossmore, to be told they were delighted to have someone in the house minding it for them all.

'I just couldn't imagine the place cold and empty,' shuddered Kate, hugging her. So now there was Uncle Eamonn, herself and the cat left.

She had phoned New York and told Diana that she wasn't coming back and contacted her landlord about the lease on her apartment. Greg had been calm and accepting when she told him of her plans to stay in Ireland. Romy hoped somehow they could remain friends. The stores she worked for were a little upset when she told them that she had no plans to return to New York for the foreseeable future but promised them that once her equipment was shipped over she would try to supply a minimum number of items each month and work on individual commissions.

Back in Rossmore, she was ready to admit

that she couldn't imagine herself living anywhere else. She had taken the keys to her
father's office in Main Street and asked Kate
and Moya and their partners for their advice.
Derry had assured her that with a little
investment and employing a good shop-fitter
she could easily convert the upstairs office
into a studio, and refit the downstairs to
create a bright display and sales area.

'Just imagine it, Romy – with your own
designs and metal art pieces on show,'
enthused Moya, 'it could look wonderful!'

'And you get to keep all the money, no
percentage to stores or split commissions,'
laughed Kate.

'Though there will be overheads,' Patrick
warned her. 'But I think it would be a very
sound investment in a town like this.'

Patrick was right: trade in the town was
good and a new bookshop and an expensive
boutique were scheduled to open only a few
doors away.

She had masses to do and to sort out, and
appointments were made with the local
bank manager, a building contractor and an
architect. Romy reckoned that keeping busy
made it a little easier to get over the loss of
her mother. She was doing a bit of a clear-
out of the house with Aunt Vonnie's help
and had the garden to tend to before the
place went wild with neglect.

That afternoon she planned to make a start by cutting the grass and tackling some of the weeding and was kneeling on the lawn when she spotted the familiar black Land Rover pull into the driveway.

Her instinct was to drop what she was doing and take to her heels and run, except that Brian had spotted her and was coming across the lawn.

'Romy.'

Shading her eyes, she blinked in the sunlight. He looked great in a pair of chinos and a pale blue shirt, while she was in a crappy pair of cut-off denim jeans and an old Mickey Mouse T-shirt.

She watched as he walked towards her, his eyes hidden behind a pair of dark sunglasses, wondering what he wanted from her.

'I wanted to talk to you before you go back to America,' he said, taking off the sunglasses.

'I'm not going back. I'm going to stay here.'

She could see the relief in his eyes.

'Good, I don't think I could stand to have you go away.'

She stared at the blades of grass. This was utterly pathetic. She was a grown woman, not a stupid teenager, and she should at least be able to talk to the guy who was her best friend for years and the one time love of her life.

'Romy, there's so much I want to say to you. I've made such a fuck-up of things between us. Years ago, I know I let you down.'

She looked up. He was being serious.

'I should never have gone away. My mother thought we were too young to be in love, too crazy about each other, that's why she sent me over to Uncle Kevin.'

'I screwed up too,' she admitted.

'Then I messed things up even more by getting involved with Gina. That broke up and then Marie and I got together. We should never have got married and I guess after a few years we both realized we'd made a huge mistake.'

Romy considered. She had to tell him about what she had done and was frightened to tell the truth because he'd probably hate her, be disgusted by her.

'Brian, listen to me for a minute please,' she insisted, barely daring to speak. 'That time you went to Frankfurt for work, the reason I tried so hard to contact you was to tell you that I was going to have a baby.'

'Oh Christ,' he said. 'I don't believe it!'

Standing on the lawn looking out over the sea, voice shaking, she told him, seeing the pain in his eyes, waiting for his contempt and anger, and for him to storm off and leave her. For him to jump into his car and forget her.

'Oh God, Romy, I'm sorry about what you had to go through,' he said softly. 'We were just kids then but I was the one who let you down!'

She looked up at him, lost in the blue of his eyes.

He bent down and touched her, his lips warm against hers. She opened her mouth and responded fiercely, kissing him back. Nothing had changed.

'It's like I thought,' he said slowly, looking at her.

Her heart sank.

'Perfect! There's always been that perfect chemistry between us.'

Romy sighed. She guessed that's why no guy she'd ever met had measured up to him.

'We're not kids any more,' he said, touching her hair, moving it back from her face. 'This time I want to take it slowly, OK?'

She looked dazed and confused.

'We're grown up now, Romy, and I want a grown-up relationship with you.'

Standing in front of the Stone House, watching the shimmering blue of the sea as, with the tide out, the waves rippled onto the beach below, Romy could feel the smile begin way down at her toes as he pulled her into his arms and held her. Romy promised there would be no more secrets between them, no more running away, for wrapped in Brian's arms, here in the place that she loved, she was finally home.

The publishers hope that this book has given you enjoyable reading. Large Print Books are especially designed to be as easy to see and hold as possible. If you wish a complete list of our books please ask at your local library or write directly to:

Magna Large Print Books
Magna House, Long Preston,
Skipton, North Yorkshire.
BD23 4ND

This Large Print Book, for people
who cannot read normal print,
is published under the auspices of

THE ULVERSCROFT FOUNDATION